HOT BISCUITS

Hot Biscuits

EIGHTEEN STORIES
by WOMEN *and* MEN *of*
the RANCHING WEST

Edited by

Max Evans *and*

Candy Moulton

UNIVERSITY OF NEW MEXICO PRESS
ALBUQUERQUE

LIBRARY OF CONGRESS CATALOGING-IN-PUBLICATION DATA

Hot biscuits : eighteen stories by women and men of the
ranching West / edited by Max Evans and Candy Moulton.
p.   cm.
ISBN 0-8263-2889-X (alk. paper)
1. Western stories. 2. Cowboys—Fiction.
3. Ranch life—Fiction. 4. Cattle trade—Fiction.
5. Working class writings, American—West (U.S.)
I. Evans, Max, 1925– II. Moulton, Candy Vyvey, 1955–
PS648.W4 H68 2002
813'.087408—dc21
2002002092

DESIGN: Mina Yamashita

CONTENTS

HOT BISCUITS

Introduction

To the Wonder of Reality

MAX EVANS

I think we are all guilty, during our lives, of putting something off that is extremely important to us. There is nothing easier to make than an excuse, and nothing more difficult to accept after it is too late.

That is the mistake I almost made while considering this collection. For over two decades I thought about gathering a group of stories from the real working West, written by the very people who performed that tough, mostly unappreciated labor. Since I had set some minimum requirements in my often-numb skull about the qualifications of the writers—I had easy access to plentiful excuses.

First I expected the cowboys to have drawn wages for, at the very least, five years. I know that ranchers can't afford to pay a hand for long if he or she can't deliver.

Since cowgirls have different chores around the ranch house, and often add cowpasture cowboying to their other duties, I decided they had to have been raised on a ranch, or joined their husbands on a double hire-out for the aforesaid five years. Simple formula, huh?

However, when I added in the gift of being able to write a short story of a certain quality my formula disintegrated.

I easily found a few who had already proven their writing skills to a degree. But I kept on making excuses such as my own writing deadlines, research trips and study, having too much fun, and endless other excuses. Now, getting fifteen to twenty damned good short stories together from the men and women who actually got down in the dirt and lived the reality seemed beyond me, since I badly needed a woman writer or co-editor. I looked for that special woman, but never felt quite right, and mainly they didn't qualify in the cowgirl department. Then, to my thickheaded surprise I thought of Candy Moulton, writer of nine fine books, writer for many magazines from livestock publications to *Sunset*. Here was a woman who had been raised on a ranch, and presently lived in the heart of ranch country a dozen miles from a small Wyoming town; her husband helped run a cattle ranch and they owned cattle and horses of their own. Not only that, she was the highly respected editor of *Roundup Magazine*.

I had run out of excuses. There was only one left. If Candy said "no" I'd probably go on dreaming instead of doing.

I was stunned when she seemed as excited as I was. I told her briefly some of the difficulties we were going to have in gathering this little bunch of real cowboy/cowgirl writers and attain the quality I'd spent so many years planning. Candy, like the good cowgirl writer-editor she is, was undaunted, pawing the ground, raring to go.

Surprisingly, we soon had in hand five or six good pieces of short fiction. Then we hit the proverbial snag: I was pursuing a couple of working cowboys who had published some pretty fair nonfiction, and one of them even had one fine novel in print. However, they couldn't seem to understand what a short story was. I tried to explain. I tried again. I suggested they go to the library and check out a collection of O'Henry short stories. I even named some of my own short stories in print.

I suppose the daily, hourly, split-second decisions they were having to make out in the brush and rocks made a short story search seem kind of silly. Of course, like myself, maybe they had been bucked off on their heads once too often.

Eventually they delivered the real working goods. We also had a couple of cowboys and cowgirls who tried to get us to accept nonfiction, and when that failed, to have us print excerpts from books they had already written. The easy way out didn't work.

You see both Candy and I had agreed we had never seen a collection with the strict restrictions ours must have. We, of course, had seen scores of *Best of the West, The New West,* on and on into the hundreds. Most were about a fantasy West that never was and never will be—but fun reading in most cases. However, we remained adamant in our choices. Why not just once in all history have a book of stories straight from the horse's mouth, with the taste and tang of horsehair, and the jolt one feels when an old pony has bucked up in the domain of birds and hits the ground driving down like a thousand pound bomb? Why not make a rodeo run at smelling the fresh cow shit and seeing the brush and rocks peel the hide? Why not truly know what it takes to survive a lifetime, a year, or a day on a real working outfit? Why not indeed.

There is plenty to fight out there, besides our fellow humans, such as wild cows, and flesh-killing droughts and blizzards, unforeseen diseases, and livestock prices below any hopes of a single dollar's profit. Five generations of bending work and sacrifice can be lost to a mortgage banker in the time it takes to sign his name. What makes these endless endurance tests worthwhile is the promise of the glorious sunrises and sunsets, the grace and stability of a good working cow horse, a helpful neighbor, a good soaking rain, a country dance, a drink in a cow town bar with those who have ridden the rocks, and popped the brush, cut and stacked the hay for winter, repaired the water gaps, fixed the windmills, and busted the ice on water tanks for the livestock's winter drinking and survival.

Then there is the prayed-for green grass of spring, the new calves, bucking, whirling, running, tails up with the promise of growth to come. These are some of the little things that cause a real working cowgirl/cowboy to listen to the irresistible call. That is what Candy, myself, and the writers have tried so hard and honestly to explore here.

There have been almost as many stories by academics about the beginning of the Western novel as the legend of that little punk killer, Billy the Kid. Folks, that is a bunch. They correctly tell us that Ned Buntline, and his made-up little dime novels came first, and then the boost or boom really began with Owen Wister's *The Virginian* in 1902.

Of course so many others followed that they are countless. Some writers such as Zane Grey and Max Brand on up through Louis L'Amour who gave unnumbered millions pleasurable escape worldwide. In fact, Louis L'Amour was the greatest promoter since Hemingway and rapidly crowded most everyone else of this genre from the bookracks. I met him a couple of times. He was a damned nice fellow. So sincere. I read his first book, *Hondo*. He did over a hundred more, but the one I'd read seemed to be his best. The movie from his book, from his treatment and someone else's screenplay, made John Wayne and associates a lot of money. Louis's books made him well known and he never let up until the day he died. At least in that respect he was similar to a working cowboy/cowgirl. Who knows, maybe he helped kill the genre. Maybe he kept it barely breathing. Whether we like it or not he became very near the sole proprietor of the shoot-'em-up Western.

Now, let us get one thing finally straight. Please. There is as much difference in writing the traditional Western and the real working cowgirl/cowboy stories as there is in fine Italian olive oil and West Texas crude. You just can't quite do the *Working West* right unless you've been there and tasted the dirt, over a long period of time.

I can hear the hurting howls now about the domain of creativity being the only source of talent projected by the human mind. Surely, that is true is some cases. Two quick examples are Honore de Balzac and the currently neglected Somerset Maugham. Those two certainly turned their observations into powerful visions of the human comedy.

In our own West, we have two obvious examples of keen observers and they are among the few exceptions, of course: Larry McMurtry and Elmer Kelton.

Larry McMurtry was born to a North Texas ranching family, but never worked five years for cowboy wages—if at all—yet wrote a first-rate western book, *Lonesome Dove*. It became what most critics feel is the greatest western film to ever inhabit a television screen. It will hold its own against any other mini-series made so far for this medium.

Where McMurtry has staked a claim on the historical North Texas, Elmer Kelton has produced several working ranch novels of West Texas that are just fine.

Elmer Kelton was born on a ranch in Andrews County, Texas, and soon thereafter moved on south to Crane, then to San Angelo to spend the rest of his life. Because of, by his own descriptions, extreme near-sightedness and glass ankles, he never took to actual cowboying himself. But like Balzac and Maugham, he was there to observe it piercingly. *The Time It Never Rained* is a top example. Kelton had a giant loop of his own over the vastness of the real ranch lands of West Texas.

On the other hand, such an internationally prominent figure as film director Steven Spielberg was quoted by Tom Brokaw in a recent *USA Today* thusly: "Steven Spielberg says he used to believe that the best stories came out of the human imagination, but after *Schindler's List* and *Saving Private Ryan* he now believes the best stories come out of real human experience."

That is certainly true in writing the real working West. You just can't do it without the lack of experience showing—too much.

It seems to me that the formula for writing our subject is *experience plus imagination plus innate writing ability*. If one of the three is missing it won't work. That is, of course, the reason we've had so few, so very few, writers of the vast working West. So few, in fact, that the important advancers such as literary academics and critics simply don't recognize it when they see it, and mostly dismiss it forthwith. Now, it is not their fault, this lack of recognition or cognition.

Most of the publishers and film producers simply don't know the difference between the Faux West and the Real West—that is the *Working West*.

So far they have not cared enough to learn the truth. So the plain reader, the academics, and the critics who are the ultimate deciders rarely get a look at these working women and men in authenticated settings that can provide as much entertaining drama, in fiction, as the wildest of shoot 'em ups. I must admit, however, that the non-fiction writers have produced and equaled in both quality and numbers any other segmented section in the world. There are simply too many good ones to attempt a list. A few are Bernard DeVoto's *Across the Wide Missouri,* David Lavender's *Bent's Fort,* Robert Utley's biography of Sitting Bull, H. H. Bancroft's thirty-six books on the West, and most recently Dale L. Walker's unique and enthralling *Pacific Destiny.*

There is indeed another urgent matter related to the people and stories included here. We have no choice but to face a terrifying fact: the working cowgirl/cowboy West is rapidly being altered into chopped up blocks of ranchettes, mobile home clusters, and little exotic game hunting parks that will soon be filled with seriously inbred animals.

It is deteriorating with such speed that every day, week, and month we have fewer and fewer down-in-the-dirt people to live or portray that very special way of life.

The Working West began with the Spanish vaqueros from south of the border and their well-trained Indian cowboys moving cattle into America to help maintain food for the religious missions their priests were building. Some of the cattle escaped or were abandoned and they bred themselves into massive wild herds, especially in South Texas.

The need for meat back East created a big, lucrative market. The gathering, trailing, and turning of the cattle into steaks and money created America's first homegrown cowboys. These herders were of every nationality and ethnicity known at the time.

Great open range cattle empires were founded. Empires of cows, cowboys, and a few extra-durable cowgirls came into prominence and made history worldwide. That was the *first* segment of the Working West. The *second* phase came with the invention of barbwire, but even after fencing it was still a horseback West. There were often huge areas of open country between fences. The *third* great change followed the vast mechanization necessary to help win World War II. The pickup truck altered it immensely yet again. This cut the time of work with horses in most places by about half, but ranches still couldn't operate without them. The *fourth* great fragmentation is the New West, as so many learned people have chosen to call it.

The gut truth—with the learned and a lot of the ranchers in denial— is that the New West comes with the break-up of home ranches, families, and so many of our valiantly earned traditions—into supposedly controlled environments.

The result of the aforesaid actions on such a massive scale is equal to an earthquake of about ten (10) on the Richter scale. Along with two-way radios, cell phones on horseback, high tech camcorders, broadband, wireless this and that, and e-mail, the electronic new New West has now arrived.

What dismays the most is the danger that the changes have barely begun.

It threatens to be as all consuming as the great plague of the Dark Ages, combined with the whamming of a huge asteroid into our precious western earth.

As the Working West shrinks with such sad swiftness, we have left a *tiny window of time.* Some of those who once lived it, and those few who are so agonizingly still working it with bloodied souls, must put it down on paper when and where possible. If we fail to act with immediacy the truth will continue to dissipate and be distorted with frightening rapidity.

In the process of assembling this book Candy and I had a surprising revelation. Almost every story had homemade biscuits included as an integral, natural, daily part of the Working West. They were possibly more important than coffee and certainly guns. I recalled so many rural kids whose school lunches consisted of three biscuits. Two of them would include some kind of meat, such as sowbelly, and one would be a dessert filled with peanut butter or some kind of fruit jam or jelly, sometimes both. I ate the above for several years with anticipated pleasure.

A woman who could make superior biscuits received more respect than the mayor and chief of police combined in the nearest town. A few men, scattered hundreds of miles around, became famous for their sourdough biscuits and bread. Of such small things came great traditions.

When I was a kid/cowboy up on Ed Young's Rafter EY on Glorieta Mesa, south of Santa Fe, so long ago, there was a cook I remember with great fondness and respect. I put it down in the introduction to my three novels in the tragicomedy included in a trilogy of the Working West called *Rounders 3.*

Here it is exactly:

Ed Young's wife was known as Mother Young. The term was used with enormous respect. I never knew why I started helping her after supper, but thanks to any and all great spirits for the privilege. I'd chop and gather wood for the next day and fill the hot water reservoir on the side of the huge wood burning cook stove, fill all the water buckets for drinking, washing, and cooking, help clean the supper table, and then the real treat—stand and dry dishes for her. We talked and talked— even about books, paintings, and sissy stuff like that.

Her contributions were everywhere. She made the rag rugs that covered the floors, built the lamp stands from tree cactus or old wagon wheel hubs, painted the pictures that hung on the walls, cooked, cleaned, doctored, washed, ironed, and in true essence held the whole damned outfit together, as thousands of others like her did, and still do.

I don't know why I left out the specialness of Mother Young's biscuits with larruping cream gravy, but I realize now that it was a thoughtless omission of a small but important part of ranch life.

So, I called Candy Moulton and asked her if she thought *Hot Biscuits* should be the title of our book. We had a few laughs.

She said, "What else? They show up in almost every story."

I was thrilled at her keen observation. All we'd asked from each of our qualified writers was a short story about the Working West set any time between 1920 and the present.

Another thrill we had coming was the unbelievable luck of receiving stories all different from one another. They covered a range as wide as the Rockies, from a murder mystery to a unique horse trainer, to a family joined in a desperate battle against a grass and forest fire, to a world famous violinist, and a gruff old man.

You will find here stories filled with all the exciting lore of reality on working a ranch, surviving the harshest elements, and the endless forms of love that come from getting down in the dirt, the soil of the soul, and the eternal song of truth.

One Man's Land

TAYLOR FOGARTY

The drive alone into that place was something a person could never forget. New snow glittered on the sagebrush, the frozen range covered in winter velvet. The world looked perfect and full of promise. Without thought, the words escaped my mouth like a prayer.

"Sure is pretty country."

Quinn, my husband of ten years, hadn't said a thing for thirty miles, but now he let out a heavy sigh.

"Folks like us got to be careful, Ivy," he said. "Don't ever dig your bootheels too deep into another man's soil."

Those words were like his creed, and I'd seen him silently mouth them at times while haying another man's meadow, or pulling a calf from another man's cow, or sitting in the saddle atop another man's horse gathering cattle in the mountains, way up somewhere in another man's blessed pines. . . . It is the ranch hand's code.

We both needed employment and we had heard the Circle Bar Vee had three openings. Ten minutes after passing through the ranch entrance gate, we were inside the main house, sitting across from Frate Grayson, the ranch foreman. The office smelled of cooked beef, leather, horse sweat, and cigars.

"There's only one opening," he said, keeping his icy blue stare locked on Quinn. Grayson sat behind a big desk in a fancy leather armchair and he held up his long, crooked index finger, making extra certain we clearly understood what 'one' meant.

"She might wanna get a job in town," Grayson continued. "My wife works in town. As a floor manager at the department store. Been there fourteen years now."

From down deep inside, my stomach began to rumble with every reason why someone of my particular talents was not at all suited to managing floors or collecting plastic gold cards from ladies with painted nails and perfect hair who purchased silks and linens just to put a dent into the mister's gains, all in a vain attempt to fill some need that wasn't otherwise being met. My needs were very different from theirs. My wardrobe, from the secondhand store, consisted mostly of faded denim and flannel. I was not a town girl.

But before I could open my mouth to argue the point, Quinn's large hand clamped down on my right knee and he gave it a hard squeeze—a hold he would not fully release until I had drifted back to the reality of our desperate financial situation. When you're broke, reality can hit you hard and pride dies fast. I patted Quinn's hand and silently sat there, soaking up every word Grayson had to offer.

The deal was $800 a month with housing and a side of beef every six months. The house, Grayson explained, was about three miles away on another section of the main ranch, near what was once the old buffalo jump. It came with a few furnishings, its own barn, pond, springhouse, chicken coops, and fenced yard. After a year of employment, the company would supply paint for the married hand's house, in case we wanted to freshen up the walls.

"Though, you might not wanna count on that last part too much," Grayson warned. "The ranch is up for sale and there's been some serious buyers on the line. Could be in six months, we're all out lookin' for work. No guarantees."

That's just the kind of news I did not need to hear. Just the moment prior, my head was busy planting perennials in that yard of ours I hadn't yet seen . . . and now there we were, once again reduced to a pair of tumbleweeds who had the hard luck of getting tangled up in the man's fence for a time.

Grayson stood then. He was a tall, thin-lipped man in his late sixties, with narrow eyes and a shiny, two-tone head, pale on top and tan from his brow line on down. The two men shook hands, the interview apparently over, and I guessed we . . . I mean *Quinn* . . . had just signed on with the Circle Bar Vee.

By seven o'clock the next morning, Grayson had hired on two more men, both drifters. That irked me since he'd said he only needed one hand the day before.

Caid, the youngest of the pair, was the first to emerge from the bunkhouse that morning. He was a blonde-haired, chaw-chewing cowboy, footloose and cocky, fresh from Arizona with a blue heeler pup, a saddle, two good ropes, and a box of clothes. Judging from his truck, a flashy red dually with too much chrome, he must have been the favored son of a moneyed man. Caid was fairly handy, but a mite prideful, refusing certain chores. Especially if a job involved using that dually of his. He kept the glove box stocked with specially treated soft cloths, which he used to wipe dust from the paint job.

The third man to finish out the crew was Willie—or as he preferred to be called, Honorable Reverend Willie. He was the huffing-est, puffing-est, drinking-est, cussing-est cowboy preacher I'd ever heard, seen, or met. At six foot four, he weighed in at two fifty, and came abundantly blessed with a gift for fixing things, from engines to edibles. He kept his Official Man of God Certificate, framed in barn wood, proudly displayed on the bunkhouse wall. It wasn't until some weeks later he confided to us that he received the certificate from some Christian ministry based out of California. All he had to do to get it was check off three yes or no boxes on a questionnaire and send it in . . . along with thirty-five dollars. (Frame not included.)

With the crew in place, we settled into life on the Circle Bar Vee.

A couple months later, in mid-July, while taking laundry down from the line, I saw a billowing cloud of red dust trailing Grayson's Ford pickup and two Chevy Suburbans down into the quiet little draw in front of the house. The little caravan was strangely official looking, and my heart skipped a beat as they crossed the cattle guard and entered our ranch yard. I rolled a sheet into a quick, mindless wad and dropped it into the laundry basket as Grayson and the strangers exited the vehicles and approached the front yard gate. Knowing they weren't the haying crew, I stretched my neck and caught the name of the real estate company on the magnetic sign stuck to the door of one of the white Suburbans. The agency was a well-known one, but the letters, no matter how they read, were interpreted in my head as 'The End.'

"Miz McKinnon," said Grayson, greeting me with a nod. "Mind if these gents go inside and have a look around?"

I was well aware Grayson's asking was just a formality, but inside my head I was kicking and screaming, begging them, *Go away! Don't buy this place! Please! You can't need this ranch like we do!*

Instead, I smiled politely and said, "Go on in."

Grayson held the door open and offered no introductions to the four men, each dressed in western-style suits and fine white shirts that were as crisp and expensive as the cologne they wore. I stood with my arms folded and nodded a howdy as each pair of sunglasses filed past me. The men glanced around the place like secret service agents and entered my home without removing their Stetsons.

I stayed out in the yard with my laundry, listening to the hay swaying in the wind. Above me, white mare's tails stretched high in the thin, pale blue sky—by tomorrow a storm would hit. I hoped it would be a good one. For some reason a good hard rain always made it easier for me to cry.

So overcome was I by the meaning behind the strangers' visit that I forgot all about those papers from the County Clerk's office that I had found in the front pocket of Quinn's dirty jeans that morning. Four of them, folded up into neat little squares, and each receipt was written at the beginning of the month, right on every payday, each month since we hired on. The receipts, stamped Paid In Full, looked like they had something to do with some kind of land lots, but at only forty dollars per lot. I couldn't imagine what kind of land in this country would ever sell that cheap.

·.· Ψ ⚘ ·.·

As the weeks passed, I eventually began cowboying with Quinn and the others; my participation went unpaid. Grayson neither noticed nor seemed to care. Nothing was said about the visitors that came looking around the ranch.

Several weeks later something important must have been going on at headquarters because Grayson lined out all four of us on the same job ten miles away. Whatever it was that was going on, Grayson didn't want us around. We loaded up one pickup with salt blocks, per his instructions, and drove to the other side of the ridge. There we laid the salt in different areas of the open mountain meadows for the Circle Bar Vee cattle. Between the four of us, that only took a couple of hours. Since Grayson had made a point of telling us he expected us back at headquarters later that evening, we spent the extra time driving around, checking on the general welfare of the herd, and speculating on what might really be going on at headquarters.

A month later, during fall gather, we came up eleven head short on the count. Worried for our necks, or at least our jobs, we rode for days and picked through the pines, the draws, the shaky trees, from sunup to sundown, till our butts turned dead as the leather we were sitting on, fearing if we didn't come up with those steers pretty quick, Grayson would next send us out on our hands and knees, hand-sifting through the pine needles if we had to!—or at least threaten as much, like most bosses would.

But he didn't. No, Grayson didn't do much of anything at all when he found out.

That night after supper Quinn got to thinking aloud about it . . . eleven beeves times a decent market value would bring a pleasant little bonus to a man—especially one left on his honor by absentee owners who only visited but once a year. But we sure weren't in the position to be accusatory.

Quinn pushed away from the table and put on his hat and barn jacket. "Maybe with these new owners, things'll change." Without another word, he walked outside.

I ran the water for dishes and started to put away the leftovers. On the kitchen floor, near the mud room door, I spotted a square of papers that must have fallen from Quinn's coat pocket. I unfolded it, revealing two more lot receipts from the County Clerk, one dated the first of this month and the other from last month. Not knowing what to make of it, I refolded the papers, staying as true as possible to the original crease order, then placed the square back on the floor where I found it.

It wasn't like Quinn to keep secrets from me, and I wondered about the change. I looked out the kitchen window. Whatever secrets he had, Quinn didn't look like he was of the mood to be sharing them. In spite of the fourteen-year age gap between us, I, being the younger, had always been quick to pick up on his ways. But right then, I was suddenly struck by how much older he looked. And tired.

And lost. He stood near the springhouse, chewing on a willow twig, his coat collar turned up against the wind, his gaze fixed to a point out over the ridge somewhere. And there he stayed, pondering and staring, well into the evening.

·⁖· 𝇋 ⋌⋋ ·⁖·

With the changeover in ownership we shipped early that fall. Next came the equipment auction. The new owners were there, along with their families, gabbing and grinning like it was a Sunday ice cream social. But it wasn't, least not to us. By the time it was over, the ranch was rid of a lot of junk and some good equipment, including most of the horses. Only four horses remained on the ranch.

It could have been five. Prior to entering the ring with the young sorrel gelding I had been using all summer, one of the new ranch owners, Kent Ellsworth, assured me he would bid enough to keep the horse for our continued company use. But as the bids crept higher, I slowly realized that gelding and I were on our final ride together.

"Sold!" The auctioneer's gavel hit the block with such finality that it made my heart sink.

We trotted out of the ring and I immediately stripped my saddle from the gelding's back. I gave him a couple of pats on the neck and told him he was in someone else's care now.

Ellsworth came up and put his hand on my shoulder. I couldn't bring myself to look him in the eye.

"Sorry about that," he said. "The bidding just went too high. *Surprisingly* high."

I nodded my appreciation and my agreement. "It was my fault. I shouldn't have ridden him in. When a man sees a female on a horse, he assumes the horse must be all gentled out—sorry to say, you're not the only one in for a surprise."

I took my tack back to the rail and unbuckled my chinks, my eyes burning with tears that I refused to let flow. That gelding was still green, but he had all the makings of a fine company cowpony. Caid told me the man with the winning bid bought the horse for his young daughter, a Denver girl who was just learning how to ride. I shook my head. The gelding would leave all this wide open and be spending his days penned up in a boarding stall somewhere, never to see cattle again.

Quinn walked up and handed me a Styrofoam cup of steaming coffee mixed with just the right amount of cream and sugar. "You look pale. You feelin' all right?"

I assured him I was. Secretly, I felt a little light-headed.

"I think she's standing up pretty good, considering she just got her horse sold out from under her," said Caid. "Think they'll keep us on?"

"They actin' friendly enough," Quinn replied. "But likely, they got their own crew sittin' up the road a piece, just out of sight somewhere. Revving up their engines."

·∗· ⚑ 🐎 ·∗·

Several weeks before Christmas, Quinn and I were putting up the new ranch sign near the highway. The Circle Bar Vee was no more. It was now Ellsworth Land and Cattle Company.

Grayson's voice suddenly blasted over the truck radio. "In case anyone cares, you are all on Ellsworth payroll as of seven o'clock this morning." The high-powered mike at home base clicked off.

Then it clicked back on. World-weary came Grayson's words. "Someone tell the girl she's expected to earn her wages, same as you boys."

Quinn threw his hat up in the air. Laughing, we hugged and did a little jig, dancing on the frozen prairie. Having that extra paycheck couldn't have come at a better time. Quinn didn't know it yet, but after trying hard for seven years and eventually giving up during the last several, I was fairly certain I was now two months pregnant with our first child.

I ran over to the truck and grabbed the mike from the dashboard. "Wo-wee!"

The ranch radio resounded with Caid's return version of my victory howl.

H.R. Willie keyed down on the cook shack radio. "We're still a crew! Good Lord, please see fit to bless this damned ragged outfit! Amen."

As the months passed, it seemed like the Lord was watching over us pretty good. Things were going along real smooth. The cows had wintered good and the calves were coming along just fine—a little early, but otherwise fine. There were only two things troubling us mortals on the ranch: The cattle market was starting to nose dive, and Grayson's wife had left him.

"Look at it this way," Caid said one day. "We lost us a boss, but H.R. Willie's gained him a drinking pardner."

We would've laughed, had it not been so true.

Not long after that came the shocker. During one of his better drunks, Grayson got to talking to the Reverend, and that eleven head of missing steers eventually come up. That's when he admitted to the Reverend how, for thirty years, he had "taken a little off the top" for himself, standing by his own twisted reasoning, figuring he had somehow earned the right to be dishonest because he had earned the owners' trust.

We kept silent about it. And I guess you could say that, in the end, we all got what we deserved.

It was the Ides of March, the kind of Spring day that was trying hard to get warm enough to melt off the spotty patches of snow, overcast and blowing. I had just finished painting the walls of the baby's room.

And for all I know, Grayson's last words were the panic-stricken ones that come blasting over the ranch radio that morning.

"Fire at Headquarters! Fire at Headquarters! Fire! Fire! Fire!"

By the time I ran from the back door and jumped into my truck, I was rattled by the explosions of the propane tanks at Headquarters, three miles away. A few beats later the fuel tanks exploded in a red-orange ball of flame. Even at that distance the sound was deafening. Trails of thick, black smoke climbed high over the range and the wild Chinook winds swiftly took them toward the mountains. I stared out the windshield in sheer and utter disbelief.

The truck mike was in my hand. "Quinn? Quinn!"

Quinn was in the company truck, coming back from checking cows in a pasture behind our house. His voice was even and dead-like. "I see it."

Caid and H.R. Willie had seen it, too. They were out feeding, pitching hay from the old flatbed. Caid keyed down on the microphone of the feed truck and slowly voiced his disbelief. "Oh. My. God."

No one knows for sure exactly how it happened, but they say the fire started in the calving barn. A carelessly tossed cigarette was to blame. Disturbing, considering Grayson had given up cigars for cigarettes around the same time he'd given up water for whiskey.

By late afternoon, the fire trucks rolled up their hoses and pulled out, quietly followed by the ambulance, which carried Grayson's remains.

The four of us, soot-covered from head to toe, stood alone in the ranch yard, feeling like orphans amid the smoldering, blackened ruins of what was once one of the county's grandest ranches. Oh, how we had fought to save her, but the wind proved too strong. All that stood intact was the main house windmill. With each rotation of the blades, the sucker rod would rise and fall, sending out an eerie and soulful moan.

Tears cut a clean path down the chubby, smoke-stained cheeks of H.R. Willie as he surveyed the ruins of the bunkhouse. "You know, that preacher's certificate wasn't worth the ink used to print it. But dammit, it was all I had."

"It was only paper," said Quinn.

"That's right," added Caid. "You'll always be the Honorable Reverend Willie to us."

The baby moved in my swollen belly, and I wondered where any of us would be by late June, that being my expected due date. Quinn must have read my worry. He tightened his hold on me and gave my belly a few gentle pats.

I think it was H.R. Willie said there were so many townspeople went to Grayson's funeral that all three flower shops within a hundred mile radius ran clean out of fresh flowers. Town folk never knew the dark side of Grayson that we did.

The owners flew in to pay their respects. Afterwards, they kept all of us on until the cleanup was completed. Seems they needed a tax write-off a lot more than they needed ranch hands.

We were handed our last paycheck on the first of July, in exchange for the promise we'd be moved out of the company housing by the tenth.

Figuring we were all due a break, we cashed our checks and drove the ninety miles to Laramie to the Fourth of July celebration. Quinn knew I didn't mind going that distance in my overdue state, for being there would only put us that much closer to the hospital of my choice in case of delivery.

The main song act that night was Michael Martin Murphey. For a crew that loved cowboy tunes, we weren't much able to draw ourselves into the spirit.

Then, midway through his act, Murphey looked around the crowd and asked, "How many ranch hands in the audience tonight?"

There's no way Murphey could ever have known how hard those words struck us. As the ranch hands in attendance all around the stadium started whooping, whistling, and raising and waving their hands, Caid looked at Quinn, Quinn looked at the Reverend, the Reverend looked at me, and not a one of us was certain if we had a right to include ourselves.

"Quinn," asked Caid, leaning a look past the Reverend. "If we've been fired and got no outfit to go to, does that mean we ain't ranch hands no more?"

Quinn sat silent for a long moment. "Guess we ain't."

The next morning it was business as usual, and I resumed packing. In looking back on my years of marriage to Quinn, I had packed all the boxes I had ever cared to pack. Usually, just the sight of them could wear me out. But that morning I felt so rested and full of energy that I had the last box packed hours ahead of schedule. With nothing left to do I decided to drive up to what I called my "special spot," located on a hill about ten miles from the ranch. Quinn had left early that morning to go check on another ranch job. Afterwards he said he would be at what was left of headquarters, helping H.R. Willie and Caid take down the big tent, which stood in place of the bunkhouse ever since the fire. I left Quinn a note on the kitchen counter, letting him know where I went so he wouldn't worry.

Before leaving the house I took one last look at what would have been the baby's room. The fresh coat of pale yellow paint I had applied to the walls months earlier suddenly struck me as being overly bright and joyous. I pulled the door shut, put on my hat, and left.

What I didn't realize, until much later, is that the note I left might appear strange. Especially if Quinn was never aware that I had often visited that particular piece of land in times of crisis. Everyone has a special spot, a quiet place where they can go to recharge spiritually and mentally. Mine, however, was slightly out of the ordinary. I didn't plan it that way, it just happened. From the moment I first came across that little cemetery on horseback, I had felt immediately at peace there. The cemetery was located on top of a hill and was well cared for by someone—and I envied him his job. Early on, I had once counted the headstones and memorized the names to the point where they all felt like family to me. There, amid the vast landscape of barbwire fences and sage, stood fifty-seven headstones in a place where the hawks and eagles regularly flew watch. Some might call it a forlorn place, lacking in lush green as it were, but up there I had always felt surrounded by a special reverence. It had always inspired within me a unique connection to the land I never could quite explain, and few would understand.

Twenty minutes after arriving, however, I realized the impending birth of our baby was evident. My water broke and things were moving along much more quickly than I had anticipated. The pains were growing intense. Driving back to the ranch now would be too risky a prospect. Seeing as the expensive two-way radios had been stripped from all the ranch vehicles by the new owners shortly after the fire, I had no way to call for help.

As a first-time mama, my initial instinct was to panic. But after a few frantic minutes I realized that I had helped hundreds of first-calf heifers with their babies, and panic wasn't going to help me . . . I mean, *us* . . . get anywhere. So I gathered myself together and got down to business, getting as comfortable as I could on the truck seat. A grove of aspens near the cemetery entrance served as my point of concentration during contractions.

Deep into labor, sweat trickled down from my forehead, perspiration soaked my clothes. Needing a cooler focal point, I shut my eyes and thought back to the day we first drove into the Circle Bar Vee. How clearly the image came to me . . . the snow glittering on the sage . . . a clear, blue sky above . . . the crunching of snow beneath my boots . . . Quinn's words escaping from under his heavy mustache, in white puffs on the air as we entered the house at headquarters. . . .

"Ivy!" yelled Quinn, running toward the truck. Caid jumped out from behind the wheel of his red dually, and H.R. Willie trotted close behind. A general commotion erupted when they peered through the open window of my truck.

"Quiet!" I snapped. "Can't you see I'm having a baby here!"

"I *see* that!" Quinn removed his hat and stuffed his long body next to me inside the truck cab. His dark eyes were wild with confusion and excitement.

He ran his hand through my sweat-soaked hair and laughed. "Well, you've shared your good news, so let me share mine. When you're done, we've got a new job to go to! And wait until you see the house!"

A renewed sense of hope washed over me upon hearing the news.

Caid, too young to be comfortable with the natural happenings taking place inside the truck, made some nervous jokes from a respectable distance outside.

In between contractions, Quinn told me more about the new ranch job. It was on a large ranch in the same county, and the position offered more money.

By then H.R. Willie caught his breath and couldn't hold back his tense question any longer. He stuck his head inside and tapped Quinn on the shoulder. "Hey, what are we doing having a baby here? Ain't it bad luck to birth a baby so damn close to the dead?"

Quinn grinned. "This is Ivy's favorite spot."

"How'd you know that?" I wondered, puffing through a contraction.

"Seen you up here a number of times, when I was checking cattle and fixing fences. Even from a distance I could tell this place was special to you."

Caid's face scrunched with confusion. "And you never thought that was weird?"

"Nope. As a matter of fact—" Quinn reached into his front jean pocket and pulled out some papers, the edges well-worn and soiled. The squares were immediately familiar to me.

Quinn pressed the papers in my palm and closed my fingers around the wad. "We can't ranch it, but we own all of Lot M here," he said. "All eight burial plots in it—ev'ry one of 'em, ours. That way, next time you come up here, you'll have a place to sit. And *nobody* can ever kick you off."

"Lot M?" Tears streamed down my face as I looked at the papers sticking out from my fist. "I want to see it. Take me to Lot M! I need to see it."

Quinn started to argue with me, but I would not hear it. The urge to push was strong.

"Lot M! *Now!*" I demanded.

H.R. Willie and Caid, who were as bewildered by my order as Quinn, cleared the way as Quinn carried me through the sagebrush and past the cemetery's tall, white iron entrance gate. Once inside, H.R. Willie grabbed Caid by the shirtsleeve and pleaded with him to participate in a spur of the moment ritual of ridding the grounds of possible evil spirits.

Caid abandoned the Reverend for a better idea. He turned on his heels and ran back to his truck, returning with the brand new fleece seat cover, which he had hastily cut free from the bench seat of his truck cab. He offered it to Quinn.

Quinn nodded his thanks and hurriedly spread it out over the vacant and bare prairie plot. He shrugged, somewhat uncomfortable with what was about to happen, yet fully aware there was nothing anyone could do to stop it from happening.

Resting upon the first bit of earth that was truly ours, I felt at home, and not even the pangs of labor could take away my smile. From Lot M, I could look down upon the country I had traveled on horseback during the past calving season through fall gather. From there I could clearly see every winding stream and tangle of willows, and every lush hay meadow amid the patchwork of fences and pastures. Best of all, Lot M was on the outer edge of the cemetery, and faced west. The unobstructed view would provide a spectacular vantage point of the many mountain sunsets yet to come.

H.R. Willie made for a fine back support. I bent my knees and *buried* my boot heels deep into the ground.

The baby's first wail came upon the cry of a hawk circling above. After cutting the umbilical cord with his pocketknife, Quinn wiped the baby clean and wrapped his work shirt around it as Caid counted fingers and toes. The baby, of good size and weight, looked so tiny within Quinn's muscular arms.

At that moment Quinn looked twenty years younger, and prouder and happier than I could ever have imagined. After clearing his throat of emotion, Quinn spoke.

"Boys," he said, beaming. "It's my pleasure to introduce Dillon Joseph McKinnon—the first McKinnon ever born in a cemetery, I do believe."

After a few whoops and hollers, H.R. Willie led us in a proper prayer of appreciation.

On that July 5th, from Lot M, the world once again was perfect and full of promise.

As I held my son for the first time, I thought more about the house and the ranch we would be moving to. If they would allow us to paint, I wanted the walls in Dillon's room to be sky blue with some puffy clouds above a jagged range of snow-capped mountains all around.

Quinn sat down beside me and explained how our new boss said his ranch is legally locked up on paper to stay ranching property.

"For as long until our new boss's great, great grandchildren decide otherwise," Quinn confirmed. "And even then, it would take a unanimous vote for them to bail and sell."

Gazing deeply into the newborn cloudiness of Dillon's eyes, I couldn't help but think about the new outfit and its owners. I would bet, even somewhere off in the third millennium, if ever it came down to selling, there'd be at least one child among them who'd hold out his vote—and that's all it would take is one—just one blessed believer among them who's figured the worth to this lifestyle and seen the gambles of this business as a challenge worth the taking, a tradition worth the hanging on.

But to keep it going, the owners would need someone who is willing to bet his sweat on another man's dream, someone who is proud to wear upon his boot heels the crusted soil of another man's land. By God, they would need a ranch hand. . . . Maybe two.

TAYLOR FOGARTY has worked on various ranches in Texas, Wyoming, and Colorado as a ranch hand, both full and part-time. She and her husband of twenty-one years have worked on sheep ranches, guest ranches, as well as steer and cow-calf operations. Taylor's ranching experience includes working with horses, calving, lambing, foaling, fencing, irrigating, and haying, as well as cooking and taking part in many ranch improvement and restoration projects. For the past eight years Taylor has worked on a large cattle ranch in North Park, Colorado, on which she and her family reside year around. She is also the founder and publisher of *American Western Magazine—ReadTheWest.com,* a monthly online magazine that celebrates and promotes the traditions, culture, art, music, films, and literature of the American West.

Cowboys Fly

J. P. S. BROWN

I loved that ranching, but one day discovered I just could not get along with the head rancher of all time, my old Pappy. He was the genius who taught me to cowboy so that I had become certain that some day I would discover that cowboys could fly. However, old Pappy kept me home too much and penned too long. He wouldn't allow much of that flying on his ranch, nor would he allow any of his youngsters to sally from the nest to try their wings without a fight.

So, I blew up and joined the Marine Corps, then saw I might make a good place for myself there and quit thinking I'd ever cowboy again, much less graduate into old age as a full blown cattleman. My job in the Marines was a lot like cowboying. I started out as a colt that got trained, then was used a lot until I became a veteran, then became a trainer of the colts myself. I worked with a herd, only this herd didn't scatter or try to get away. This herd could understand English in low or harsh tones, even responded to arm and hand signals and answered the telephone. This herd didn't run over me, or hook me with its horns, blow snot on me, kick me, or ruin my paycheck when it fell down dead.

Even though I was afoot all the time, I figured I was doing just right. Hell, I wasn't the only one afoot. Nobody else had a horse to ride. In fact, every Marine was *happy* to pack everything he and five other men needed and do the work of both horse and rider all day.

What a lie that was. I'd been a cowboy all my life and was a darned good horseman and that wasn't a thing like being a packhorse. I'd been taught racehorses don't run with mules. Not only that, I was supposed to know the difference between a soldier and a cowboy, because cowboying was in my blood on both sides. My mother's and father's people had been horsemen and cowmen clear on back before any of them came to this continent. I'd read that back in the old country some of them wore metal suits and rode down the faggot gatherers just to get firewood for their camp. I couldn't get away from it. My Pappy knew that. All my folks knew it. My Pappy had never in his entire life lined out to go more than ten yards afoot.

I'd been back from overseas a year and was training colt Marines near Bridgeport, California, a bad place for a cowboy to be stationed if he wants to stay in the Marine Corps. That's cow country and some great cowboy playgrounds like Reno, Tahoe, and Bishop are right close. I could wear my boots and hat when I went on liberty. I could rodeo and visit with other cowpunchers on the weekends and on leave. On Sundays, on my way back to the base from liberty, more and more, I began to look way off over the fences. Every single time I did that I saw somebody pushing a little bunch of cows up a draw, smelled the puredy cow whether I was downwind or not, and missed being in their dust.

That little glimmer in the back of my mind that told me cowboys could fly began to grow. My heart warmed to it again and I began to hope I might possibly prove my theory that someday every cowboy took that quantum leap and never had to come down unless he wanted to.

When I had gone in the Service I had been as earthbound as any fledgling could be. Then after I began to serve seriously as a Marine, something of that state of being afoot and disgusted by it snapped and I gave my soul to God, and my butt to the Marines, as ordered. In fact, I gave myself up for dead. As a Marine, I was given to know almost absolutely for sure that the God who had given me body and soul and all the little glimmers of hopes, knowledges, and loves that went with it, in all probability would at any moment take it all back. Now, I began to hope that I would have a life of my own as a cowboy again and the ways a man could soar at that were unlimited.

I had one month before I came up for reenlistment after my first hitch as a Marine and I'd even sort of promised my commanding officer that I would reenlist, when my Pappy called me. The first thing out of his mouth? "How much longer you gonna be held up there with them Marines?"

I was so glad to hear from him after four years that I sure didn't think it was a good idea to wave another red flag in front of him, that red flag being the Marine Corps, the last red flag I'd waved in front of him when I'd left home. So, I said kind of under my breath, "Maybe a month or so."

"What's that? How long?"

"A month."

"Well, that suits me, because we'll have steers coming out our ears in a month."

That was it for me and the Marine Corps. I have to tell you, during that last month, I was so anxious to be turned out, I almost forgot everything they'd taught me about duty. If anybody had changed his mind and said I had to stay one minute over one more month, I would have gone AWOL. Cowboying was all I'd ever wanted when I joined the service, all I'd hoped for down in my heart while I was rode and packed as a Marine, and all I've ever wanted since. Hell, it's all I want now that I'm in my seventy-year-old geezerhood.

I'd been active as a Marine, but now it was time to get busy. I flew to El Paso to receive fourteen thousand steers from the Terrazas family and Alejandro Prieto of Chihuahua, weighed them, paid for them, then cut them, and shipped them to eight different destinations stateside. That was during my first three days out of the Service. In fact, I'd broken my ankle a week before I was discharged and Pappy put me to work so quick, I didn't even have a chance to unpack and change clothes. I went down to cut cattle in the alleys of the stockyards with crutches in both hands and that first evening when I was finally through, I looked down and I still had my dress greens on. Still wore my barracks hat.

Even my very raiment had been joyously transformed by cattle again. Only a semblance of the mirror gleam of my spit shine could be seen through the dust and manure on my shoes. The splatters of manure on my trousers and blouse exactly color-matched the Marine green and therefore were practically invisible and totally tolerated. When I found myself that day about to take off that uniform that had never in its entire history even known a smudge, I knew, sure as goodness is in the air of Texas corrals, that I was only one alley away, one more corral, or only one horse to mount and one canyon trail to follow, from flying.

Thousands of cattle crossed into the United States out of Mexico each day. In those days the El Paso Del Norte Hotel was where all cattlemen stayed and did their business while in town. Ranchers and feedlot owners who were there to buy, speculator-traders who bought and sold the same day for a profit of $1 dollar a hundredweight, cowboys who received, weighed, and shipped cattle for the traders, and a whole lot of their wives, children, and girlfriends poured in and out of the lobby of that hotel.

I swear, when I first walked in with Pappy, I knew everybody there. It took me two hours of hand shaking and *abrazos,* hugs, before I could even send a bellboy up to our room with my seabag. We went into the bar at midday for dinner, put several tables together, and fifteen people sat down to eat and drink with us. Not only that, but a lot of the people who were there at the beginning left to do business and were replaced with new people. The best thing about it? Everybody there had cattle in their blood, even the bellboys. Everybody was full of stories and none of them were about prices, weights, or margins of profits. They were about theirs and their family's constant endeavor to stay joyfully ahead of the cattle for which they made themselves responsible.

A whole lot of cattle were being crossed, and a whole lot of good business being done. Cattlemen can't ever be happier than when they're moving cattle, because when cattle move, cattlemen earn their daily bread, or at least they are given the prospects of a payday.

I could not have had a sweeter homecoming. I'd been staying in cattleman hotels like the Del Norte, the Adams Hotel in Phoenix, the Gadsden in Douglas, the Santa Rita in Tucson, and the Montezuma in Nogales with my folks since I was born and all the same folks that I'd met there were still there. Steak and eggs and cold beer never tasted better any time in my life than it did that day, and I knew it would keep tasting better and the company would always be good.

And another thing, I'd liked those places, but never really appreciated them, because I'd been kept haltered as a youngster. I'd been there to work in the stockyards and about all I'd liked about town was the picture show, the pulp magazines, and the hamburgers and milk shakes. I'd not appreciated the hotels much, except as places to eat and sleep and have conversations with old folks in the lobby. I sure did now. I'd just been turned out and was as juiced up as a race horse who'd been trained on hot feed and kept in the same pen for four years and I darned sure knew what to do when a girl promenaded through that lobby and gave me the eye.

For the first time in my life, I was given a good taste of that trading life. I just flat came alive, and believe you me, I had the stamina for the all-day work and the all-night play. I discovered I had another full-blown cowboy talent and that was how not to pull up for work in the day, or stop that running and playing at night with my own kind. Believe me, it was no life for anybody who got drunk, sick, or tired easy. The more cattle I could look at and run by me in the day and the more prancy, two-legged, long-legged things I could run with at night, the better I liked it.

I made some awful good girlfriends, too, because I worked just as hard in the springs where the humans watered and danced at night as I did the stock pens during the day. I ran those girls By and In, culling them By and keeping them In, and there were plenty to pick from. After awhile, though, I kind of settled on three special ones. The funny part of that was, two of them were named Darlene. One of the Darlenes was an airline stewardess, so her schedule just fit in when the other Darlene and I could not get together, so those two worked out just right. The third lady had come down with her father to buy a bunch of cattle they wanted to put out on Northern California grass, so she kind of had the same kind of schedule as me. The best part of that, we saw a lot of each other while we worked during the day, so we got to eat together and party a little in Juarez on our way back from the pens at night. The longer I ran with those girls, however, the more complicated the juggling act I performed to keep them apart. I managed it though and didn't get caught and didn't hurt anybody's feelings. I was starting to strain at it, though and I began to kind of drag my feet because the more fun the girls had, the less fun it was for me. When the time came for Pappy and me to leave with the herd he wanted to keep for himself, I was ready. I could see the By and In girls were about to collide with me inside the mill.

That year, in payment for the work I did for him in El Paso, Pappy staked me to 250 head of steers. I didn't like that way to get paid, but it was the way Pappy always did me. He liked to work me hard and pay me in steers. Then, when it came time to sell the steers, he'd get the money for them and put it into another bunch of steers for me. If the steers made money, another bunch of the same number of steers were bought and the profit put away for me in some kind of very nebulous account and I kept working for him. If the steers lost money, after a vigorous accounting, I was told how much I owed Pappy and made to sign an IOU and to keep working. Then one day, he would make me sit down for a clean-up accounting and I would be shown that the amount the one bunch of cattle had made was not enough to pay back the amount the other bunch had lost and I would have to sign another IOU.

I had not minded his accounting methods for a long time, but that was one of the reasons I left him to join the Corps. Now, he sent 1,031 steers to the Mesa Redonda ranch at Concho, Arizona, and put me out in a camp to look after them, because he knew how much it suited me, knew I would stay. The longer I could stay out with a herd, the more I wanted to. My 250 head were part of that bunch and I made daily circles on the cattle. I saw every one of them at least once a week and my horse tracks never went dim on any corner of that ranch. Under the two hundred days of my care, the cattle gained 365 pounds apiece. Any time young cattle who have just been weaned off their mammies are shipped as far as those were, to country that is different from their birthplace, cattlemen can expect a minimum of a six percent death loss. We only lost six head, but not one to sickness. Lightning killed the first one and in that way went the rest, by the sure hand of God.

During those two hundred days I broke eight two-year-old colts for my Pappy. They were good foundation quarter horses from a great Texas herd owned by Buck Pyle. Pappy gave me my pick of the colts for breaking them. On the first day when I unloaded them off a boxcar and drove them down the highway to the ranch, I picked the horse I wanted by the sure and straight way he stepped upon the ground. I could tell there was nothing permanent about the way his hooves touched the ground. Horses' hooves are slick enough, but that colt's feet did not adhere to the ground in any way. Before I ever mounted him, I knew that he would be my top horse of all time. I named him Pajaro, because I was certain he would one day be the Bird who flew with a cowboy.

The name Pajaro fit him for another reason. He had the most awful roman beak anybody ever saw on a horse. He had a wonderfully typy little short quarter horse head with big round jaws that flared, pin ears, and a tiny, delicate muzzle. He was the color of a red ant and when he was worked and fed well and all his hair shed down in a warm climate, every other little hair on his hide glinted and glimmered pure gold. His mane was fine as lace, but each hair strong as catgut. His chest and rump were wide and shiny-muscled, his back was short and his barrel round, but his withers were right to hold a man's saddle in place for any kind of work. His walk was a wonderful kind of foxtrot that covered ground like tapping for a dance, and from sixty yards off a standing start I was sure he could outrun anything that used four legs on any kind of ground and could stop and turn his face into his own tail to go the other way. He had everything that any cowpuncher could ever look for in a top horse, the kind of horse anybody would keep until his dying day, but you had to look out. If you weren't ready for it and he turned his profile to you when you didn't expect it, the sight could make your heart stop.

At the end of that season at the Mesa Redonda me and Pappy sold those cattle, traded two months in El Paso again, and shipped three thousand to be turned out on alfalfa and barley pasture at Brawley in Imperial Valley, California. Of those three thousand cattle, 250 were mine, again.

This time, I decided not to hang right with Pappy and go to another ranch. After six months by myself on the Mesa Redonda, I was full of juice again. I called the man in Brawley who would be paid for the care of our cattle and hired on to cowboy. Those cattle would pasture on green feed for one hundred days, then be turned out on sugar beet tops for another hundred. I'd get to do what I liked to do most and earn a good paycheck, because the company that furnished the care paid $100 a week. That was at a time when cowboys out on ranches earned $100 a month. I'd also be right close to town where all the good springs were easily found and ladies watered.

As a cowboy I was smooth again. A whole lot of cowboying is athletics that involves timing, reflexes, and observation at a run in the open field. I figured I was ready for anything, but I really had no idea of the pace or the volume of work that I was in for. I found out quick that a ditch bank cowboy in Imperial Valley saw more cattle, turned back more cattle, saw more sicks, roped more, and did more of everything else that had to be done with cattle horseback in one day than a ranch cowboy did in six months.

I was lucky, because I threw in with a forty-five-year-old cowboy named Tom Ford. He'd been born and raised on the Matadors near his birthplace in Vega, Texas. His first ten years as a cowboy had been on the Mats and he'd left there in his thirties as a top hand.

Tom was as much a genius as any Einstein and right quick I saw, if I was to catch up and make a hand at the pace and volume of work on the ditch banks, I had to keep him in sight. I learned by watching, for nobody had time to tell me what to do. On a ranch a cowboy walks his horse out and turns one back into the herd with a lot of space and time to help him. Beside the irrigation ditches, every time he turns one he multiplies it by the thousands that hurry right in behind him and snort on his tail.

Tom could put me in the right place at the right time with a look from across the herd without making a sign or a sound. Every man on the crew knew the cowpuncher-horseman axioms and rules, but Tom fearlessly invented new ones as they were needed. He also made sure he learned something new and vital to cow work every day as geniuses like Einstein do. He rode good horses and they were geniuses, too.

I had never learned that cowboying was work. To the men in my family it was life and you were either given to love it with all your heart from the first step you took in boots or barefoot, or you were not. It was born in you, or it was not. It was your life lived naturally, or a job of work that made you tired, but not both. In those days I bragged that I'd never been drunk, sick, or tired. It didn't matter how full of whiskey I was, how sleepy or germ-ridden, if it was time to cowboy I got ready and shed it all. The worst thing that could ever happen to me was to be left behind when there was cowboying to do. I was never any better at being left behind when I reached the age of seventy, than I was when I was a three-year-old.

When I got to Brawley that year I was no different than any youngster who leaves his place on a ranch to rodeo. Youngsters leave when they're full of juice because they don't want to be stuck way out with no audience, no background music, and no ticket sales ALL THE TIME right when their skills are the sharpest, they make the most dashing picture, and they want most to show off for the girls.

Most cowpunchers don't of their free will go looking for old cows to take care of out by themselves on ranches forever until they are ready to settle down. That is usually long after they have been forced to admit that horses and cattle are slower than they used to be when they were young and full of juice. Slower? Sure. Cattle and horses get slower when a cowpuncher gets older. How else do you explain the reason he doesn't get run over, kicked, outrun, blown all over with slobbers, hooked, and bucked off the way he did when he was young?

The same siren that calls a cowboy to the excitement of performance in rodeo had even more of an appeal for me there in that Imperial Valley. There was enough cowboying stacked up there for a thousand top hand cowboys, and more than enough for any top hand to keep getting better. The best part of that job in Brawley was, I saw the same kind of action fifteen hours of every day, seven days a week as rodeo cowboys saw a few seconds a day for three days a week. I was horseback with cows in front of me and having the same fun every hour of the light of day and some at night.

We worked seven days a week 3 to 11. A lot of that time was 3 in the morning until 11 that night. We didn't get very close to the springs where girls watered, but were given no time to worry about it, either.

For recreation, we invited wives and girlfriends to come to our corrals with potato salad, filled a tub with ice and beer, built a fire, roped a trainload of bulls by the head and heels to castrate them, then roasted and ate their oysters with the beer. Then on lean but full stomachs we all moved the cattle out in separate bunches of 250 head to fields of alfalfa and barley, or sugar beets.

We moved cattle miles past wet lettuce, cabbage, and carrot fields, used the paved roads and stopped traffic, threw them into pastures fenced by one strand of barbwire that was kept hot by car batteries beside freeways, malls, and private homes. We found out quickly what happened if we did not get in the right place at the right time to keep cattle together. In one beat of a heart, a spilled herd could make a lot of bad tracks on a wet lettuce field. Every track hurt hearts and pocketbooks, a lot. The sound of a hoof on a cabbage head was like all the other sounds of sure death.

In spite of the awful characteristic of Pajaro's visage, a characteristic that I even now hate to tell about, a characteristic that made me as defensive about my horse as I would have been about myself had I been born with a beak so bent, I had made up my mind that I would make Pajaro into the greatest horse any cowboy ever rode. I loved that horse. I worried about him when I was away from him. He was also my most valuable material possession, and I was never separated from him except on his days of rest when he was safe with good feed in the corral. Before I left Imperial Valley he became a good rope and cutting horse, a quiet horse around a herd. I used him for everything. He was so darned handsome, I even used him to woo the girls. I gave him away to every new girl I found hard to bluff, so that was every girl who would run with me. That always inspired unconditional surrender. Usually a girl, knowing how stuck I was on the horse, or just because she was too darned mad at me, would not demand that I hand him over when she'd had enough of me. However, one time I had to load him and haul him away and hide him in the middle of the night from a darned little old thing that I think had run with me awhile just to get my horse.

That job on the ditch banks was over after two hundred days and nights. It had been hard, but so was graduate work at Oxford under Albert Einstein. If you survived it, you were better and would always know how to keep getting better at your work.

Pajaro and I pulled out for Sonora, Mexico to buy *corriente* cattle. In those days, a heavy Mexican Customs duty on geldings made it prohibitive to take them into Mexico, but breeding stock could be taken in free. Pajaro had given up his stones when I broke him on the Mesa Redonda, but he was so good-looking I was used to bluffing livestock and folks with him, so I tried again. I obtained a permit to cross a stud, and at the inspection station no one thought to look for the credentials he should have been carrying between his legs that qualified him as one. I drove away from there with Pajaro up in the back of my pickup in the most extreme bliss of temporal glory anyone can enjoy in this life, on my way to cowboy in the country where *la vaquereada* was invented.

I was only hitting the ground now and then when I touched down in the town of Navojoa and stopped at a watering place for cowmen. The first tall *vaquero* I met said he raised *corrientes* in the Sierra Madre of Chihuahua. His name was Rafael Russo and he had just come down over the trail with a herd of young bulls that were resting in San Bernardo, at the foot of the mountains. They were for sale and I could go look at them the next day.

Carnaval was underway in Navojoa. That's like Mardi Gras, the week of party before Lent begins. Russo had been in his dry, brushy mountains six months and he was thirsty for fun. Cars could not get within one hundred miles of his ranch. If he wanted beer, he had to pack it in on mules. He had worked cattle horseback every day for the past six months. He was trying to dam up and drink everything that tried to run by him. I threw right in with him, even though he was way ahead in the jubilation. I was in the prime-your-engine stage and he did not mind it at all that his engine was about to flood out. He was also having an awful good time with the things he said to me. I began to smart under what I perceived as near-insults. To distract him, I told him I needed to feed and water my horse. When he heard that I had an *Esteeldos,* Steeldust, horse out in my truck, he and his seven vaqueros surged outside to look at him.

I climbed up on the back of my pickup and untied Pajaro, then opened the gate and backed him out. I watched Russo as the horse stepped away from the truck. Appreciation for all the great traits of my horse put a shine on his face. He had been loud in his near insults to me, the *Gringo*. They had not quite been full-fledged insults, so I had not frappéd him. I waited for him to have a good look at Pajaro's profile and insult him, so I could frappé him. I turned Pajaro this way. I turned him that way. Russo had not said a word since his first sight of my horse. I couldn't understand it. He now was being given a good chance to see and insult me about Pajaro's awful profile. I turned the horse's head so the man could see it from every angle. Finally, he looked up at the right time for the full impact of the awful sight to land on him, but he took only a very brief note of it. I was confounded. Russo's eyes flickered with only enough of a tiny amount of pain to tell me that he had taken note of Pajaro's roman nose and he did not say one word about it. Neither did any of his vaqueros. That day the man became my friend and partner for forty years and he never once mentioned Pajaro's awful profile and neither did any vaquero of the region who ever worked with us.

The next day Russo and I began our association in cattle. A week later we rode into the Sierra Madre together and he began to share his genius with me. He had been born in the Sierra, had strapped his spurs on his naked heels and worn huaraches all his life. He knew the term for every weed, grass, and clump of brush, knew the use of every tree. If a tree was no good for lumber, or did not own roots, or leaves that would cure an ailment, it was good for *sombra,* shade. He always mentioned a tree's goodness for its shade, even if it did not have any other use, even if it was poor for firewood. He knew the centuries-old names of every canyon, trail, and spring that were too small, or too hidden to be shown on any map, and he took the time to share his genius in these vaquero ways with me.

One summer day he we were on a high trail above a place called *Arroyo Hondo* and he stepped off his horse and picked a fern off the ground, handed it to me to crush between my fingers and told me it was *anis.* The juicy debris of the crushed stem smelled strongly of licorice. The Sierra was rich in treats like that, and he knew them all.

About a year later, Russo and I were on our way into the Sierra to buy cattle for the third time. As we rode into a canyon called *El Cajon de la Virgen,* Russo moved ahead of me, because he wanted me to be able look around and appreciate the place again. The canyon was so narrow in places that only one horseman could pass, the bends in the trail sharp and blind, the walls one hundred feet high and black as obsidian. We stopped in the place where strong water gushed straight up out of the bottom of the canyon in the *cajon,* or box, where the cattle we drove out of the mountains could be held and watered, a place considered sacred by everyone in the Sierra. We dismounted for a drink and squatted to mix water in our cups with *pinole,* a paste vaqueros make of cornmeal and brown sugar for a collation on the trail. Pajaro drank a few sips of water and then turned his head toward me with bright drops of it shining on his whiskers. He did not raise his head, he only turned it off the water and looked at me with his eyes at my level and sighed and I realized that we had long since taken flight. His sigh caused my next breath to shudder right down into the deepest corner of my soul. Joe Brecker and his horse were on the wing, and had been for a long time. How else could we explain being where we were and on our way to places we already knew well called *Los Mezcales, Ojo de Agua, Las Animas, Guasisaco, Gilaremos, Gausaremos, Tepochici?* How else could we have come so far, so effortlessly?

J. P. S. BROWN has spent all but three of his seventy-one years cowboying in the United States and Mexico. His first novel, *Jim Kane,* became the movie *Pocket Money,* with Paul Newman and Lee Marvin. In 1999 the Will James Society gave him the Big Enough Award for achievement as a writer in the cowboy tradition. He makes his home in Arizona.

Guiding Light

WILLARD HOLLOPETER

"Looks like we're gonna spend Christmas in the hills," Shorty said, as he put a chunk of wood in the stove, which was struggling mightily to drive the night chill from the cabin. Christmas came tomorrow and the boys had planned on going down to the ranch headquarters for a genuine honest-to-goodness woman-cooked Christmas dinner with all the trimmin's. But the wind rattling the windowpanes and what snowdrifts they could see in the first light of advancing dawn told them that the storm was just getting up a good head so it could really turn loose and they likely wouldn't be having Christmas dinner anywhere; they'd be out hunting cows.

They had sat and talked far into the night, trying to get a grip on some understanding that a man could hang onto. Being in a line camp in the dead of winter, they were so to hell and gone far from the beaten path that they would be the only ones to see that winter can do that to a fellow, get him to trying to figure out just exactly why he's here and where he is going.

"Been married?" Shorty had asked.

"Naw, you?"

"Yeah, not for six or seven years."

"Got any kids?"

"Two; haven't seen them for quite a spell. I know they are all right though, she's a good mother, got purty churchy. I s'pose that's the biggest reason why we split up, kept wantin' me to go, too. She's too good a woman for a man like me."

Slim was some younger than Shorty and surely needing to dally up some comprehending.

"My mother used to tell me about the reason for Christmas, s'pose there's anything to it?"

"Don't know, seems kinda far-fetched; a star leadin' some shepherds across the desert right to the door of a stable to see a baby."

"Ma shore made it sound convincin', way she told it, but it's easier to believe somethin' like that when you're a kid. Anyway that would be some kinda miracle."

The boys hadn't gotten any closer to getting a handle on things that night but Shorty had lain awake thinking most of the rest of it. He went out into the morning storm to give the horses a bait of grain while Slim cooked up some biscuits and steak for breakfast, then they rode out to hunt storm-drifted cattle.

They rode all that day, driving scattered bunches down into the willow brakes along the river, coming back to camp to change horses. The blizzard increased in fury as darkness caught them that Christmas Eve, miles from the cabin. They were afoot, their horses having played out a ways back; and they were lost.

"Looks like we might not make it back," Slim said.

Then they saw it—a faint light a long ways off, shining through the dark and the snow, growing brighter as they watched. Maybe it was the northern lights. No! Couldn't see no northern lights in a storm like this.

"Don't know what that light is," Shorty said, "but that's all we can see and I reckon that direction is as good as any."

They took dead aim on that unwavering light and walked, floundering through waist-deep snow. They were getting so frazzled that they were beginning to get the notion that the easiest and most sensible thing to do would be to just lay down and rest, when Shorty bumped smack-dab into the cabin door.

WILLARD HOLLOPETER ran a cow/calf operation for many years in the Nebraska Sandhills, "but in an effort to cut down on work, to find time to pursue other interests, to get out of debt, and because I just figure I'm getting to the age where it is time for change, I have sold most of my cows and am leasing my land and taking cattle in to pasture. I've still got my horses though." He writes for the *Midland News* of Valentine, Nebraska, the *Nebraska Fence Post*, and *Cowboy Magazine* and has also had his work in *The Nebraskan, Nebraska Life, Rope Burns,* and *Cattle Country News*. He has one book of poetry, *So Many Winters,* and is a cowboy poet and entertainer on the Nebraska Arts Council touring program. He is an organizer of the Nebraska Cowboy Poetry Gathering and Old West Days in Valentine, Nebraska.

The Violinist's Story

Elaine Long

Sara parked the rented car on the road in front of the motel because dried weeds standing in a pool of dirty water obstructed the driveway. No telling how many pieces of broken beer bottle were hidden under the oily slime on top of the puddle. She slid out from under the steering wheel and stretched. Funny how a rental car never became like your own even if you'd just driven 350 miles.

What made a thing one's own? Some violins she had played fit the curve of her chin, nestled close to her neck, and arched their own necks to her hand—Slim's old fiddle was like that; but other violins stayed stiff, uncomfortable, until she sold them or gave them away.

Anyway, she was stuck with the unyielding rental car for the return trip. There wasn't any other means of getting away from Dust, Colorado. The Interstate was eleven miles back along the misnamed frontage road—the frontage road that didn't front the Interstate, but angled away following the track of the old highway, making a blue-black mark through Dust before becoming a grey streak that went up and down across the rolling prairies and faded into the watery lines of heat mirage on the horizon.

She walked gingerly along the remains of a concrete walk, hating the weeds that poked her legs and clung to her stockings, until she came to Unit Five. She peered through the screen of the unit's lone window, but the window itself was so dirty she couldn't see through it. She knocked on the screen door, then pulled on its handle. It was stuck tight. A tall sow thistle, which had pushed its way between the screen door and the door, had dried there into a cluster of brown knife-shaped leaves with serrated edges. Unit Five was obviously not occupied.

Sara looked around the L-shaped motel. Most of the windows were boarded up; only those on Unit Two had shades at half-mast. She opened the screen door on Unit Two and tapped on the door, but there was no response. She knocked louder, waited a moment, and then started to turn away, but the door opened suddenly.

She turned back and smiled at the old man who stood blinking in the sunlight. His eyes were bloodshot, the lashes and brows grizzled. A skinny arm reached to the door, holding it in defensive position.

Sara said, "I'm sorry to disturb you; I'm looking for Slim Miller. When I was here in August, he lived in Unit Five."

The old man raised his other bony hand and rubbed his left eye. "Slim's been gone all winter."

Sara's heart beat a little faster. "Gone?"

"Yeah. He moved on back over to Mabel's jist after Thanksgivin'."

Sara laughed with relief. "I thought he and Mabel were on the outs."

The old man grinned, showing scraggly teeth that bent inward like the teeth in a wilting jack-o-lantern. "Aw," he said, "you know Mabel. Soon's she figured out that Slim wasn't going to give in, she got to missin' his rent money real bad and come suckin' and cooin' around that old cowboy. Wasn't long 'til she turned his head and snagged him back."

"I'll go over there, then," said Sara. "Thanks."

"You his niece?" the old man asked. "The one he taught to ride and to play the fiddle?"

Sara said, "Yes, I'm Slim's niece. He gave me his old violin and my first lesson when I was seven." Slim had given her more than that old fiddle; he had given her a way to escape from the prairies.

The old man opened the door a little wider and relaxed against the jamb. "He goes on about you a whole lot, like you was a genius or somethin', playin' violin in that concert orchestra and travelin' all over the world."

"Well, if you've known Slim long, you know how he can stretch a story. My father used to say, 'Slim could see a sage hen in moult and convince you it was a peacock.'" The man grinned again, but before he could start reminiscing about other Slim Miller stories, Sara turned away, thanking him over her shoulder.

After forty years, she still remembered the rise of hope she had felt on the days when Slim gave her violin lessons. She had grown up in a cross, crowded world of tired parents, chicken-house dust, and greasy kerosene lamp chimneys. Washing those chimneys was one of her chores; the water was always cold, the soap, a slimy blue film on top of the water. But she hated the chicken smell worse. Her older brother whacked her with his fist when he wanted help cleaning the chicken house and pushed her out of his way when he didn't need her. Her sisters gave her their hand-me-downs, but begrudged her every inch of space she used in the bedroom she shared with them. Her mother was too tired to notice, and her father was a remote force, unapproachable. Slim's music was the only thing she could claim as her own—the only thing that wasn't half worn out when she got it.

Sara left the car parked where it was. Everything in Dust was within walking distance. Dust, Colorado. Sara didn't know who had named the town, but she'd bet it was a woman; a woman married to some raw-boned farmer who, when he spoke at all, spoke only in facts: "Wheat's up in the north field." "Old Brindle's lookin' poorly. She may lose that calf." "Busted the coupling on the harrow again and got to take it into town." Town was Limon or Hugo. Dust was just a joke the woman had told herself to keep from dying of starvation while her plate was heaped with facts.

There had been nothing *but* dust on those prairies for years during the thirties. The good land blew away, and the dust settled in its place, sterile and worthless, choking even the weeds. So the woman called the place Dust, Colorado. Sara didn't think she said it in despair; it was just part of that strange humor that some country women hid behind their tight, weather-beaten faces. But the menfolk took her seriously and also began to call the old place Dust; and when the farm died of dust pneumonia and was buried in dust, the little settlement that hung on there kept the name. Someone put up a sign. "Welcome to Dust. Population, 79."

Sara walked along the frontage road toward the second cross street. Mabel's rooming house was on Second Street. It loomed up two stories high above the little frame houses on either side, its dandelion-yellow paint a gaudy argument against their gray asphalt shingles.

The original owner of the yellow house had built the motel, too. He'd had a few good years renting units to travelers on the old highway; then he rented the motel and the rooms in the house to the road crew that came along when Peter Kiewit and Sons built the Interstate. After the construction workers left, no more travelers came. Finally, the owner sold the house to Mabel's mother, put the motel under the management of Pete Riley at Riley's Bar and Cafe, and moved to Denver. Mabel's mother died, and Mabel, divorced by then, came back home and turned the place into a rooming house. Sara climbed the steps to the porch of the yellow house and knocked on the door, which opened so quickly Sara knew that Mabel had been watching her.

"Whaddya want?" Mabel peered through the screen, her face red and unfriendly above her pink cowboy shirt, which was stuffed into lime-green stockman's pants. Her bleached hair frizzed around her forehead.

"I'm looking for Slim Miller."

"You one of his women?" Mabel asked. Sara knew that Mabel knew that she wasn't one of Slim's women. They'd had perfectly straightforward business conversations three years ago when Slim had caught pneumonia and Sara had paid Mabel to nurse him. Sara ignored the question.

"Is Slim here?" she asked.

"No. He went up to the post office. Leastways, that's where he *said* he was going, but he's probably over at Riley's." Mabel shut the door in her face.

Sara turned and went down the steps. Darn it. She'd hoped to arrive early enough to catch Slim before he'd gone to Riley's. It had been years since she'd seen him when he was totally sober.

She couldn't leave on a six-month tour without making different

arrangements about Slim's money. She needed someone who
would hand his check over right on time, but not too soon. Not
Mabel. Mabel would starve him to death. Probably she ought to
give the money to Pete Riley. Most of it ended up at Riley's anyhow.
Maybe the postmistress. Sara sighed. The postmistress would be
best, but she was such a gossip. Slim, who hated for her to know his
business, delighted in keeping her guessing about the contents of Sara's
weekly letters.

Sara was fairly sure that he eventually shared every letter with
anyone who would listen—and *everyone* would listen. There wasn't
much to do in Dust except to watch television or one's neighbors,
and the citizens of Dust preferred to watch their neighbors.

Sara had lived on those prairies long enough to know how little one
could hide; no such thing as a real private life existed. Until recently, all
the phones had been on a party line; the postmistress knew where every letter came from; and a stranger wasn't in town an hour before the
statistics of origin, relatives, and destination were known.

Sara went into the post office, which was in the only other two-story
building in town, sharing quarters with the general store. The post
office was also shingled with gray asphalt siding, like the houses near
Mabel's and a good two-thirds of the other houses in town. Some
siding distributor must have been a super salesman.

The wealth of asphalt siding reminded Sara of Slim's old joke about
the small-town proprietor of a general store who had one hundred
bags of salt crowding his shelves and filling up floor space. A stranger,
passing through, remarked, "You must sell a lot of salt."

"Naw," said the old man. "I find it hard to sell five pounds a year,
but there was a feller in here last week—he could sure sell salt."

Sara was smiling as she stepped up to the mail window.

"Hello, Mrs. Layton," the postmistress said, smiling back at her.
"Mabel said you was on your way over here looking for Slim. He was
in a little bit ago. I gave him your card telling him you was coming
down this week. So you're going on tour again. You must have been
near 'round the world by now."

Feeling annoyed about the card, which hadn't been a card, but a fold-over letter sealed with a sticker, Sara said, "Yes, as you know, I'm going to Australia and New Zealand."

The postmistress didn't seem to notice the insult. She said, "It will be hard to get Slim's check here every week from Australia. I don't see how you've managed to be so regular as it is, gadding about the way you do."

Sara said lightly, "Oh, Slim and I will think of something. I guess he's up at Riley's."

She couldn't make money arrangements with this old know-it-all. Slim would never forgive her. She turned away. The wide wooden boards, dark with oil and age, creaked as she moved. The postmistress's answer followed her out the door. "Yes, he's out early. Been up at Riley's an hour already."

"Damn, damn," Sara said under her breath.

Riley's, which was on the old highway with the gas station and the motel, was a low tan-colored building with brown paint on the window frames. In the front window, an anemic light spelled out "Cafe" in watery red neon. The Coors sign, bright red in its blue oval, was more positive. Sara opened the brown wooden door and stepped in. It was dark inside; the front window was the only window. She waited for her eyes to adjust to the light and then looked around.

Pete Riley was leaning on the bar looking at her, his double-jowled face red and coarse-grained. All of him that she could see was dressed in white. Above the soiled apron at his waist, a white T-shirt pulled tight across his chest where the bulging fatty-tissue gave the impression of big, loose breasts. The last time Sara had played in Aspen, she had seen girls without bras whose breasts looked the same way under their T-shirts as they jogged down the street.

Pete Riley didn't jog. He scarcely walked. His progress around the bar and to the grill in the open kitchen at back was made with a jerky rolling motion, as if he paused between steps to consider what part of his bulk to shift next.

Just now, he rolled his right half back from the bar and then lumbered around the cash register toward her. "Hello, Sara." Pete used everyone's first name. "Slim's in the back booth. He said you was comin'."

Pete smiled at her, his eyes warm and appreciative as he looked her up and down. "When you gonna quit lookin' after that old fart and get yourself another husband to take care of?"

Sara smiled back. At least Pete said right out what he was thinking, or almost what he was thinking—his eye lingered a little too long on her body before he looked away and hollered, "Hey, Slim, you got company."

Sara walked toward the back as her uncle maneuvered his gaunt frame out of the varnished-pine booth near the pinball machine. He was all angles, tall and skinny and gray in complete contrast to Pete's fat, red body. He tilted slightly to the left. Somewhere along the way, a bronc had fallen on him, breaking a leg, which healed short.

As Slim turned toward her, she hurried into his arms, hugging him close, feeling the sharp wing-bones on his back—his cowboy shirt a thicker covering than the layer of skin over the bones.

She stood back and put her hands on his shoulders while she studied his face: his poor marked face, one eye missing, the other one bloodshot and watery, but still blue as the prairie sky, blue as his cowboy shirt, which she had sent from Dallas because she knew he liked remembering himself as that blond, blue-eyed fiddle player, even if his hair was gray now, sparse on top, and too long in back.

Sara was used to his empty eye socket; its story, old family history, made in another bar back along the years, when Slim was wild and young and had picked up the wrong man's woman.

The jealous husband had cut Slim's eye with a broken beer bottle, and they couldn't save it. After the surgeon had removed Slim's eye, Slim had worn a glass eye for a while—a shiny blue glass eye which stared straight ahead in a disconcerting way. But the eye socket got infected, so the doctor took out the glass eye, too. The socket healed inward, leaving a little nest of wrinkled skin, which oozed matter from the corners.

Slim said, "By God, you're looking pretty, Sarie. Jeezus Keerist, am I glad to see you."

Sara smiled and looked him up and down. His blue shirt had an egg stain near the third mother-of-pearl snap button. She hoped that meant he'd had breakfast. He wore Levi's, held up on his thin hips by a wide leather belt fastened with a silver buckle. His cowboy boots were old and run-over at the heels.

"You look good, too," she said and stretched up to kiss him. His kiss tasted of whiskey and chewing tobacco.

"Sit down, sit down," Slim said. "Hey, Pete, bring my girl a drink. What do you want, Sarie?"

Sara didn't want a drink, and she didn't want Slim to drink any more. The liquor took so much of him away.

She said, "Let's have lunch, Slim. It's a long drive down here." She took the menu from its wire bracket and studied it while Pete waddled over to the booth. "Just give me the chicken-fried steak and a salad," she said to him.

"How about you, Slim?"

"That's okay, Pete, but bring us a couple of shots of Jim Beam first." He turned to Sara. "Jeezus Keerist, we've got a lot of catching up to do."

"Well," Sara said, "there wouldn't be so much catching up to do if you'd answer a letter once in awhile."

Slim grinned at her and gulped the shot Pete had just set down. He pushed the glass toward Pete. "Fill 'er again. We've got to celebrate."

Sara said, "So you're back at Mabel's."

Slim laughed. "Oh, I give her a run for her money, damned if I didn't. I held off for over five months, and by that time, that damned bleached hussy was just begging me to come back. Hell, I made her paint my room, and *then* I didn't move until she cut my rent five dollars." Slim emptied his glass and hollered at Pete, who came out from the kitchen and brought the Jim Beam bottle to the table.

"Just leave the goddamned bottle here," Slim said. "Put it on my tab."

Pete's eyes narrowed. "Now, Slim," he said, "you know this is a cash-on-the-barrelhead operation."

Sara said, "It's all right, Mr. Riley. Leave the bottle." Better to keep the bottle than to give Pete an excuse to be eavesdropping every few minutes. She turned her attention back to Slim. "When I kissed you, you smelled like Grandpa's chewing tobacco. Have you quit smoking, or are you chewing and smoking both?"

"Aw, hell, the doctor had such a fit when I had pneumonia in January, I just gave up on cigarettes and took to the chaw. Jeezus Keerist, here I'm seventy already, and the old bastard thinks something's going to kill me."

Sara hadn't known about the latest bout with pneumonia, but she let it go. "Whenever I smell chewing tobacco, it reminds me of times when I was a little girl, and we went over to Grandpa's ranch. I always dreaded Grandpa's big hug and his kiss because he smelled of that tobacco, and there were little brown puddles at the corners of his mouth, but I had to kiss him. He was always so good to me. I didn't want to hurt his feelings."

Slim had his hands curled around his glass; he swirled the liquor around and around. "He may have been good to you—you were his grandchild and a girl at that—but he was one tough son-of-a-bitch to have for a father. Your dad's a lot like him, too."

Sara sipped her whiskey; so soon the conversation was sliding into the rutted tracks they'd traveled a hundred times before. Slim hadn't even asked about her new tour.

Slim looked up and went on. "Your dad's only two years older than me, but he took to that hard work like a new calf takes to its mother's teat. God, how many cold mornings he rousted me out of bed to help with the milking before we went to school. He'd be whistling and stomping around, busting the ice in the stock tank with a two-by-four, hollering at me to hurry and get the cows in the stalls.

"Then he'd pat an old cow's rump, 'So-Boss' her a couple of times and settle right in to steady milking. Meantime, the old cow I milked . . . Jersey or Daisy or Maggie . . . didn't make no difference what their names was, they all done me the same. I'd just get set on the milk stool, the bucket between my legs, and start milking, when the old lady'd have to pee. She'd hunker up and half squat and lift her tail and let fly, all hot and steamy and stinking, and I'd jump up and hold the bucket high and cuss her for splattering my boots."

Slim emptied his glass and looked at Sara. "You know, I can't remember one time when your dad's cow peed in the barn." Sara smiled and Slim continued. "He had a way with horses, too. He'd harness two teams and get 'em both hitched to the plow in no time at all. Then, he'd call me to help hold the damn thing in the sod. I liked breaking horses and I didn't mind working with the cattle, but, God, how I hated farm work. I was always bone-tired. If it hadn't been for my fiddle and a bit of booze now and then . . ."

Pete lumbered over to their booth with tableware, napkins, and two plastic bowls of tossed salad. Sara took the cellophane wrapping from a soda cracker and began to eat. Slim poked at the lettuce with his fork, took a bite, and chewed slowly.

Sara said, "You lived with Prohibition from the time you were twelve until you were almost twenty-five. What did you do for liquor then?"

"Oh, hell, Sarie. Prohibition didn't make no difference. Your dad and me made many a batch of moonshine. Jeezus Keerist, you think the Feds cared about a bunch of dumb prairie kids? There was never a dance I played for without somebody furnishing a bottle."

Pete was back again with their dinner—dark-brown slabs of crusted meat, a hump of mashed potatoes, canned peas, all floating in yellowish gravy. It made Sara's stomach queasy to look at it. When Slim filled his glass from the bottle, she held hers out for a refill.

They ate silently; neither ate much. They let Pete remove their plates. Slim took the round tin from his shirt pocket and put a chunk of tobacco in his jaw. He looked at Sara and said, "Is it still good? Even though Joe died? Does the violin make life worthwhile?"

Sara reached out and put her hand on his. "It's still good," she said. "From the time you first taught me, and through all the tough times since, it's always been okay. As long as I can 'fiddle.'"

He squeezed her hand. "I'm glad for you." He looked down at the table. Sara thought of the day, years ago, when Slim had talked of music as another dimension. "Music has more than height, width, and depth, Sarie. There's a part of music that reaches into another world, a world of more light, more . . ." He had faltered, looking for the right words, but Sara hadn't needed them.

"I know, Slim," she had said then, "Music extends you until the beauty almost becomes pain."

At Riley's, the silence stretched out between them. Finally, Slim looked up at her. "I was so goddamn dumb. I had to go and get a country girl pregnant. Maybe if I'd run off to the city with my fiddle, it would have been different—even if I'd got a city girl pregnant. But, no, I knocked up a little old ranch girl who thought the city was full of sin and wouldn't have left the country for nobody. 'Course my dad made me marry her. I liked her all right, but I wasn't in the mind to get married to nobody—not until I'd played that fiddle in the city. Oh, Jeezus Keerist, how could anybody be so dumb and live?"

Sara moved in the booth, almost squashing Slim's Stetson, which was on the bench beside her. She picked it up and turned it around and around in her hands. "You were young, Slim, that's all."

"Naw, I was dumb. I went out to that old place, tried to raise a few cows, break a few horses at five dollars a head, but I was too dumb even to support us. I did day labor on surrounding ranches. In those times hardly anyone could pay a cowboy monthly wages. I could never do nothing like your dad could. My wife helped some, raised chickens, sold cream." Slim hit his right fist on the table. "By God, she sold *all* the cream. And then she'd set that pitcher of skim milk on the table for me and the kids. I hated that pale-blue slop; made me sick to think of my kids drinking that. No wonder they was puny. We didn't feed 'em right."

"Stop it, Slim," Sara said. "The dust storms weren't your fault. You couldn't help it if there was a depression."

"Jeezus Keerist, what times to live in. If I hadn't been a fiddler . . ." Slim grinned at her. "But, girl, I *was* a fiddler!"

She smiled and said, "I'll always remember the way you played."

"I'd get those tired sad folks to tapping their feet and clapping their hands," he said. "I'd get 'em to dancing, then fiddle 'til the sparks flew. One night, those sparks of music got caught in the ladies' hair and lit up the Grange Hall with wildfire. And then . . ." He stopped talking and took a deep breath, "And then, I threw it all away."

Slim held up his left hand. The little finger was bent in half, a stiff gnarled bone that angled in toward Slim's palm. A crooked scar ran up the side of the finger.

"Did I ever tell you how I ruined that finger?" Slim asked.

A hundred, a thousand, a million times, thought Sara, *and you can never make the ending different.* She nodded at Slim, knowing he was going to tell the story again.

"There was this rich guy come down home and bought up a bunch of little ranches," Slim began, "bought dirt cheap from folks that couldn't do nothing but sell or lose their places anyway. And that son-of-a-bitch wanted a fine new barn for his fine big outfit. My wife, who sold eggs and cream over to their place, told him I could build a barn. Hell, your dad built most of *my* barn. I just followed along behind him and did what he told me to do."

Slim filled his glass from the Jim Beam bottle. "Anyhow, your dad had taken your mom and you kids up to Denver where there was work building barracks at the military base, and my old lady tells some big city guy I'll build him a barn. She was bound and determined to get her hands on that cash."

He drained his glass and continued the story. "So I went over there every day after I did my own chores, and I got started on a pretty good barn, but that old bastard kept urging me to work a little faster, get it done a little sooner. He pinched every goddamned nickel. Jeezus Keerist, I had to beg him for every nail." Slim looked at his empty glass.

"Generally," he said, "I didn't drink while I was working, just nights, some, when I played the fiddle; but that son-of-a-bitch got on my nerves something fierce, so I got to taking my bottle over there and stashing it in my tool box. Seemed to help me work faster just to take a little nip when he wasn't looking."

Sara nodded. She could have told the story herself—word for word.

Slim went on. "And the barn did go up pretty fast; I got the studs up and the siding on the lower part, and I was half-way done with the roof—first set of trusses built. Had to haul the lumber up one board at a time, but I built those trusses right up there on top of the barn. Of course, that part was kinda slow going, and the boss nagged me whenever he came near the barn. Got so every time I climbed down to get another board, I'd take a swaller from that bottle, just to ease the sting of his tongue-lashing."

Slim poured himself another drink. Sara put her hand over her glass.

"Anyway, I was working on the second set of trusses, and I'd just tacked one of the angle boards up at the top. When I got ready to set the bottom nail, I held it between my thumb and first finger and kinda looped my little finger over the side of the joist to hold my hand steady. Well, I guess I hadn't tacked the top half of the board just right, 'cause when I hit that nail to set it, the vibration loosened the whole board—a big son-of-a-bitchin' two-by-eight, and it swung out and then slid down, catching my little finger and crushing it all to hell. And do you think that old bastard was anywhere to be found when I really needed him? Naw, he'd got tired of bitching and gone into town. I pried my finger loose and then sat up there and bled and puked all over his barn. He hired somebody else to finish it; never did pay me all my money."

Slim propped his left elbow on the table and looked at the crooked finger. "They couldn't fix my finger. I never played the fiddle again." He shook his head from side to side, swallowed his whiskey, filled his glass and emptied it, and then just sat, looking at his left hand.

Sara said, "I'm going to have my agent send your checks from New York while I'm gone, Slim."

Slim glanced up at her. His lone eye didn't seem to focus. He grinned a loose grin and said to her. "The devil was a fiddler." He emptied the bottle into his glass, stared down at the whiskey, and turned the glass around and around for a long time without speaking. Then Slim held up his left hand.

"Did I ever tell you how I ruined that finger?" he asked.

Sara reached out and covered his hand with her own. The small crooked finger was knobby and hard. "I have to go, Slim. I've got a long drive ahead of me. I'll see you next time. I'll write."

Slim took his hand away and put both hands around the

empty bottle. He nodded, but he didn't look up when she rose and paid the bill.

As she walked down the frontage road toward the car, she could still feel the stiff crooked finger like a stone in the hollow of her hand.

———————

ELAINE LONG was born in 1935 in Logan County, Colorado, where her great-great-grandfather settled with his family in 1875, and where her grandparents filed homestead claims in 1906. Her father worked as a hired hand for several small ranches in northeastern Colorado before moving the family to Timberlake Ranch in southeastern Colorado. On that ranch, Elaine learned to ride horseback, milk cows, run the separator, make butter and cottage cheese, garden, cook and can using a wood stove, iron with sad irons heated on the same wood stove, and help with all the chores expected of a ranch woman. Memories of those years include severe blizzards and loss of cattle when stock walked out on the frozen lake, broke through, and froze to death. In 1961 and 1962, she worked for her father on a small ranch northeast of Gillette, Wyoming. Her duties included riding roundup, riding fence, helping with calving, and branding. On visits to relatives' ranches in Montana and Wyoming, she helped with lambing and sheep shearing. Now a resident of the rural area near Buena Vista, Colorado, Elaine is the author of the novels *Jenny's Mountain* and *Bittersweet Country* as well as numerous short stories and articles.

The Rough String Rider

Sinclair Browning

It was hotter than Hades that June. We hadn't yet hit old San Juan's Day and true to Mexican superstition, we hadn't had a drop of rain yet either. The whole country was suffering. Luckily we were running some cross breds and they had the good sense to browse. So the land was not only hurting from our lack of rain but also from the cow's instinct to stay alive. The creeks, once filled with snowmelt from the mountains, had been dry for weeks and even the dirt tanks were low. We went about our work pretty much the same as always, and although we didn't talk about it much, we were all snakebit with the thought of hauling water to the cattle.

It was late afternoon, right before chores, when the ranch dogs started carrying on. From the sound of their barking we knew we had company coming. Years of living with the dogs, and their pups, and their grandparents before 'em, had taught us well, for they all talked the same lingo. Today it was "Get off your butts, there's company acomin.'"

I stood on the porch and watched a dim speck grow larger. I could tell even from the distance it was a horse. It took him a long time to come in, which didn't surprise me, for the desert heat sucked all of the spark even out of a good animal.

And this one was that.

An old man and a young kid had doubled up on one of the best-looking studs I'd seen in a long time. In fair flesh, the horse was wet but not lathered. He'd seen his share of hard work I guessed. He was a young horse, steel gray, with a large jaw and small ears.

"Steel Dust?" I asked.

The old man nodded as the skinny kid slid to the ground. The boy stepped up to the horse's head, and although it didn't look like he was going anywhere to me, he held the cheek strap of the bridle while the old man got off, his right leg brushing the horse's butt.

Once afoot he wiped his right hand on his chaps before extending it to me.

"Hank Tuck," he nodded to the kid, "my grandson Twig."

"Cap'n Eddy," I said.

"Pleased to meet you, sir," the kid said. He looked like he was almost all of fourteen. His voice hadn't yet deepened and near as I could tell a razor hadn't touched his face. A crust of peeling skin drifted across his nose. He looked like a pilgrim dressed in his Levi's and a flat, low crowned hat. He had a red rag tied around his neck, and the shirt must have been his grandpa's. Garters kept the sleeves from slidin' over his hands. In spite of the heat he was wearing an old stained cowhide vest that looked like it'd been skinned off somebody's old milk cow. His grandpa wasn't dressed much better.

Near as I could tell, the horse was the most prosperous thing about the outfit.

"You hirin' on?" the old man asked.

I shook my head. Hell it was all we could do to hang on through the dry season, and while we could use the help if it went to hauling water, I knew in a few more weeks the rains would come and save our souls once again.

"No. But we can spare a meal or two if you're in need."

The old man nodded and swatted his battered felt hat against his leg. Puffs of dust filled the air, which set him to coughing and hacking. He bent almost double in an effort to catch his wind.

The boy called Twig was loosening the horse's girth.

"And I suppose we can spare some feed for the horse," I offered.

A look of relief passed between the man and boy.

"You got any horses that need work, he can do it." Hank said.

I looked at the skinny kid again. He looked too soft to be much good.

"Rough string rider," his grandpa explained.

"Rough string rider," I repeated.

Charley Gibbons, our rough string rider, was in the bunkhouse with a broken leg. He was gonna be laid up for a few weeks at least, and we had a contract with the cavalry over in Fort Huachuca to supply thirty colts by fall. It was a sure bet that not all the colts would be pussycats and we were already drawing mental straws to see who was gonna fill Charley's place. None of us relished the job.

"He's a good 'un." Tuck said.

The boy rubbed his foot in the dust and I could make out a sock through a small ragged hole in the toe of his black boot.

I'll work a man as hard as anyone I know. I think I'm fair. And I've run more than my share of young kids. But my rough string riders were usually older with a bit more seasoning on them. And while it was tempting, I wasn't keen on getting the kid hurt.

"No work," I said. "But you can bunk for the night."

After supper, we were all sitting around the bunkhouse, amusing ourselves as cowboys do. Slim Dodger was tryin' to read the old newspaper on the walls and a couple of the boys were playing some card game that Two String Smith had quit because they'd lost one of the red queens.

In spite of the heat, it was a little cold, because of the two strangers, but then Red Curry started in on some of the places he'd worked. When he got to the Double Quarter Circles, old man Tuck nodded.

"You know that outfit?" Red asked.

"Two winters ago, we worked it."

A jackrabbit had nothing on my ears.

"You worked for the Double Quarter Circles?"

Tuck nodded. "Me and the boy."

A snort came out of Two String Smith. He and some of the other cowboys had already decided the pair I'd drawn to wasn't much.

Tuck ignored him.

"Cowboyin'?" I asked.

Tuck hooked a thumb in Twig's direction. "An rough string ridin.'"

A hush fell over the bunkhouse. We all knew about the Double Quarter Circle horses. They ran a stud that was one of the rankest in the country. Most honest outfits would've cut him long ago. But he had a ton of bone and threw a handsome colt. When they worked out, there weren't any better. Trouble was they were a lot like mules, you had to go through a whole string of rotten ones before you found the one you could live with.

Red spat a string of tobacco out an open window. "Couldn't cut it, huh?"

"Ran out of work." Tuck said with a big grin.

The cowboys broke into a heavy round of laughing at the old man's joke.

Twig, so far, had said very little.

After breakfast the next morning the kid saddled up the Steel Dust stallion while the old man packed up their gear and rolled up their bedrolls.

We had pretty much said our goodbyes when they rode by the *estacada* corral where Red and Two String were working a tall roan colt. The horse was saddled and Red stood up near his head, on the offside. Since it was pretty obvious that the colt was about to be ridden, the two strangers stopped for the show.

Two String grabbed a handful of bridle and cheeked the colt before trying to step on. He hopped around on one leg, the other in the stirrup while Red tried to steady the horse. Finally Two String got a good shot and he launched himself from the ground to the saddle. The horse was madder than a rained-on rooster but with his head cheeked to the left all he could do was spin in circles. Red tried to bring him back the other way to confuse him but the roan horse wasn't having much of it.

"Let 'er rip." Two String said and Red stepped back.

The roan horse flat came apart. His front feet came flying forward as he struck the earth. He squealed like a mare before taking off around the corral at a dead run, his tail tucked tight against his butt. Two String was no longer cheeking him, and his lines were short as he tried to keep the colt's head up.

But the roan was too strong, and seemed ignorant of the fact that he was carrying a bit in his mouth as he ignored the pressure of the reins and jerked them through Two String's hands allowing his huge thick neck to plunder downward into the earth. His head rooted between his front legs as his rear end went airborne.

Some horses, when you first ride them, never buck. Others do it kind of halfheartedly, but the roan colt was serious about his work. He twisted and bucked hard and the fact is old Two String did OK for a while. Then the colt took off at a dead run, roared up to the far end of the corral, slid into the fence and ducked back hard to the left. He had about as fine an action as I'd seen in a colt, in fact he could flat cut a gopher from his hole, but this same maneuver is what had broken Charley's leg.

Two String, like his predecessor, sailed off the right side of the roan, and landed in a heap in the dust. The colt ended his success with a series of bucking jumps around the pen, finally sliding to a stop at the far side. And as he spread his front legs apart, he glared at us, his sides heaving.

Two String was sitting up now, tugging on his boot. Red hopped the fence and gave him a hand with it. I groaned. I knew it had to be serious for a cowboy to be pulling his boot off in the middle of the day. Better to pull it off though before the swelling came up and the boot would have to be cut off. They don't come cheap.

Red and I got Two String under the armpits and helped the limping cowboy to the bunkhouse.

"Cap'n, sir? Can I have a try at him?" The boy called Twig asked.

"You can do whatever you want with that son of a bitch, just don't get on him." I said. Two cowboys in two days was a pretty good score for the roan.

By the time I got back to the corral I found Twig and the horse's empty headstall in the middle of the pen. The roan colt still wore the saddle but there was nothing on his head, not even a halter.

"You're gonna have to rope him again to get that halter back on him," I yelled in disgust. We'd had to wrestle the colt to put it on him and the way things were going I wasn't sure our prospects were gonna be any better the next time.

Twig ignored me as he coiled his rawhide rope.

"Whoosh," he said as he threw it in the direction of the roan.

The colt took off like a shot around the pen.

Ain't much of a roper, I thought as I saw the rawhide laying like a dead snake on the dirt.

The horse, also seeing the dead rope, dropped to a trot.

The kid gathered the lariat up again.

"Whoosh!" He threw it out, again missing the horse, which galloped off. This time when the colt started to drop to a trot, Twig stamped his boot in the dirt. "Whoosh!" he repeated and the roan broke into a lope.

The rope was gathered up again and when the horse dropped to a trot, Twig slapped the lariat against his Levi's, spooking the horse again into a run.

Just before the roan passed Twig on the fence, the boy stepped in front of him and held the hand with the coiled rope up in the horse's direction. "Whoosh!"

The roan put on his brakes, rolled around his rear end and took off in the opposite direction. He ran about one and a half times around the corral before Twig repeated the gesture, again stepping in front of the running colt to turn him back the other way.

"Why he ain't trying to rope that horse a'tall, Cap'n." Red said.

The horse had figured that out too. Where it had been a game before, and the roan had been in control, he was now paying a lot closer attention to the boy on the ground. Something had clicked in the horse's mind. His instincts as a prey animal had kicked in and there was no way he was going to let the predator get the jump on him.

The rope flicked out toward the horse, and he took off again. This time when the boy went to turn him, instead of going up to the fence, he stayed out away from him and slapped the coiled rope against his pants. Again, the horse rolled back on his haunches, only now he was facing the boy as he did so.

This was repeated several times and then Twig went back asking for the outside turns.

I was snake bit. I'd seen a lot of cowboys work horses, but never one in this manner. So far the kid hadn't even gotten close to the roan, except to pull his bridle off, yet here he was controlling the horse from thirty feet away. He was making him turn and roll to the outside and then to the inside. While the boy hadn't said anything, I had a pretty good notion that he was playing some kind of game with himself and he knew exactly where the horse was going to turn. The horse's attention never left the kid, and even when he was running around the pen, one ear was always cocked toward Twig, waiting to see what he would ask of him next.

The boy stood in the middle of the pen and made a noise that sounded for all the world like a kiss. It stopped the horse in his tracks as he halted and turned his head to look at his tormentor.

Twig stepped back to the rear of the horse and kissed again.

The colt bent his head a little deeper to keep looking at the boy. When the horse's attention wavered, the kid brushed the rope against his Levi's or rubbed the toe of his boot in the dust. I could tell he was doing just enough to keep the horse mindful of him.

Finally the kid stood way behind the horse and the roan was bent almost in a horseshoe trying to keep his attention on the young cowboy.

Pretty soon his neck must've wore out because the horse finally turned his whole body to face the kid. After working for another fifteen minutes or so in this manner Twig reached out and touched the roan on the forehead.

"Good boy," he said. They were the only words, other than "whoosh," I'd heard him say for two hours.

By now we were all setting up on top of the mesquite-stacked corral watching the kid work the horse. We'd never seen anything like it before. Even Two String, hearing about this new system of breaking a horse, had hobbled out of the bunkhouse. Finally that danged horse was following the kid around the corral like a newborn chick to its momma. The kid would stop, the horse would stop. The kid would do an about face, the horse would follow on his heels. The roan was tired and lathered but he had learned that as long as he watched the young cowboy, he didn't have to work.

The Steel Dust stud was sleeping on his feet when the kid

gathered him up and brought him into the corral.

"This oughta be amusin'," Red offered. "Two of them studs in the same place."

Twig crossed the Steel Dust's reins over his neck and the horse stayed there. Then he went to the middle of the pen and kissed to the roan.

The horse looked at the Steel Dust stud and then back to the kid, as though he was trying to choose between the two. Twig kissed again and the roan walked to the center of the pen and the kid picked up the horse's bridle and put it on him. Then he kissed to the Steel Dust and held his hand up. The stud, as though on some kind of an invisible line, walked up to the boy, ignoring the roan stallion, who was watching him like a red-tailed hawk on the hunt.

The only sound from the top of the estacada corral was the noise of Red spitting tobacco into the dust and the old man's coughing.

Twig mounted his horse and ponied the roan around the pen for a moment or two, then he stopped in the center, well away from the mesquite wood that could have caught a stirrup or rein or leg and began sacking the colt out from up above. He took his battered felt hat off and flapped it all over the roan's neck, ears, and head, across his rump. Then he lifted up the cantle of the saddle and dropped it back on the horse and he tugged on the horn and leaned on the pommel.

I figured maybe he was gonna slide from one horse to the other but I was wrong.

He got off his horse and led it back out of the corral and returned for the roan.

Again he led it to the middle of the pen and began playing with the saddle. He pulled on the saddle strings and lifted the cantle and the pommel. He tugged on the stirrups and lifted them up and dropped them back against the horse's sides, then he went to the other side and did the same thing. He stepped one foot into a stirrup and then put it back down on the ground. And over and over again.

He checked the cinch and the bridle and we all waited, we knew what was next.

Truth to tell I coulda stopped the kid. Two of my men were already busted up. But it was a nice colt and one I knew the boss wanted broke. Besides I'd gone this far with the show and I wanted to see the end.

The kid walked up to the horse's head and bent his own. I couldn't see exactly what happened and we all talked about it later, but honest to Pete it looked like he was blowing through his nose into the wide flared nostrils of that roan colt.

When he gathered his reins in his left hand there was only a little less slack in the left rein. He wasn't going to cheek the colt. Finally he grabbed a hunk of mane and placed his foot in the left stirrup. I've seen a lot of cowboys get on a lot of horses for the first time and there's always a little pussyfootin' around. But not with this kid. He got on that colt as though he was gettin' on the most broke horse in the outfit, and as he swung his body up over the colt's back, his boot even brushed the horse's rump which will usually send a colt skitterin', but the roan colt stood long enough for the kid to catch his offside stirrup.

We waited for the explosion but the colt just trotted off. The kid just sat up there, never asking the colt to change direction or go faster or slower or stop. He was just along for the ride. Finally the colt broke into a lope, and again the kid just sat him. He had a little slack in the reins and he looked as unconcerned as a sleeping dog. The roan loped around the corral for a few times, his ears back as he focused on the kid riding him.

Finally the colt cut across the center of the corral, gathered steam and took yet another run at the far wall of the pen. We knew what would happen next. He ran straight for it, the way he had done with Charley and Two String, slid almost into the fence, and rolled back on his haunches hard off to the left. And the kid just sat there, never losing his seat as the horse came out of his hard left turn. The colt took a few more strides at the lope, dropped down to the trot and finally stopped, sides heaving.

Twig Tuck worked the colt for another hour or so and his work was always the same. There never seemed to be an argument. He'd give the colt a little pressure and then release it before the roan came unstrung. By late morning the horse was giving well to the left and to the right. Twig nodded to his grandpa, who opened the corral gate and the kid and the colt rode off into the desert.

That afternoon, although San Juan's Day was still a couple of weeks off, the thunderheads started building toward the east. Great angry growling mountains of rolling clouds. We were all happy to see them but we knew from our years on the desert that it would take at least a week of threat before any rain would fall. In the meantime the stock tanks just kept gettin' lower.

Along about chore time Twig and the roan came back. The kid looked pretty much the same as always, the colt looked tired, but not at all abused. Twig stepped down and handed me the reins.

"He's all right," the kid said and as he said it a fat drop of rain landed on his sun-scorched nose before rolling to the ground. It was followed by millions more as the rainy season began in earnest.

And I, of course, gave him a chance to fill in as the rough string rider until Charley's leg got better.

It went on pretty much that way for the next few weeks. Where we'd been breaking several colts a month in the past, now we'd just give the kid a new horse every morning and by evening the horse was ready to be ridden by nearly anyone in the outfit. And almost every afternoon the monsoons hit. Where most cowboys get goosey about riding in lightning it never seemed to bother the kid and on more than one afternoon I'd spot his tattered yellow slicker through the thick mist before I could make out either horse or rider.

Red and Two String and the others didn't have much truck with the kid 'cause he spooked them a little. Before when a young 'un came on board he'd be like a young colt chatterin' his teeth before the old hands, but this one was different. He never said anything, never asked for advice or offered any. Clearly the kid knew more about horses than any of them. The colts he started were all honest and had a pretty good rein before the other cowboys ever stepped up on them. While they liked riding the horses Twig had started, they still didn't much like being showed up by a snot-nosed kid who hadn't even slapped a razor to his peach fuzz yet.

Although the old man was sick with the cough, he still tried to pull his own load. He was able to do a little cowboyin' and help out around the place and truth to tell I would have kept him on even if he'd been plumb worthless just for that kid's way with a horse.

Twig wasn't much on talkin' and the old man seemed to encourage this. Even in the bunkhouse, the kid's bedroll was sandwiched in between the old man and the wall. It was almost like his grandpa was trying to protect him from the rest of the outfit or something.

Sometimes, though, I'd catch the kid carrying on some kind of conversation or another with the horse he was workin' on, but as far as people went, he just didn't say a whole lot.

I was coming back from checking one of the tanks late one afternoon when I met up with him. He was on a piebald mare he'd started that morning and she was just going across the desert as though she'd been ridden all of her life.

"Twig, where'd you learn about horses, son?" I asked.

He grinned. "Well for starters I just like them, fact is I like 'em more'n most people." His voice was high and thin.

His mare came to a little creek, normally dry, but now swollen with the rain. She sucked back from it and where most cowboys would've gone to beatin' and spur-in', Twig just sat. I could see that the mare was trembling with fright, either from the running water, or the vision of having to haul her load across it.

The boy reached down and patted the mare on the neck. I was beside him so I could see when he squeezed gently with the calf of his left leg. She approached the creek again. Twig let out her lines as the mare stretched her neck out toward the running water. The kid sat her as though he was on the most broke horse in the world, not a green colt started that morning that could just as easily cut and run. The mare dropped her head and sniffed at the water, snorting as she did so. Twig sat.

After a minute or so the mare's neck came up and she shifted her weight, resting a hind foot. Twig pressed her again, and this time the mare went across the water without a fuss. It was the easiest water crossing I'd ever seen on a green colt and I've dallied and pulled more than my share of them across runnin' water.

"I learned a lot from my grandpa," Twig said when we reached the other side. "He gave me this vest as a prize for starting my first horse right." Twig rubbed his free hand lightly across the belly of the old cowhide vest like it was a Sunday go-to-meetin' suit.

I was surprised, but said nothing. As near as I could tell the old man was an all right cowboy, but nothin' to write home about. I thought the horse talent rested with the younger generation.

"He always taught me to find the oldest cowboy I could that weren't draggin' a leg, or had a broke arm, or his teeth knocked out by some bronc. He said that cowboy was doin' things right. The one who'd been around horses all his life and wasn't too busted up."

"Well, Twig, your granddaddy's right," I said. "It don't take much to get hurt by a horse."

"No sir."

While none of us ever talked about it, it was clear that the old man's cough was getting worse. The humid air carried in by the rainy season wasn't helping any and some nights his coughing got so bad he'd leave the bunkhouse and we wouldn't see him until morning. The kid never talked about it.

By the end of July all the colts were well started. Charley's leg wasn't healing as well as expected and after a trip to Tombstone, he was ordered by the doc to stay off of it for another month, which gave me a little leeway on this rough string rider business.

Already all of the cavalry-promised colts had been broken out and they were easier to ride than most of the horses on the ranch. Some of the cowboys were actually picking the colts to ride, said they handled better than the older horses.

When there was slack time, which was rare, Twig would work on the roan colt, the one he'd started that first day. Now the colt was doing sliding stops and rollbacks. He could cut a cow quicker than a flea hopping on a dog. Fact was he was so handy I took to ridin' him myself.

I expected Charley Gibbons to be riled over Twig's replacing him as the rough string rider, but he never said a word until he'd been up and about for a week or so.

"Kid ain't bad," he offered.

"He's a hand with a horse," I said.

"Well I guess we ain't all bulletproof." Charley leaned against the porch post. "Not enough work for more'n one rough string rider."

"Nope." I wasn't ready to make a choice. Twig was good, but Charley had been with the outfit for three years.

"Fact is, Cap'n, I'd be happy goin' back to cowboyin'."

Gibbons had let me off the hook.

"Gettin' busted up gets a man to thinkin'," Charley continued, "I'm gettin' a little long in the tooth for it."

I nodded. My own body was also doing a lot of kicking.

So that's how it was settled. Although nothing was ever said, Twig Tuck continued as the rough string rider and Charley Gibbons went back to being just a regular dirty shirt cowboy.

When the quartermaster from Fort Huachuca arrived at the Rocking K in September we trotted out the thirty head of horses we had contracted for. They were all fat and sassy from the grass the rains had brought. When the boys started working the colts through mock cavalry drills, the quartermaster's eyes lit up.

"Good horseflesh, Cap'n. As good as I've seen."

I grinned. "Too bad we don't have a bugler." Once the horses had been used for any time they would quickly learn the bugler's calls for right and left turns, retreats, walk, trot, and canter. Now they did the maneuvers because they were told to by their riders.

Because the cavalry preferred solid-colored horses and didn't want mares, we held back the roan, the piebald mare, and a few others to work on the ranch. They took everything else broke we had. Before the quartermaster left, he contracted for another twenty head. It was a good start for 1930. We had no way of knowing that in just one more decade a man named Hitler would cause the demise of the horse cavalry. It would all be mechanized to match his might.

So Twig's work was pretty much set.

His cough had gotten so bad by Thanksgiving that old man Tuck was unable to ride. He tried to help out around the headquarters but he was blowing hard after not much work. Even mucking out the bunkhouse would get him hacking and gasping for air.

By the first of December he was in his bedroll all day. Twig would sit with him in the evening. They didn't talk much, even to each other, the boy would just sit there holding his hand. Two days before Christmas the old man finally died. We buried him that afternoon. No one saw Twig after supper so I went looking for him.

I finally found him among the remuda in the holding pasture. In the moonlight I could see him sitting on a large boulder surrounded by horses picking at dead grass. He had his arms crossed across his chest in an effort to fight the chill of the evening.

"Sorry about your grandpa, son."

"Yessir." His hand brushed his face and I looked away fearful that he would catch me catch him cryin'.

"He was a fine man."

"Yessir." His breath escaped in white clouds into the frosty evening air.

"We need twenty colts ready by the middle of next month. Do you think we can do it?"

He turned his wet young eyes to me. "Plus the ones for Huachuca, sir?"

I nodded. I'd secured my contract through some pretty fancy price-cutting, taking fifteen dollars less a head than a Phoenix seller. But the horses were a sure bet. Cash on delivery.

"Yessir, we can do it."

And that was the end of our evening conversation. It was just my way of telling him he had a place on the Rocking K for as long as he wanted to stay. Far as I knew, the only family Twig had was the old man. They never talked about anyone else.

The kid was definitely a loner. He stuck to himself and when the rest of the hands teased him, he just got quiet and never took their bait. Whenever anyone asked him anything it was just "yes sir" or "no sir" and the longest conversations he ever had were with the horses.

It was just after the first of the new year when I was getting ready to check the warm springs pasture. The roan was tied to the estacada corral and a spiral of dust was coming from the center of the pen so I knew Twig was working a new colt. Any more, we just kind of let him be. There were no cowboys perched on the top rail this morning to watch him work his magic. We'd all seen it many times before and fact is the new had pretty much become everyday.

As I untied the roan I saw that Two String Smith was in the middle of the pen with Twig. He had his lariat out and was flicking it at the stout bay gelding galloping around the corral.

"Whoosh!" Two String whooped. "Whoosh!" He stepped in front of the horse toward the inside. I knew enough about Twig's program to realize that Two String had asked for an inside turn.

As the gelding turned to the outside, the kid said, "turn him back the other way, don't let him git away with that."

Two String stepped in front of the horse again and sent him back around the pen before again asking for an inside turn. This time he got it.

"Looks like we're gonna have us a whole pile of rough string riders if we're not careful," I said as I tightened the cinch on the roan.

"Well Cap'n we don't even have a rough string any more," Two String offered.

"Keep it up boys, keep it up," I said before riding off.

By the time the Bowie quartermaster came for his twenty head, Twig was workin' horses in the morning, Two String in the afternoon, and we had already started on a small round pen so we could start twice as many colts. Red and some of the other hands were also learning Twig's revolutionary method of colt breaking.

The accident happened in mid-March. We were on the *bajada* gathering a group of cattle that hadn't been worked in a while and they were wild, runnin' all over the countryside in every direction but the right one. Cowboys were scattered like startled quail, crashing through mesquite and catclaw trying to turn the cattle back.

Twig was a little ahead of me on the Steel Dust stud trying to turn a rogue cow and her calf when the confused calf rolled back under the chest of the huge horse. The stallion scrambled to regain his feet but it was a cat's cradle of animal and man as the three of them went down in a cloud of dust. The calf somersaulted and crashed on its side, rolled once and was on its feet before its momma could charge.

A ton of horse came down on Twig, smashing him into the desert floor. The horse lay idle for a moment as he pinned the boy beneath him. Suddenly he began to get up and it was like watching a mother hen settle her chicks. In spite of the horse's great size, he rose from the earth with care.

As I ran up I saw one of the stud's rear hooves touch the boy's back and as quickly as it touched, it was withdrawn. I never knew a horse could or would want to be that particular with a man. But clearly the Steel Dust stallion did not want to hurt his young rider. The horse stepped across the boy's body, shook, and stood quietly as I rushed to Twig, who was as still as a June noon. I rolled him over on his back.

His face was the color of milk. His eyelids were closed and although I could see chicken tracks of blue veins running across them, nothing fluttered.

His arms lay stretched across the desert, one of them cradled in a prickly pear cactus, the other flung outstretched as though reaching for something.

I stared at the small face below me. There was no movement. No breath. His lips were turning an ugly shade of blue and his thin young body did not twitch.

I struggled with the rag wrapped around his neck and loosened the laces on his shirt. I tore open the horn buttons on his beloved cowhide vest and shoved it aside as my hands began pushing hard against his chest in an effort to bring some breath back into him. I pushed and pushed and it was only when his thin chest began to swell with air and pump up and down that I realized something.

Twig Tuck was a girl.

"Twig!" I yelled.

Eyes still closed, his lips tried to mutter something but I could not hear it. I didn't care. He was breathin' and for now that was enough.

His eyes began rolling behind his eyelids as though they wanted to buck out of his head. Finally he opened his eyes.

"Cap'n, what happened?"

"You took a fall. Twig, you're gonna be all right."

"My horse?"

I looked at the stud who had wandered off a ways and was

picking at the dry desert grass.

"He's all right."

Twig retrieved his hand from the prickly pear as a wince of pain darted across his face. He stared at his hand, now covered with faint white thorns that looked finer than frog hair. Slowly he sat up and patted his body with his good hand.

"Guess I'm of one piece."

"Looks like," I stood and walked over to a mesquite tree that had caught his hat, dusted it off against my chaps before turning back to him.

Twig was buttonin' up the cowhide vest.

She must have seen it in my eyes.

"You won't tell the others, Cap'n?"

I shook my head. "It'd only cause trouble."

"Yessir."

We got on our horses and continued gathering the cattle.

From that day forward we never mentioned Twig's accident or my discovery. She went on working as our rough string rider and kept to herself as she had always done.

And the Rocking K horses began making a rep for themselves. All over the country people were talking about the fine young colts that were coming off the Rocking K. Of course they were the same horses we'd always had, only we had discovered a new way of break- ing them out and the horses had responded with honesty and hard work. All of the Rocking K cowboys had come to using at least a little of Twig's tricks.

Just before San Juan's Day of the following year, the Steel Dust stud stood saddled and packed with Twig's gear. She was moving on and all of us, myself, Two String, Red, Slim, and the others gathered to say goodbye.

"I wish you'd reconsider Twig, we could use you here."

She grinned and pointed to the rest of the boys. "You got yourself some good riders here Cap'n."

"But no rough string," I said.

"Nope." She grinned. "Guess I run out of work."

This time no one laughed as the slim young cowboy on the Steel Dust stud rode off.

SINCLAIR BROWNING of Tucson, Arizona, spent her childhood on her belly in dry arroyos hunting sand rubies, converting her propane tank into a stagecoach and exploring the Sonoran desert on her horse. Summers were spent on the family ranch in Southern Arizona. Her cowgirl mystery series *(The Last Song Dogs, The Sporting Club, Rode Hard, Put Away Dead,* and *Crack Shot)* features Trade Ellis—part Apache, part rancher and all private eye. Sinclair has also written books, including two historical novels: *Enju,* about an Aravaipa Apache and the Camp Grant massacre, and *America's Best,* focused on World War II and set in the Philippines. She is the co-author of the best-selling horse-training book, *Lyons On Horses.* Browning lives with her husband and assorted menagerie outside of Tucson, Arizona, where she still breaks her own horses and works cattle.

Night Ride

SLIM RANDLES

The magic crescendo of day's end took forever to come, but it finally happened. The packer could look up to the west, above the tired ranch house, above the shady, whispering black locust trees along the alfalfa fields, and see the peaks of the eastern Sierra transform.

From the hazy-hot mountain range of the summer day, the peaks now became vertical battlements backlit by the flooding of a setting sun. Each snowfield seemed larger at this time of day. Each peak strained upward through the sun blasts as if to declare then-sovereignty before night cloaked them in mystery.

And the packer saw, as well, the blazing Inyo Mountains to the east, lit with the burnishing brush of evening, the rock spire of the Paiutes' sacred Winnedumah now absorbed by the mountains.

"Chores done?"

It was the boss.

He nodded.

"Can't eat the scenery," the boss said, chuckling. "Get some food. Time to go." It was already getting dark when he began the saddling. Five horses, six mules. He tied the stirrups over the saddle seats with the saddle strings on the horses and checked each animal for shoes. Then he strung them together, being careful to get the right order.

You led the horses and tied the mules on behind. If you had trouble with the stock, he knew it would come from the horses, not the mules. You led first the slowest horse, then the ones who caused you trouble, then the good horses, then the slowest mules, then the faster mules. Each collection of stock required some thinking before it became a functioning pack string.

"Lead ol' Jim," the boss said, unnecessarily. "He's the slowest. Always lead the slowest."

The packer nodded and ran lead ropes through the stirrups hanging on the near side of the saddles, and then tied large bowlines around the necks of the next animals. Six mules first, then the mules to the horses and finally to ol' Jim. One by one in the alkali dust and salt grass smell of the big corral until there were eleven head in one long string and ol' Jim's lead rope was dallied to the horn of his own rough-out saddle sitting on Brownie.

It was going to be another of those nights. Another of those special nights, he knew. Another gem in the necklace of a life he hoped would become heavy with such treasure.

He realized he wasn't talking tonight, except for a few words to each animal in the string as he worked on them. It made him smile, because the packer was naturally talkative, but talk could only profane a night like this, and he needed this night to be pure. Being silent was this mule packer's attempt at religious sacrifice. He would never say anything about it to the boss or the other guys in the bunkhouse, though. If any of them had similar thoughts, they wouldn't talk about them. There is an unspoken holiness in silence.

He tied his jacket behind the cantle, despite the sweaty hot evening and its brassy taste. He knew the winds coming off Kearsarge would bite deeply before he reached the pack station up there in that blackening canyon at 9,200 feet above sea level.

The boss stopped traffic on the highway as the packer rode Brownie and led the jittery, trotting string of animals across the pavement and up the start of the dirt road then through the sage toward the night fastness above him. And then it was quiet but for the footfalls of the horses and mules as they once again figured where their places were and what their speed should be and turned from a herd of tied-together animals into a pack string.

As the road became a trail, and the trail went up into the mountains, the packer could look back at the ranch lights at the fort, and then look the two miles farther down the valley along the moving pearl string of headlights to the town lights of Independence, his adopted

home. It's strange how those lights mean so much, huddled together
in the face of such awe, gathering as if for company and support
against the overwhelming mountains and the secrets of the night.
He became aware of the moon only gradually, as he realized an hour
later that he could make out Brownie's ears before him. Then he
turned back to see each silvery animal work the slow switchbacks
in turn, and he paused each animal length ahead of them to let
them make the corners. There is a thrill and a pride in handling a
really long string of stock, he thought. During the days in the high
country, he seldom had more than five or six head behind him. But
a man who can handle a pack train this long has reached the elite
status of packer in this eastern rugged tall-nasty High Sierra country
of California. A string like this one, on a moonlit night, alone, can
earn a packer a doctorate in this unique craft.

During each of the summer days, he led the mules and took the
dudes over the rocky, wind-snapped passes to the fishing lakes. He
chatted with the people, reset errant horse and mule shoes, enjoyed
the scenery. But these night rides were special. The boss's stock truck
could climb the switchbacked dirt road to the pack station in the
meadow they called Onion Valley, but not if it had any stock in it. So
on the days when some of the stock wasn't needed for the high trails,
it was taken down to the ranch in the stock truck where grazing was
a lot cheaper than feeding alfalfa.

And when the time came to go back to the mountains, the packer
had to ride at night to return them "up the hill" for the next day's work.

This meant riding all day, riding all night, then riding all day again,
but it didn't happen often and the packer didn't mind that much,
really. There were things on the night ride, he knew, that somehow
paid the ticket for the fatigue.

And it made him smile. The stock didn't seem to misbehave as
much at night, either. Maybe they, too, sensed what he did, that this
was somehow a privilege and not just another long, dusty trail up the
mountain.

At Tubbs Springs, he tied the string to an oak and went down the
string, one by one, checking cinches, whispering reassuring words,

making certain no saddle pads had slipped. Four cinches needed tightening. Not bad. The percentage was getting smaller each trip, he thought, and he felt pleased.

Then he swung back aboard Brownie, picked up the lead rope to Jim and yelled "Mules!" and they obediently swung into line again and headed for the brushy saddle known locally as Tubbs Summit.

By this time, the moon turned the horses and mules silver with its magic. It gave the packer an unspoken pleasure to look back on a sinuous Sierra snake of eleven animals stretched in a flexible line nearly 150 feet long behind him. And he looked up, straight up on the peaks of Kearsarge where the snow fields always left behind shady patches of dirty white, up where the Inyo moon splashed them with a dream brush and made old secrets come to life.

˙₊˙ ✦ ☾˙ ˙₊✦

"You've heard of the ghost of Kearsarge," the old man said. "Everyone knows about her." The packers at the table at the ranch looked at each other.

"What ghost?" one asked.

"Just the old lady," the old man said, with laughter in his dark Paiute eyes. "She doesn't hurt nothing, you know. Just sings a little."

The evening was dark at the ranch, and the table lamp splashed shadows of the assembled weary cowboys on the kitchen walls as they sipped coffee. It was always good to hear the stories the old man told, coming over from his own small cabin here on the reservation.

"I never heard nothing about a ghost lady up Kearsarge," said the cook.

"That's what they say," said the old man. "Ever since there was a town up there. Used to be the mine up there, you know. Big one. Then there was a big dance in town one Christmas time, it was. Long time ago. Before my time.

"Anyway, everybody went to Independence to dance, you know, except the caretaker and his wife. Avalanche got 'em. They were the only ones. Everybody else went to the dance. Can't remember what year it was. That mine was working then, though."

Nobody spoke while the old man sipped some coffee. "You boys ever hear her up there at night? You can hear her. That's what they say, anyway. Avalanche took her head off, you know. Never did find it. They say she calls for her head at night when there's a moon."

"At Kearsarge?"

"Yeah, you know where those old foundations are? That's where the little town used to be. Where the stock trail leaves the Onion Valley road. Looking for her head. That's what they say. Looking for her head."

⋆ ☽ ⋆

The first foundations of Kearsarge glowed in the moonlight, little more than deliberate rock piles and scattered timbers now. The packer steered Brownie around the first and left the little stretch of dirt road again to follow the creek up the canyon. More foundations glowed, their old stones like age-worn teeth, and the wind came down from the snow patches cool and quiet. The packer thought he heard something, once. Just once, but he wondered about it, anyway. Maybe it was a night bird. Maybe. Looking back, the cluster of lights that was Independence had now shrunk to a small glowing nucleus in the moonscaped miles below.

He rested the stock on the first switchback above the old ghost town and pulled on his jacket. It helped.

⋆ ☽ ⋆

"Your granddad told us there was a spook up at old Kearsarge," the packer said as they a walked along the irrigation ditch that one night, a time back.

"Grandpa knows a lot," she said, squeezing his hand. "It's probably true."

He saw her eyes then, in the glow of a nearby streetlight there in town, as they walked. The desert night warmed them and made them both think of things long past and yet to come.

"You don't think he was just trying to b. s. us into being scared?"

"Not Grandpa. He knows a lot."

"Umm," the packer said.

"You like him?"

"Sure. Great guy."

"He likes you, too. He likes you a lot, I know. So does my mom and dad."

"Very nice people, your mom and dad."

She smiled up at him and he could see the pretty eyes again, the ageless eyes that spoke so much of generations of desert and mountain people, despite her youth.

"You like kids?" she asked.

*　·* ·· *·*
(·
· ·* *·*

The creek crashed down the mountain, heading for its ignominious ending in the Los Angeles aqueduct far below. The packer took the rocky crossings slowly, stopping often. The longer the string, the slower he must go, until every part of this long silent snake had negotiated every obstacle smoothly. Brownie was used to the stop and go of the night rides with long strings and didn't argue.

And there was the magic, of course. The seductive sorcery of night in the place where desert collides with mountains. It makes the longest nights shorter and the hardest rides easier.

He found the first of the pine trees at about 8,000 feet and listened once more to the breeze in the needles. And every now and then, in spite of himself, he listened for the voice of the lady without a head. Most of the horses were eager to get to the corrals and the hay, but the mules seemed content to look for moon-splashed grass clumps along the trail, clumps they may have missed on the last night ride.

The packer looked back each time the trail offered a view of the long string behind him.

The saddle horns on the horses and the forks of each packsaddle seemed to be straight up. No animal was hanging back on its lead rope. No one had stepped over one. He could see this clearly, all the way back to the caboose mule. Sometimes he felt like the engineer on a train, except that each of his boxcars had a mind of its own.

Then, as the peaks surrounded them in moon shadow, the wind turned cold and the weariness hit. He pulled his hat down farther on his face, turned up his collar, and shamefully admitted to himself that he looked back less often. That's when he heard the lady. Just once. He was sure of it, but he'd never tell anyone. It was too private. Too special.

The moon was behind the crest of the Sierra as he rode Brownie into the blackness of the pack station yard. The boss was there to help him unsaddle.

"Everything go okay?"

"No problems," the packer said.

"By the way, happy birthday."

"That's right, isn't it. Thanks."

"How old are you now?"

The packer stopped to think for a second in his early morning weariness. Then nodded.

"Seventeen," the packer said.

———

SLIM RANDLES is an outdoor novelist, newspaper columnist, and hunting guide. He spent eight years in the eastern High Sierra cowboying and packing mules for Sequoia-Kings Pack Trains and the Burkhardt Ranch.

Natural Causes

LORI VAN PELT

Carl Walker's patience wore thin. The lost man cost him time. Lambing was a hell of a time for Johnny Shale to disappear. Frigid air stung Carl's nostrils, smelling like metal and burning his lungs. April in this valley at the base of the Wyoming Sierra Madres yielded blizzards more often than showers, and this year felt colder than most.

He'd already returned two ewes to the shed. He'd left them in Anna's care. Anna suggested he ride out to look for Johnny. He was addicted to her homemade biscuits and never missed breakfast, most especially when he knew she planned to whip up a batch. When he hadn't arrived by eight o'clock, Carl began his search.

"Maybe he's staying away because of—"

"No." She spat the word. They looked at each other for a long moment. Carl saw something he didn't recognize in his wife's eyes. Normally they shone as silvery blue as the water rippling down Kayley Creek. As she spoke, her eyes glinted like the steel of the butcher knife hanging in the rack by the window above the kitchen sink.

"Carl," she said, "something's wrong. Bad wrong. I can feel it."

He had drunk the last of his cup, walked to the sink to stand beside her, looked out the window. Viewing the sky, a man might mistake the season for spring. The sun shone in a docile blue sky, reflecting on the snowdrifts piled by yesterday's raging blizzard. The brightness blinded him. "This storm was a bad one. Maybe he's holding the herd near the wagon."

Anna took the cup from him, and began filling the sink with hot water. She wiped her hands on her gingham apron, and said, "Let's hope so."

Carl dressed warmly, and Anna patted his heavy wool winter work coat when he pulled it on. He put on his hat, secured the woolen scarf she'd given him for Christmas around his neck, and bent to kiss her before facing the cold.

To her credit, Anna hadn't wavered when he brought the ewes in. She'd dropped her house chores, layered sweaters beneath her coat, and prepared to sit it out in the lambing shed. He hadn't even had to tell her what he was thinking. Since he'd returned alone, she knew that he hadn't found Johnny.

The sheep wagon hadn't been used in the night. There'd been no tracks except the ones that his own horse, Scout, made as they approached. When Carl dismounted and shouted, no one answered. No smoke escaped from the chimney pipe of the little wagon, and when he pushed open the door, he saw messy quarters but no one inside. Johnny'd eaten beans but hadn't cleaned up after his meal. A partially filled pan sat on the stove next to a dented enamel coffeepot containing a cup or so of the bitter brew. A few books lay scattered about near the rumpled bed. Carl smiled when he noticed Pearl Buck's *The Good Earth*. Anna lent the book to Johnny when he'd admitted he liked to read. The gesture was a kind one; the book was Anna's favorite—a Christmas present from Carl.

Carl shut the door. Finding the vacated sheep wagon knotted his stomach. Johnny hadn't planned to leave, or had he? Maybe he just stayed the night in town and hadn't returned. And maybe Carl didn't know his hired man as well as he should. Nothing had been stolen, at least nothing that Carl knew about now. Johnny's sudden disappearance was plumb odd, that's all there was to it.

Carl remounted, patted Scout on the neck, and turned toward the west pasture. His sheep were scattered. Some had frozen during the blizzard yesterday when they'd lost their way. He'd have to do the best he could in rounding up the remaining ewes. Damn, but he'd needed a good lamb crop this year. As he squinted across the white snow, breathing sharp air, he prayed that he'd save enough to meet the mortgage payment on the ranch. If not, well, he didn't want to think about it just now.

"Johnny, you damn fool! Where are you, man?" he shouted to the snow-covered hills. He received no answer. He expected none.

Carl spent the rest of the morning rounding up the survivors and penning them near the house. Even then, his eyes watered from the exposure to the blinding sun and snow combination and he couldn't be certain he'd found all the sheep.

Anna proudly showed him the efforts of her morning—two healthy lambs produced by two healthy ewes.

Carl hugged her but could not smile. "We've lost more than we should have," he said.

Anna blinked back tears. She coaxed him into their house for a hot lunch of chicken and dumplings and an apple crisp. "You'll feel better after you've eaten," she said.

"I'll go to town after lunch and see if he's there. Maybe he stayed in town for the night."

Carl's words sounded hollow. Johnny Shale had worked for the Walkers since last October. He'd never missed a day. He'd been good help up till now, but Carl had dealt with hired hands who appeared to be good workers and left at the worst times before. Some spent most of their nights at the bar in town. Not Johnny. He only partook of the drinks once a month. At least that's what he'd told Carl. Odd that he hadn't collected his pay. Most hands who left insisted on being paid all that was owed before leaving.

Carl considered their unusual argument of the previous day. He'd stopped at the bank in town, then had found Johnny in the bar. Carl didn't like that, but he couldn't stop the man from seeking his fun on a Friday evening.

"I expect you'll need your wages, Johnny," Carl said, sitting on a stool beside him.

"Why, hello, Carl." Johnny took a swig from a beer bottle. "I've been thinking about improvin' our arrangement."

"How so?"

Johnny suggested keeping the sheep near the wagon. "That way, they'll be in the lee of the hill if a storm comes up."

"And they'll be farther from the shed." In the corner of his eye, Carl noticed a young woman dressed in a ruffly dress and stockings and heels a few spaces away from them. Johnny paid no attention, but Carl wondered if she was the reason for Johnny's sudden bravado.

"Ah, Carl, sheep crowd together and keep themselves warm and cozy."

Carl shook his head. "No, Johnny. We ought to move them on down to the corral nearest the house. I don't want to take chances on some of them smothering. And a ewe giving birth—the herd might smother the lamb, too."

"Well, if you don't mind my askin', who's the sheepherder? Me or you?"

Carl managed to contain his anger but he felt his jaw tighten as he spoke. "Well, if you don't mind my askin', Johnny, who owns the sheep? Me or you?"

Johnny frowned. "You may as well pay me then."

Carl handed him an envelope filled with most of what he owed. He paid the amount he could. The banker kept pestering him about the ranch debt. He needed a successful lambing season to appease that man. And he needed Johnny to help with the lambs.

The argument left a bitter taste in Carl's mouth. What a lame-brained idea the man had. He couldn't believe Johnny had left over their dispute. Yet the sheep wagon stood empty. Why would he leave so suddenly if he had earlier planned to keep the herd nearby? And without collecting the rest of his pay?

Anna said, "Do you want cream on your dessert, Carl?"

Carl shook his head. "No, thanks. Cream's too heavy for me today."

She smiled at him and dished up the apple crisp. Handing him his portion, she said, "I warmed it in the oven while we were eating."

He took a bite, letting the cinnamon caress his nose and savoring the soft warm apple slices and brown sugar's crunchier texture. The sweetness soothed him. He said, "Mm, Anna, this is good crisp."

She thanked him, said, "Better than bride's crisp?" They both laughed at the joke he'd made when they'd been newly married ten years before. Carl's way of complimenting her cooking was to tell her the meal was "better than bride's cooking." He'd complimented her often for her tasty cooking since, especially her homemade biscuits. He never tired of eating them. Sometimes for breakfast, she'd fry up some ham and make gravy to go with them. He savored the taste of those light biscuits doused with thick, creamy ham gravy. For morning snacks, he usually covered a biscuit or two with a good helping of salty butter and a healthy dollop of Anna's sweet chokecherry jelly. A fresh, warm pan of Anna's golden, airy biscuits gave a man the strength to go on, especially when things looked bad.

She got up to pour him another cup of coffee. She stood beside the counter for a moment to pick up the coffeepot. She turned toward him, and he wondered again why Johnny would leave without his money, without even telling Carl he was going.

Unless it was the incident with Anna. Carl watched his wife. She continued eating her lunch, taking careful bites, blowing on the hot food before tasting each. Her hard work in the cold air made her hungry.

Carl had walked into the house mid-morning one day last week. Johnny had been reaching around Anna's waist for a biscuit, and Carl had been on the same side of her, so he didn't see the man's face, just the shaggy cut of the dark hair on the back of his head. But Carl could see Anna's. Beads of sweat formed on her forehead, dampening the blonde curls she worked so diligently to maintain. Tight lines cut the edges of her thin mouth. She faced Johnny, her right hand behind her gripped the counter. Her left hand was lifted behind her, its palm extended in an awkward position, out of Johnny's sight. Her hand halted in that distorted way within inches of the handle of the butcher knife. Viewing the scene, a man might have mistaken her movement. Maybe she was reaching for Johnny.

"Carl," she said, and exhaled.

Johnny spun to face him.

"She makes mighty good biscuits, Carl. You're lucky to have her."

Carl said, "I believe I'll have one myself." He walked closer to Anna as Johnny walked away. "We'll plan to take a break in the mornings from now on," Carl said, careful to keep anger from his face and his words. "I'll bring the biscuits with me so you won't have to bother Anna in the house."

Anna's hand, still gripping the counter, trembled. She turned her gaze to her husband's. "Here, Carl, I'll get you one." She turned shakily toward him and lifted a biscuit from the pan, handing it to him. Unsteadily, she reached for a napkin. Carl was certain from her actions that Johnny had made an unwanted advance. He forced unwelcome thoughts of the even more disturbing possibility that they were together in the house for another reason from his ravaged mind.

He vowed he would not ask her. Anna would not have done anything to jeopardize the success of lambing season. They needed the money too badly.

Johnny remained silent through their exchange. He ate the biscuit, after spreading some spicy apple butter on it, and drank coffee as if nothing had happened. Anna never spoke of it again. Carl did not ask questions. He needed the hired man to help them get through lambing. But the memory lingered in his mind.

No one remembered seeing Johnny in Chalk Bluff the night before. Carl inquired at the post office, the Hotel Goldwin dining room, the bar, the grocery store, the newspaper, and finally found the deputy sheriff at the town police office and told him all he knew. Pat Branson shook his head. "I'm sorry, Carl. Rough time to lose a hand."

"Sure is. Know of anyone who'd care to help us with lambing on short notice?"

Pat shook his head. "If I run across someone, I'll send him your way."

"Thanks, Pat." Carl started to leave the office, then turned back. "And you'll tell me if you find Johnny?"

"Sure."

As Carl rode back to the ranch, the newspaper reporter jumped on the story, seeking out Pat Branson for the sensational details. He needed a story for the next week's issue, and this would be a good one. He could tie it in to the blizzard, too. Though Pat told him that Carl Walker was an upstanding citizen, a quiet sheep rancher who kept to himself with a wife who attended church regularly, the reporter also checked in at the bar. There, he heard the tale of a heated argument between the hot-tempered Carl and his hired hand, Johnny Shale. The bartender had seen money exchanged. The information provided the balance he needed to write the article fairly. He envisioned the story being carried in the 1933 yearly wrap-up, and the thought of a reporting award crossed his mind while he worked.

By Sunday, when Carl and Anna had lambing under control as best they could, and the cold air abated some, Anna attended church. Carl watched the sheep.

Instead of finding her singing in the kitchen, as was her usual way following church, Carl found her in tears at the table. He poured himself a cup of coffee and joined her.

"Carl, I overheard something at church today. I think you should know."

"What, Anna?"

"People were saying they thought you—," she muffled a sob in her handkerchief and started again. "That you got rid of Johnny so you wouldn't have to pay him."

Carl stood abruptly. He struck the oak table with his flat palm with such force that the dishes rattled.

"I'll be go to hell, Anna," he said. His quiet, rage-filled tone frightened her. She stood.

They looked at each other for a long moment across the round oak table that had belonged to her grandmother.

"Anna," he said, "what do you believe?"

"Oh, Carl," she said, turning away toward the stove.

"Anna?" His voice was soft now.

She turned to him. Silvery hair slipped down across his forehead. His face was burned by the wind and the snow and the sun, and the unanswered question trying to burst through his skin.

"Carl, you know better than to even ask me."

He blinked, pressed his chapped lips together.

April and May finally melted into a spring-like June. Carl and Anna managed the lambing chores alone. No word came of Johnny Shale. Folks around town instead focused on Carl. He'd soon tired of suspicious glances and whispers behind his back. People he'd thought were his friends spread rumors that he'd killed the hired man to save money. The newspaper report let the story dangle in people's minds. The reporter couldn't decipher the true story, so in telling the tale, the open-endedness of it pointed to Carl. The report explained the facts—Shale turned up missing; lambing time was the worst time he could have gone missing; Carl and he had argued in public; Carl had handed Johnny money in the bar. Though the sheriff's comment had been to explain that Carl had reported the man missing and had cooperated with his efforts, the sensational aspects overshadowed the facts. The money, however, was not explained. A second report a week later had reiterated the story. Johnny Shale could not be located, and he had worked for Carl Walker at the time of his disappearance. Sheriff Branson admitted that Johnny had been a regular weekly customer of the local bar. That comment angered Carl. Johnny had told him otherwise. He'd once told Carl he'd rather read a book than gallivant around at the bar in town. Maybe they were better off rid of the man, even with the scandal he'd produced.

Carl knew of the nasty rumors because Woody Martell told him. Woody built houses and had helped Carl build his and Anna's. Woody and Carl had been friends since elementary school. Carl told Anna, "A true friend will tell you unpleasant things. Those who don't tell you the things you'd rather not hear are not your friends."

Anna searched his face with dull eyes. A long moment passed. "Some things are better left unsaid, Carl," she said.

The town talk wore on Anna's nerves. She jumped when Carl entered the house and called her name. She dropped plates as she washed dishes in the evenings and then had to clean up two messes. She picked at her food. She lost weight. Carl began to wonder if she had taken the butcher knife to the man. Out of guilt? Maybe she believed he killed Johnny. If they'd been having an affair, she might have imagined the worst.

Carl thought it odd that she seemed so shaky in the house but she bore her lambing chores cheerfully, as if a weight had been lifted from her shoulders.

In mid-June, Carl rode around the ranch, fixing irrigation ditches as best he could and keeping tabs on his grazing sheep. He rode near the sheep wagon. He'd cleaned up the mess but left it sit where Johnny had last left it, thinking the man might return for his things. The wagon was parked in the lee of a rocky hill Carl started calling "Johnny's Knob." As he crested the hill, he could see the house. On the fence hung a white dishtowel—Anna's signal that she needed his help.

Carl returned home, greeted by Anna and a neighboring rancher, Ben Thompson. Carl took off his gray felt work hat, smoothed the locks of sweat-curled hair at the nape of his neck, twisted the length of leather that he used to hold his hat on his head, and stuffed the leather inside the crown, placing the worn Stetson upside down on the counter. He looked toward Anna, seeing first the bloody butcher knife on the counter. She moved toward him. Near the knife, pieces of chicken lay in disarray, pale skin pulled back to reveal white protuberances of bone where cuts had been made.

Ben stood, but Carl motioned him to sit.

"Ah, sit still, Ben." He shook the man's hand. Ben remained standing.

"We found Johnny," he said, voice quiet and somber.

The room was hushed as if covered by a heavy wet spring snow. The only noise was the bubbling sound of the coffee Anna poured into Carl's mug. The lid clanked against the porcelain-enameled pot. Anna held the knob, covered by a red gingham potholder, with her middle finger. The lid shook in her hand.

Carl stopped, midway through removing his winter overclothes. Though the calendar indicated late spring, the outdoors remained chill. One hand, still gloved, held the empty glove. He tapped it in his palm. "I'll be." He looked at Ben over the table for a moment. Carl sighed, pulled out a chair and sat down. "What happened?"

Ben followed suit. "We don't know. Found him out in the sagebrush flats—on my land. About four miles from here as the crow flies."

"Dead." Carl didn't ask. He stated the fact.

Ben nodded. "Not much left I'm afraid."

Anna gripped the counter top, and stood still, her back to the men.

Ben picked up his cup of coffee, and as if becoming aware of Anna again, said, "Sorry, Anna."

Carl's gaze rested on his wife. "You all right?"

"Yes," she answered. She turned to face them. Her pale face belied her words. Carl reached for her hand and held it in his own. To Ben, he said, "I expect you've gone to see Pat."

Ben finished another sip of coffee. "No, Carl. I came here first. I thought we should go together."

Carl squeezed Anna's hand. He blinked. Ben's kind treatment of him lifted a weight from his shoulders. Ben said, "I'll take you out to Johnny first if you'd like."

Carl said he should go and Ben explained how he and his son stumbled across the body. They had been out riding fence, checking to see how much of it had held up through the winter. The horses caught the scent in the wind and shied.

"Raised quite a ruckus," Ben said. "We had to approach on foot. I wonder how he got way over there?"

"Guess we'll never know," Carl said.

"I bet he was out in the storm and got disoriented." Ben explained that the body was hidden in a draw. The wintry snows had buried the corpse and so it hadn't been easily visible.

Carl nodded. "Makes a crazy sort of sense, don't it?"

The three of them were each lost in their own thoughts for a moment. Carl broke the silence. "I expect we'd better go." He released Anna's hand, unaware he'd held it through the whole sorry tale. "Anna, you'll write his mother, then?"

She closed her eyes for a moment as if gathering strength. "Yes, Carl. I'll write Johnny's mother. She'll be anxious to know."

Ben said, "His mother?"

Carl explained, "We contacted her when he first went missing. I sent her the rest of his wages and such then. She lives in Nebraska. Maybe she'll want to come out or want a service or something." Carl paused to take a sip of coffee. "She's been ailing. She hadn't seen Johnny since he'd left as a teenager. He sent her money from time to time. I don't think they got along." He took another quick sip. "Still, it's right that she know." He rose from his chair and Ben did the same.

Anna said, "Yes. It's right that she know."

A draft of cold air made Anna shiver as the men left the house. She watched them drive Ben's red Dodge pickup down the muddy road toward town, past Johnny's Knob. She stood at the kitchen window looking at the knob. Suddenly, she realized that the earthly bulge was covered with the green grass of summertime. She turned back to the oven, wiping her hands on her apron, and began thinking about what she could cook for supper to go with a big, golden-crusted pan of Carl's favorite.

LORI VAN PELT writes regularly for *Roundup Magazine* and the *WREN* (Wyoming Rural Electric News). She has written numerous nonfiction articles for a variety of regional and national publications and is the author of the *Dreamers and Schemers* book series published by High Plains Press. Her short fiction has appeared in the books *American West: Twenty New Stories by the Western Writers of America* (Forge), and *White Hats* (Berkley). Lori grew up on a wheat farm/cattle ranch in Banner County, Nebraska, and now lives with her husband on his family's cattle ranch near Saratoga, Wyoming.

The Stormy Blue Jitney

GREM LEE

Will Stockton's thoughts were elsewhere as he sat tapping a matchstick on the edge of the supper table. The old cowman pondered over what he knew to be inevitable. He had strong feelings, but that didn't matter. He was trapped of his own doings. There was no turning back.

Surrounding him like a den of starving coyote pups, his four boys were unconsciously devouring every last morsel of the evening meal. Sarah, their mom, hummed softly as she moved about by the dancing flicker of a coal oil lamp.

"Boys!" Will busted in. Immediately the boys trained their eyes and ears on the man at the head of the table. It was really the old cowboy's quirt hanging on a saddle horse way down at the barn that got their attention. "I made ya'll a deal earlier this spring and I aim to keep my word."

They knew what their Dad was talking about. Everybody, including Sarah, got big grins on their faces. Everybody except Will.

Will Stockton had told his four strappin' boys that if they could put up a winter's worth of corn for his livestock that he would get them some kind of old jalopy to drive. The boys had stayed hooked up short all summer and had just one task left to do. That was to get the matured corn out of the field and into the barn. They were anxious and so was their mom, Sarah. She had an important reason why.

Will said, "Tomorrow I'm pulling out with the horses for the C Bar N. If everything goes well, I should be back within six days. That ought to give ya'll time enough." His sons also knew what that meant. He expected the entire field of corn to be taken care of by the time he returned. The bargain was almost complete. The boys focused on the prize, not the backbreaking work that lay ahead. They all envisioned the fun times to be had with an automobile.

It was barely crackin' dawn when Will slid the light aspen poles back so he could enter to wrangle his horse herd. He and his boys had constructed from one bluff to another a rock and log barricade across the narrow mouth of Bear Canyon. It was virtually the only way in.

Behind this passageway opened up several square miles of sub-irrigated meadow. Side oat gramma grass covered the hillsides. Lots of gray oak, too. The perimeter was walled up by a malpais rim rock that was tree-top high. The natural enclosure was broken open by only a few thin crevices here and there. Indians and wild animals had made steep trails through these. They had been used eons and eons.

This cosmic-created fortress was the perfect protection for Will's select livestock. This was his world. He wanted for nothing else.

On the upper end of the ground, the boys had built a round corral for Will. The posts were of alligator bark juniper and all set deep in the dirt. In between each of the solid posts spanned eight quaking aspen poles. The corral grew with their dad's rigid words in mind. "The right way to do anything is always the hardest way."

Inside this stronghold, ranch horses were made and Will's cattle branded. The place was a stockman's paradise. How in the devil could the boys see more in a machine or any fancy new invention than they could in this? He would never understand.

Today, Will and Ol' War Hatchet led the way as thirteen fine young horses followed. Past the cabin they went. As Will had gotten into the habit of doing and would forever do, he tipped his hat toward a well-kept grave. The boys were already at work in the field. They all paused to wave and one even hollered, "Adios, Pa!" Will waved back.

The eldest son, Bill Jr., was the head honcho for the work detail. In reality, however, the brothers needed no boss. This wasn't their first time in a cornfield. Bill's hardest job was going to be in keeping the twins, Burt and Curt, out of a knuckle-bustin' fist fight. After all, the two exchanged blows a handful of times a day. The middle brother, Charlie, was a worker when he wasn't being a clown.

It had been a hard struggle all summer. The boys had done battle against a cold, heartless phenomenon known as Mother Nature. First there was that strange late freeze, then a hard-hitting hailstorm in June. Two rows were missing from when that crazy one-eyed mule cold jawed with the cultivator. And all those damn critters. Big and small. There were caterpillars and grasshoppers. Rock squirrels, raccoons, deer, and one sneaky, self-indulgent black bear. The thieves just kept coming and coming. Hooter, the bellowing hound, was wore to a frazzle in his quest to protect.

The boys absolutely hated the farming end of a ranch. Hooter, too. What they'd rather be doing is cowboy work. The riding! The roping! The branding! The working with Will's horses, but not if it was trailing behind a dang plow. However, for an automobile, that was a different matter. For that, the young cowboys would plow.

Better than a week ago, the boys had cut the ends off the ears of corn. These were called nubbins and would be fed to the milk cow, hogs, and chickens. The ear left on the stalk would now dry and the kernels get hard and be good for cow horses the year around. This morning the boys were breaking the dried ears off the stalk and packing them into a wagon at the edge of the field. It would take most of the day.

They halted when they heard familiar singing flowing down Apache Creek. It could only be Slack, the Irish whiskey maker, from up Yankee Gulch. "If the ocean were whiskey and I was a duck, I'd swim to the bottom and never come up."

Slack rode his burro up to the boys. "By guineas lads. She looks to be three gallons to the acre!" he exclaimed. Then he turned his trusty mount and pointed him down the creek. "My regards to Will and your dear sweet mama." The jovial man then continued on with his song.

Slack and Will had come to these mountains at about the same time. These two tough hombres had become good friends. Also, through the years, they had stumbled into a business arrangement.

Will's boys delivered sacked corn to Slack's hidden spring in Yankee Gulch. On their return they would carry home a two-gallon keg of moonshine whiskey plus all the fermented mash that the horses could haul. The hogs would be drunk for days. Some of Sarah's chickens, too.

It just so happened that Sarah wasn't far from the cornfield now. She was beginning her daily ritual. Every day of every season for close to a year, Sarah had faithfully visited the grave. The emotion was still there as she slowly walked the well-worn path. She wasn't crazy like some would think or even say. She was just a normal grieving mother. It was her way.

At the end of the path stood a stately oak. Beneath it a simple headstone that had been made by a sister's four brothers. Crudely chiseled on it was a young girl's name, Stormy.

Sarah sat on the board seat of a rope swing hanging from the tree. This had been her daughter's favorite place. Sarah talked softly and only of good things. She smiled and teared some, too. She didn't stay long. "Your dad said he'd be home later in the week. He gave the boys his word on the automobile. I hope. See you tomorrow, sweetie." Sarah then started back for the cabin.

Several days later, Will and Ol' War Hatchet were already most of half way home. Ol' War Hatchet was the best horse Will ever raised. His best friend, too. Will had just delivered and sold to the V Cross T thirteen of the most muscled-up and rock-wise mountain horses in the country. They had a good handle on them, too. The cow sense would come with a savvy cowboy atop.

Will was anxious to get home and check on his stock. He had a sneaking suspicion that Harlan Hooper and his outlaw boys were still prowling the hills like a pack of savage wolves. Also, the mean old man, Henry, with his hungry passel of kids lived just down the creek. It was a sure bet that even a poor bony milk cow's life was in bloody danger.

Suddenly Ol' War Hatchet's ears shot straight up. Will could see something in the wagon trail ahead. They were only a few miles east of Horse Springs. The strange object turned out to be an automobile.

As they passed by the newfangled contraption, Ol' War Hatchet snorted and shied sideways. "Yeah, I know ol' pard," Will said in disgust. "I don't like the damn things either." The vehicle was jacked up and one wheel was in the front seat.

Back home the boys were exhausted. The strong incentive of a possible automobile had kept them busy. The cornfield job was close to done. It had not been easy.

The stalks had been shocked and the bundles stacked in the barn. The husks on every ear had been peeled back to expose the rich yellow kernels. Then, all of the ears had been poked through a hand-cranked sheller. They saved the best of the crop to be milled into corn meal for their beloved mom. She'd put it to good-tasting use. The remainder was all shoveled into a rat-proof corncrib for Dad's livestock through the winter. Jim Crow, the family's milk cow, had been turned out to graze on the stubble. The boys basically had this deal cinched.

The long demanding days weren't the only reason for the boys' fatigue. Half their nights were being spent whispering about the automobile. Sarah would act mad and tell them to hush up and go to sleep. The silence wouldn't last long. Her voice didn't have the sting to it that Will's did. Didn't matter. She was getting a big kick out of their grandiose plans for the automobile.

Down the road a ways, about midmorning the next day, came the singing Irishman. He was heading to the Apache Creek Store for another sack of sugar and some yeast. "Rye whiskey, rye whiskey, rye whiskey, I cry. If I don't have rye whiskey, I'm sure I will die." He had just departed from introducing himself to the new school marm and was rather excited. His voice gave it away.

He rounded the bend when he bumped into Will. Will had already heard his happy buddy coming. "Why, top of the morning to ya, Will. Jolly, jolly good to see you!" Will thought he sounded like a crowing rooster. The two friends shot the breeze for a bit, but both needed to get on.

As they parted company, Slack held his burro up and called back, "Oh, Will, me boy. The wild grapes up Yankee Gulch are purple and plump. Plumb full of juice. Tell Sarah and Stormy that . . ." Slack shut his trap in a heartbeat. His ramblin' mouth had let the girl's name slip out before he realized it. "I'm sorry, Will," he said. "I shorely weren't thinking."

It had been almost a year since the tragedy. Sarah and Stormy enjoyed each other's companionship and were close to inseparable. The two pals had a favorite fall pastime. They loved to pick wild grapes together and then make jelly. There was none better. Slack raved about

Stormy's wild grape jelly.

The sadness came when the lively little Stormy hopped up on a loose rock above a grapevine. It slid out from under her quick and the innocent kid hit the ground hard. The nasty black-tailed rattlesnake struck her instantly right on her tender face. Stormy was everybody's doll on Apache Creek. She was barely fourteen. Mother Nature has her cruel ways.

The accidental mention of her name by Slack hit Will like a hard fist. His body felt as if his life's blood had been sucked away. He hadn't forgotten. He'd never forget, but he knew the day was almost here. Will kicked his tired partner on. Ol' War Hatchet obliged him willingly. Sarah. Will had to get home to check on Sarah.

Up Apache Creek, the cornfield had been completely taken care of. Even so there were other chores to be done before winter. The boys had been raised to do chores without having to be told. Again, it was the quirt that kept them on their toes, that got their respect.

Since Stormy wasn't there this year, the boys had faithfully been helping their mom put up her garden. What they didn't pickle or can, they dried. That included the fat little forked-horn buck deer that was helping himself to Sarah's fall turnips. She had a big heart, but enough was enough. From the cornfield the boys had heard her Winchester go off. It only took one shot and they knew the hunt was over.

This morning their efforts were on making the woodpile bigger. All that the boys could talk about, though, was the automobile. It was the epicenter of their lives now. An automobile would be nothing but fun, fun, and more fun. Their dad would see.

Sarah had just walked out on the porch to holler "lunch" when Hooter went to barking. Here came Will and Ol' War Hatchet at a fast trot. The boys and their dog raced out to meet them. They swarmed Will and his horse like a wad of happy gnats. All of them jabberin' at once.

"Howdy, boys," he said as his big hand pawed their heads, hats and all. His eyes, however, were locked on Sarah. She stood at the edge of the high covered porch drying her hands on a towel made from a cotton flour sack. At the top of her slender willowy frame was a simple smile. As always, she was steadfast.

Will rode up and stepped down from his horse. The boys were already in a big growl over who got to lead Ol' War Hatchet to the barn and who got to unsaddle him and who would grab the brush and who would get the bucket of corn. Will never heard the squabble. He just walked up the steep wooden steps, gave his wife a kiss, and hugged her tight. Then at arms' length, he held her back and tried to look into her heart.

Sarah knew he worried about her. "I'm fine, Will," she gestured. "Don't worry, honest, I'm fine."

For lunch, Will was more filled up on questions from the boys than he was on Sarah's good cooking. "When, Dad? When are we gonna go get the automobile?" The boys kept digging at Will despite knowing this was shaky ground to be on.

Will slowly finished his plate and reached into his shirt pocket for a match. He didn't smoke, but he always whittled himself a toothpick after every meal. Will didn't get his pocketknife out now, though. He began tapping the blunt matchstick on the tabletop. Everybody got quiet knowing Will was thinkin'.

"All right, all right!" Will finally said. He knew he had to bend. "Day after tomorrow we'll go see Demetrio." Will then began to talk at length that the boys better be sure about trading off Steamboat for the automobile. The loyal horse was part of the family. "Ever one of you knotheads learned how to ride on that little rascal. You better be sure."

They were boys to the bone and never even flinched. Heck Fire! This was darn sure no time to be getting sentimental. After all, they were in dire need of an automobile. "We're sure, Pa," Bill Jr. piped up. The other boys nodded in agreement.

Sarah grabbed Will's hand and smiled. She knew he was fighting his head over the deal. It didn't make any sense. There was no way he could have traded off his horse when he was a kid, not even for a bucket of gold.

That night Will held Sarah close. He told her about his trip and how well the C Bar N cowboys liked his horses. He mentioned meeting

Slack and how Stormy's name had been said. The parents then reminisced about the fun times they'd had with their daughter.

Will almost forgot, but before they fell asleep, he told Sarah about the broken-down jalopy that he and Ol' War Hatchet had passed by at Horse Springs. He laughed and poked fun at how the driver had probably had to walk. "Worthless dang things," Will grumbled.

The air in the dark room got still and quiet. Will drifted off. Now Sarah's thoughts began to stir and gain strength. She wanted the automobile, too. What if they would have had it back then? Could they have gotten Stormy to the doctor in time? Maybe, just maybe. She would never say this to Will, but she would always wonder. The mother never wanted to go through that again.

It was two days later and a small Mexican man had been toiling in his field since daybreak. He was pulling up his bean plants and placing two or three to a pile to dry. Frijoles were his life.

Demetrio paused for a moment to straighten the aching bones in his bent back. He became aware of the Stockton gang coming at a fast clip. The boys' direction fixed on the rusty object at the edge of the field. The old man walked over to meet them.

The unused machine hadn't moved in years. Not since Demetrio had run it out of gas on this very spot. Never in his life had he forgotten to feed his animals. However, he constantly forgot to pour fuel into his automobile. "Very, very goot to see you Weel," he said.

"Good to see you, too, Little Dee," Will said. "Here's that horse I told you about." Will told Demetrio that he was one of the best horses he had ever raised. Of course, he said that of all his horses. Will quizzed Demetrio one last time, "Are you sure you still want to trade?"

"Oh sí, sí Señor Weel," Demetrio said. "Me *esposa*, I mean—me wife, likey the caballo and buggy more better. Some Sundays we come from church. We stop by the creek for some lunchy. Maybe I get a cookie from Mama!" Demetrio got a big toothy grin and winked at Will.

The boys were engrossed in their newly acquired treasure. Like inquisitive young raccoons, they probed over every inch of its iron anatomy. "Hey, Dad!" Curt hollered. "All the tires got air in them, too."

Will remained sitting on Ol' War Hatchet and murmured to himself,

"Yeah, but they'll all be flat someday."

Demetrio had told Will beforehand that the automobile would have to be pulled. As he said in his broken English, "The macheen no worky no more."

For that reason, Will had brought along his dependable draw horses to do the job. "Okay, boys, hook 'er up! Let's get this hunk of junk to movin.'" The boys sloughed off Will's remark and hitched the team in a hurry. Everybody took his place. Bill Jr. was in command at the steering wheel. Charlie stood in the shotgun seat and held the lines to the actual horsepower. "Hey horses!" he yelled. Huck and Fletch, the two gristle-headed tuggers, laid into the trace chains. The big wooden spoke wheels of the 1917 Buick sluggishly began to roll.

Burt and Curt sat in the back seat and slapped the sides with their floppy hats. Hooter began barking like a lunatic dog and commenced to run idiot circles around the circus. It was onward to the good times ahead.

Will and Ol' War Hatchet started as this raging wash of excitement moved forward. The happy Demetrio held on tight to Steamboat. The two sun-baked men simply smiled at each other. Their unspoken wisdom said it all. "Adios, Little Dee," Will said as he and Ol' War Hatchet took up the trail behind.

That night around the supper table, there was a special glow. The boys were lit up about ready to explode. Sarah gazed at their ecstatic faces with pure pleasure. The family had an automobile now and it was right outside.

Sarah's dark ebony eyes grabbed their attention as she began to speak. "A year ago tomorrow is the day that Stormy passed away. It was the saddest day of our lives. I never want to feel that way again." Sarah went on to inform her brood that from now on, the date was to remind them of how full of life Stormy had been, instead of a reminder of her death. She knew with certainty that her spirited daughter would want it that way.

Sarah said she had ordered and received four quarts of paint from the Monkey Wards catalog. It was Stormy's favorite color, royal blue. Slack had been by earlier in the day with a bucket full of wild grapes.

She said, "Slack and Stormy were best pals, so I invited him down for dinner tomorrow. I want you boys to paint your automobile."

Will had work planned, but that notion had changed now. He'd never utter a word about it. Some things are just better left unsaid.

It was a fine autumn day. The fall had been mild on Apache Creek and the lovely Indian summer was being gracious. The animals gained life from the heavy mast of acorns, pinions, and berries. The grass was curing. The water flowed and the mountain birds sang.

Sarah made certain this day would be special. She had the boys dress out three pullets over by the woodpile. Along with the fried chicken, there would be snap beans and roastin' ears, mashed potatoes and gravy. For dessert, peach cobbler and hot biscuits with wild grape jelly. All of this grown, or gathered, on the Stockton Ranch.

Slack showed up about midmorning. He had brought along a jug of his homemade beverage, too. White mule, he called it. He and Will sat on the porch and visited. Slack again apologized for the blunder made a few days earlier.

Directly in front of the two men was a drastic look of the changing times. Around the automobile and at the end of four wooden-handled paintbrushes were four excited boys. In their eager adolescent nature, the blue paint was laid on thick and in haste. Crude as it was, it was done. A zenith in their young lives.

As they finished, Sarah hollered, "Come and get it!" The aroma of her dedicated cooking had preceded itself. All of them washed with the warm water at the wash pan Sarah had set out on the porch bench.

The whole bunch gorged on the feast that Sarah had prepared. Afterwards they sat in pure pleasure. Everybody stared through the wide plate glass picture window. Outside against a backdrop of the earth-toned fall foliage was the brightest blue Buick in the country. It was indeed an impressive sight. The boys were proud as full-feathered peacocks. Will was tapping a matchstick.

Slack cheered up, "By guineas, Will, me friend, a toast we must make." He raised his mason jar of corn juice high and let it rip, "Here's to the lads with the Stormy blue jitney and here's to my new acquaintance with the plump new school marm, Miss Maggie

Magee. Jolly be!"

For the moment they all laughed hysterically. As the laughter quieted, however, an eerie noise was heard. A threat. It penetrated through every opening of the Stockton cabin. The group at the table froze and listened. They had heard this familiar sound before.

Sssssssssssss! It was a snake. A twisting, breathing snake. Sssssssssss! Slowly, it crawled off the high rimrock and hunted its way down into the deep canyon bottom. It poked and prodded for game. With prowess, it easily passed over the barn and then slithered through the woodpile. Unrelenting for carnage, it crept closer and closer and closer. Suddenly, the victim was spotted. Hurriedly, the cold heartless phenomenon coiled and readied for the strike. KaBloooooeee! The whirlwind, Ma Nature's dust devil, hit hard.

The nasty, whirling monster completely engulfed the sticky blue prize. Immediately, it spit the cold, lifeless object out and then vanished as quick as it had appeared. Left behind remained the ugly spoil of its poison: leaves and twigs and dust and white chicken feathers galore.

The lunch party was flabbergasted and sat in silent shock. All at once, the boys hit the screen door in an angry mob and scrambled off the porch to size up the damage. The adults followed. They all milled around the automobile in a daze. Suddenly Slack began laughing like a braying burro.

Will just shook his head, "I could have told you boys something like this would happen. Wonderful meal, Sarah. Ol' War Hatchet and I are headin' up Bear Canyon to check on the cattle."

Sarah had to turn her head away as a grin washed over her face. She honestly felt bad for the boys, but she couldn't hold in her mirth. She started down the path toward the grave. On this day Sarah would definitely have a special story for Stormy.

In sickening disgust, the boys began to pick feathers from the skin of their pretty blue baby.

Slack busted out hootin' again, "Ah, ha, ha! Whoa ho . . ." Catching his breath, he was finally able to gasp, "By guineas, lads! I bet she be the first jitney to ever have her feathers plucked. Golly, golly!"

GREM LEE is a fourth generation New Mexico rancher who has been surrounded by the trade since the day he was born and named Oliver M. Lee IV. His boot leather–tough Dad, Sato, taught Grem and his two brothers, Tommy and Michael, how to deal with the everyday hardships of life and death on the range. Grem says, "Ranching will ground you in reality." He is the great-grandson of pioneer cattleman Oliver M. Lee, a solid individualist, who built a ranching empire and refused to be intimidated by the likes of Pat Garrett and the Santa Fe Ring. Grem is an award-winning artist and writer, and continues to work despite having the vicious disease of M.S., or B.S. as he calls it. He currently lives with his wife Debbie and daughter Tana on the family ranch that's located in the high cedar mesas of west central New Mexico. The Lee ranching tradition endures.

Open Winter

CANDY MOULTON

The only bad thing about an open winter is a dry spring followed by a summer when the water springs go dry. With her house on a ridge that formed foothills like a piece of ric-rac at the eastern flank of Wyoming's Sierra Madres and located a mile and a half above sea level, Emma always said whenever she went to Laramie, Denver, or even to Montana it was always downhill. That year even when they headed upcountry to summer pasture, Charlie said it was downhill.

They'd spent twenty-three years sharing the same bed and the same name, and for their efforts had two kids, S.R. and Marie, and a few dozen cows of their own plus a couple hundred Charlie took care of on the ranch his boss owned and two other places he leased.

Charlie's boss was typical for the times, a gray-headed dentist-turned-rancher who knew more about fixing teeth than he did about herding cows, which was a good thing, otherwise he'd have never gotten the money together to buy the Home Place down on the river, what with land selling for twenty times its worth.

It was a melding of cultures. Emma stood only five foot three when her long black hair was in a pile on top of her head, but she was strong-willed and had an argumentative streak. Charlie said she got it from her Belgian grandparents. Charlie topped her by a mere four inches, had no hair to help him achieve that lofty height, and was a perfectionist who'd spend hours making sure the fence was fixed exactly right, or that the door on a medicine cabinet he built for the barn fit like a new glove. Emma said that came from his English forebears who had the temerity to travel to Utah with a Mormon handcart company in 1856. Neither one drank coffee, though they downed tea by the gallon.

The Boss was a high-strung, generous-to-a-fault Greek who wore a sweatshirt year around. He downed coffee by the potful. His wife Dee was a city gal, but born to ranch with a natural understanding of the land and the livestock. She kept to herself, spinning mohair from goats she raised, riding her horse, and making sure there was plenty of tea and coffee to go around.

The open winter made feeding easier because there were no snow-drifts to move with the ancient tractor that hadn't had much power even when it was new, forty years earlier. The only big snow of the winter came a week before Christmas. Almost twenty inches of pure white powder coated the meadow above the house and Emma itched to put on her skis and take a run up across the fields. But she'd hurt her shoulder lifting a sack of grain and couldn't raise her arm high enough to open the gate to the meadow, let alone break a cross-country trail in fresh powder. So she sat in the house watching the powder and nursing a cup of the green tea she'd started drinking after seeing a story in the newspaper claiming it was better for you than black tea.

There was barely enough snow left to call it a white Christmas.

"I don't care if it don't snow down here," Charlie said one February evening as he read the *Fence Post*. "So long as it falls above the ditch."

"Doesn't look like it's doing that though," Emma replied from her seat at the table where she worked a jigsaw puzzle.

"There's a little snow up there above timberline. There's still time," Charlie said.

But it didn't snow as he fed the cows. And when the heifers dropped their calves every day was filled with sunshine, the nights not even cold as they should have been. It was a good open year. They lost only a couple of calves and had three sets of twins, making it a hundred percent calf crop.

The high country had a real spring for the first time in fifty years. It warmed up. There were a couple of days with a soft rain, but no mud. The crocuses and four tulips in Emma's untended flowerbed under the picture window bravely poked their heads out, spreading new petals to the sun. Robins landed on the pole fence. Ten-year-old Marie weeded the iris patch and planted some petunias and carnations. Fifteen-year-old S.R. washed the rickety old Jeep he'd bought with last year's wages earned helping on the ranch. The lilac leaves poked out a full month before they should have and the L-shaped snowbank on the mountain that marked the end of high water melted before mid-May.

Then winter arrived. The temperature plummeted. Hoarfrost coated the flowers, the fences and the trees. When winter concluded its four-day run, the petunias wilted and drooped. The lilac leaves turned black.

Emma didn't yell at Charlie, S.R., and Marie about tracking mud into the house. There wasn't any. One day of sunshine took care of that. By early June she thought a little mud would be good, that would mean it had rained, that some moisture had fallen. Instead it got cold at night, nipping the alfalfa as it tried to grow. And the soil, usually moist, turned to hardpan. It cracked and curled up at the edges, making a cup to capture any stray drop of rain that fell.

In the evenings, as they'd done for two decades, Charlie and Emma walked up the road to check out the flow in Beaver Creek. S.R. and Marie joined them occasionally, but usually it was just the two of them, Charlie walking quickly, Emma trailing along trying to smell the roses. Only there weren't any roses this year, they'd withered and died in the winter of May and the dryness of June.

The evening walk was a social outing as much as anything. All the neighbors made their own trips to the creek to see if there was enough water so they could take an extra measure for their fields, knowing even before they left their old ranch houses that there wasn't.

Wilbur dwarfed his four-wheeler as he dropped it out of gear and killed the engine beside Emma and Charlie on the road.

"See you got some longhorns down on Section Seven," Charlie said, twirling a piece of hay in his mouth.

"Ya, we branded those old cows the other day," Wilbur replied.

"How do you get them through the chute?" Charlie asked recalling the wide horns of the multi-colored cows.

"They're amazing, they just twist their head and go right through," Wilbur replied.

"Heard you took non-use on your forest permit," Charlie said. "You taking 'em to McCarty Canyon again?"

"Nope. This might be a big mistake, particularly as dry as it is this year, but I'm gonna run 'em right down to home, on Section Seven and over in the hills. Can't afford to pay for pasture."

"Gonna be tough."

"That's why I switched to longhorns, heard they could adapt to conditions better than those black baldys I had." Wilbur removed his Centennial Livestock cap and scratched his head before starting the four-wheeler and kicking it into gear.

The news exchanged, Charlie and Emma resumed their walk.

Every year in June Emma and Marie took a week and went to a Cattlewomen's meeting. Charlie and S.R. stayed home and fixed fence on the Bensen place. One of two ranches the Boss had leased, the Bensen had better fences than the Indian Creek operation, but only by a nose.

The river served as a fence down at the Home Place and even that failed. The lack of runoff left the river low and an old one-horned cow led fifty of her companions over to the island, a grazing area that would hold them about three days. But before Charlie could get them back across the river the little bit of snow in Colorado's Never Summer Range upstream in North Park melted and the river rose. It was too risky to try to get the cows back across the channel. True, the cows could probably make it and Charlie on his horse. But he'd lose calves for sure and he had a hundred percent calf crop going so he didn't want to take the risk.

Fortunately for the cows, but not for the irrigators, the high water lasted less than a week and the feed held out until Charlie got the cows and their calves back to the home pasture.

"I tell you with this dry weather, people aren't kept busy enough this summer. You hear what Frank's boys did last week?" Charlie asked as he piled his chipped china plate with lasagna.

"No, what?" S.R. replied, filling his own plate. He aspired to be like the two older boys.

"You know those two big old Simmental bulls Frank just bought?"

"Sure."

"Well, they were lying in the corral up at the barn, butt to butt. Butch dared Carl to tie their tails together, and he did it."

"What happened?" Emma said pouring iced green tea into tall mis-matched glasses. She figured if it was good for her, the whole family ought to be drinking the green brew.

"Those old bulls decided to get up. One went east and the other headed west. It was a helluva ruckus when they got their tails all stretched out. They started pulling each other all around the corral, knocked one pole gate down, broke through a fence in the round corral and roared into the calving shed before they finally got apart. By that time the shed itself was darn near wrecked."

"What happened to their tails?" Marie asked.

"That big old bull with the white splotch on his rump just pulled the tail right off of that little sandy-colored bull," Charlie said. "Now that little guy looks like he's on the prod all the time and could give it to those cows from two different directions."

"Charlie!" Emma said. "Not around the children."

"We're not kids anymore, Mom," S.R. said with his mouth full.

"You're my kids, and don't talk with your mouth full."

"Frank was pretty mad about the whole deal and I bet it'll be a good long time before those boys pull such a prank again."

"Why's that?" Marie asked.

"'Cuz he made 'em clean the chicken coop the other day when it was hotter'n blazes out."

"Oh, yuck," S.R. replied, his mouth still full, his nostrils sucking together as he thought of the smell.

"Yep, there's nothing like the aroma of a hen house. Just the smell of ammonia when Oma mops the kitchen floor will remind them of their prank," Charlie said.

What grass grew wasn't green for long. It never got very hot at 7,500 feet, but this year the mercury had soared to the high 80s and the grasses cured quickly. No bluebells had bloomed and the lavender pasqueflowers remained dormant, perhaps knowing instinctively there wasn't enough water to sustain their brief lives.

"Wilbur shipped his longhorns out yesterday," Charlie said one evening as he forked a piece of beefsteak into his mouth.

"You're kidding?" Emma replied cutting her own meat.

"Nope. He sent 'em over by Medicine Bow someplace. Guess they've got better grass than we do."

"By the Bow? No way, it's always drier over there than it is here," S.R. said.

"Guess not. I heard Don took some of his cows over there, too."

"If only it would rain and not be so blasted hot," Emma said.

"If only this, if only that, like the Boss always says, 'if your aunt had a nut then she'd be your uncle,'" Charlie grinned as he said it.

"Charlie! I told you, not around the children."

"Mom, we're not kids. Besides I hear it every day at work," S.R. said as he stood to his full six-foot height. He apparently got his genes from his mother's uncles.

"Sit down at the table," Emma snapped, changing the tenor of the discussion. "How's your pasture holding up?"

Charlie's blue eyes glinted but he followed Emma's switch, "We're moving everything up to Indian Creek tomorrow."

"You need me to ride?"

"Not this time. We got it handled. The Boss or S.R. will bring the trailer up so we have a way home."

Day after day the sun baked the land. It had been a month without rain when the anticipated invitation arrived in the mailbox.

"We're invited up to A Bar A for the Fourth. Looks like they won't have any fireworks," Emma said at supper that night.

"I wouldn't want to set any off, it's too dry this year," Charlie replied.

"I'm getting tired of eating steak every night," Marie muttered as she cut through her T-bone.

"Don't complain, a lot of kids would love to have a steak. It's what we've got in the freezer and we have to eat it before it's time to butcher again in the fall," Emma said passing the biscuits to S.R.

"In our health class we learned you shouldn't eat so much red meat," Marie said. "It has too much cholesterol and isn't good for you."

"Listen, my grandpa and your grandpa ate beef damn near every day of their lives. My grandpa checked out when he was eighty-five, dying the first time he ever went to a hospital. Your grandpa is darn near that old now and he's still working, so shut up about cholesterol and eat your meat. As long as you work hard everyday the exercise will more than counter any effects from cholesterol. If you don't think you're working hard enough, I'll find something more for you to do."

"Okay, Ma, don't get so upset," S.R. drawled.

"Don't you call me Ma. I told you, I am your Mother or your Mom. I am not your Ma. I am not like Ma Ingalls on those Little House reruns."

"And I ain't your Pa either," Charlie slipped in edgewise, knowing that was the only way to stop Emma when she was on a tirade.

Emma snapped her mouth shut, but she couldn't drop it.

"Maybe this fall we could trade some beef with Aunt Lea for some of the buffalo they raise. They might like some beef for a change."

"That's a great idea, Mom," S.R. said quietly. "I love buffalo."

"Me, too," Marie said. "Buffalo is lower than beef in cholesterol." Like her mother, she always wanted the last word on a subject.

"The party start at four?" Charlie put in another edgewise comment.

"Dad, you know it always does," Marie said, determined to be the last to speak. Her mother had taught her well.

A dust snake marked the road to A Bar A on the Fourth. Nearly everyone in the valley got invited to the ranch party and the vehicles stirred up the dirt. Tiny was singing and Mack was playing his fiddle to get everyone in a festive mood. They had to work harder than usual this year. Cowboys holding cans of beer and women with cold glasses of Jack Daniels and Coke huddled in groups talking about the dry weather, while kids dirtied their shirts with barbecued ribs and corn on the cob.

"I've never seen that little creek dry up," Wilbur said as he wobbled to a chair beside Charlie.

"I know, some of those springs up in Dufunny have completely quit flowing." Charlie replied settling into a rickety chair. "We're gonna have to move our heifers out of the BLM allotment because there's no water for 'em."

"My goodness, Emma, I didn't realize how dry it was," Mary Rose said. She had on white cotton slacks, a white shirt, white tennis shoes, and a white straw hat with a red rose tied to the side.

"You gotta get out of town once in a while, Mary Rose," Emma said, slapping dust from her faded Wranglers and wiping manure off the toe of her scuffed boot by dragging it across the grass.

"All our lawns are just so green and my flowers have never looked better. I didn't realize it was so dry out this way," Mary Rose looked like cool perfection.

"Fifteen miles and no lawn sprinklers make a heck of a difference, don't they?" Emma said, drowning her parched throat in Jack Daniels straight up.

"I understand that Rob has had some sprinklers going out on the pasture all week so we can have fireworks tonight," Mary Rose said.

"He's braver than I would be," Emma replied. "I'd sure hate to see a fire get started this summer, it might burn til it snows."

The wind did it. There wasn't any so Rob figured he could have his cowhands set off the fireworks and any that went up and came down unburned wouldn't drift, but would fall on the irrigated pasture. Before the explosions began only four little kids got burned on the sparklers they lit and waved and ran around with on the lawn, which was a better record than last year when a dozen grabbed the hot sparklers. Then the fireworks shot up, lighting the canyon sky at the ranch, and fizzled before touching dry grass so everyone went home relieved that they didn't need to conclude the party as firefighters.

"Listen to this," Emma said, looking up from the paper. "It says here that some researchers at the University of Montana have done a study—no doubt paid for with government funds—that shows there will be less buildup of forest fuels if sheep graze a particular area."

"You're kidding, right?" Charlie said, plucking the strings of his mandolin as he played "Old Joe Clark."

"Nope. Can you believe it? Some environmental researcher spends probably years and thousands of dollars to find out something any self-respecting rancher has known for decades."

"You know those environmentalists won't listen to ranchers, they think we're out to take advantage of public land. They don't recognize the value we provide in the way of water hole improvements and reduced fuels to prevent fires. Not to mention feed for wildlife all winter."

"How's your pasture, anyway?" Emma changed the subject.

"Short. We're moving the cattle to the Bensen Place tomorrow. We'll drop 'em in Cottonwood and some will likely find their way on over to the Encampment River."

"It's pretty early to move them over there, isn't it?"

"Yep, but there's nothing left for them to eat at Indian Creek until we get the hay up, then we can put 'em on the meadows."

"Fox told me the other day at the Sugar Bowl that he's worried about having enough pasture for his herd."

"He ain't the only one whose stomach is tied in knots," Charlie replied, letting his fingers flow over the mandolin.

As if there wasn't enough to worry about, dry lightning started marching across the valley on a nightly basis. It was only a matter of time before a bolt became flint to tinder. Charlie saw the plume of smoke and headed toward it, to find Frank and his boys already shoveling like mad to get a line around it. S.R., who'd fixed miles of fence there with Charlie, showed the fire trucks the way in and the combined force of ranchers, their kids, and volunteer firemen battled the blaze until dark, when they went home having knocked it down and out.

Or so they thought.

Emma got up before daylight and saw the red glow. By the time Charlie, S.R., and the Boss arrived the glow had become an inferno and the wind drove it across the pasture toward the Indian Creek Homestead cabin. The hundred-year-old cabin still cowered in the cottonwoods and aspens the first night of the fire only because of the determination of firefighters who drove their trucks on unroaded hillsides and who got a break when a slurry bomber dropped a load of retardant on the ridge just back of the cabin.

Charlie and the Boss thought they'd be pink before it was over, parked as they were in the old Ford, which was right in the bomber's path. If it would have been napalm, they'd have been scorched, too.

Fires burned all over the West. They'd blackened New Mexico early, leveling hundreds of homes after a Park Service wizard started a controlled burn that—like most things started by the government—got out of hand. Then the fires had marched north, burning huge chunks of Idaho's Salmon River country and Montana's Bitterroot Valley. Wyoming wasn't immune as blazes broke out near Casper, Meeteetse, and Laramie Peak.

There were so many fires troops were training at Camp Pendleton to help battle them. And it was hard to get resources for smaller fires like the Indian Creek blaze. But the Forest Service and Bureau of Land Management did their best and found a couple of slurry bombers and a SuperPuma helicopter with a 1,000-gallon bucket used to dip water from Frank's reservoir to drop on the hottest spots of the fire. But it just kept burning, heading first one direction then swinging around in another, torching hundred-year-old pine trees, junipers, aspen groves, sagebrush, and grass. And sending plumes of smoke into the sky.

The agencies called in some experienced fire managers and they set up camp at the rodeo grounds until the school principal got back into town from a pack trip he'd been on in Huston Park Wilderness.

"Here's the keys to the school. Use it for showers. You can bunk in the gym, or on the athletic field," he told the head fire manager, dropping the ring into the amazed manager's hand. The guy was from

Denver and didn't understand how small towns worked.

Even so it's doubtful the principal expected the fire managers to use every high school classroom, the playground, and the athletic field. But there were as many support people as firefighters brought in to battle the Indian Creek fire and they virtually doubled the size of the town so they needed all the space. The firefighters took over the football field and the National Guard used the playground and tennis courts for their camp.

One old woman called the police chief to see if he knew about all the soldiers in town.

"Yes, ma'am," the chief said. "They aren't causing any trouble."

Day after day the blaze burned, eating summer pasture, then devouring fall feed, as the wind pushed it toward the north and the Indian Creek Homestead cabin, then drove it back to the west where Charlie had the cattle in the Cottonwood drainage. The smell of burning trees and sage wafted across the valley, settling into every drainage and every corner of Emma's house.

Smoke boiled over the ridge, stinging eyes as Charlie, Emma, Dee, S.R., and Marie looked for cattle. They'd had to talk their way around a roadblock set up by the BLM Ranger, in order to come up and check on the cows.

"There's flames on the ridge, right there," Emma said, coughing as she gulped in the smoke and then pointing to a blazing tree on the skyline a half mile away.

Like ants in a pile, Charlie's guts twisted. Was the hundred percent calf crop in jeopardy? "We gotta get these cows out of here," Charlie muttered, as he turned toward the horse trailer. "Emma, I think you better ride with us. If we have to get near that fire, I don't know how these horses will act and I don't want anybody hurt," Charlie said as S.R. unloaded the horses.

"S.R., put Mom's saddle on Brownie," Charlie said indicating his daughter's horse.

"Marie, can you drive the pickup down the mountain?" Charlie asked as he threw his saddle on Custer's back. Dee was tightening the latigo on her own saddle while Emma popped a lemon drop into her mouth and then tied a handkerchief around her neck and pulled it up and over her mouth and nose. She'd been coughing for days from the smoke.

"I'm not old enough," the girl said, her ponytail flipping in the wind, as she rubbed red streaked eyes. "What about the Ranger?"

"Tell him we had to move the cows and we couldn't leave the truck up here. When you get down to the bottom of Cottonwood, take that road to the right and you can cut across to Indian Creek without getting on the highway."

"I've never pulled a trailer, Dad," Marie's wide eyes dominated her small face. "And I'm not very good with the clutch."

"I know, Honey, but you can do it. Just put it in granny until you get to the bottom of the hill. Take it slow."

"And when you get to where you have to turn, swing real wide so you have plenty of room for the trailer," S.R. threw in as he closed the trailer door then stepped into the saddle on the sorrel he was riding.

"Daddy, I don't know . . ." the girl's voice quivered as she climbed into the pickup.

"You have to, Honey. I know you can do it," Charlie said, eyeing the burning ridgeline. "I'll watch to be sure you get started all right."

"Well, okay," Marie said as she stepped on the clutch and turned the key in the ignition. Cows and calves were already bawling as Dee and Emma rode through the trees toward them when Marie put the truck into gear, pulled the emergency parking brake, and popped the clutch. The truck lurched and bucked, but didn't die as Marie started down the mountain.

Later that same day Marie raced through the door of their house, field glasses in her hand. "Mom, you better get out here."

"What's up?" Emma said stirring the chokecherries she'd just put on the stove to cook. She'd filled a bucket with chokecherries from a tree down by the creek as soon as they got the cows moved and she wanted to get the juice out of them to make syrup. She didn't really

care all that much about the syrup but hoped the tangy scent of the
cooking chokecherries would overpower the acrid smell of smoke
that permeated every inch of the house. Everything reeked of smoke,
the mixed smells of juniper and pine, of grass and the pungent scent
of sagebrush burning.

"The fire seems way out of control," Marie fidgeted from one foot
to the other.

Emma slapped the wooden spoon on the counter and ran out the
door. "Give me the glasses," she said, reaching for the binoculars from
Marie who'd followed her outside.

"Oh, my hell. It looks like it's racing right toward the Indian Creek
buildings." The telephone jangled setting Emma's nerves on tighter
edge as she fled toward the house.

"Ya!" she yelled as she grabbed the receiver on the third ring.

"It's coming right at us. Can you get ahold of Charlie? He's
moving cows down on the river. We gotta get these out of here, too."
The Boss didn't have to identify himself.

"We're on our way," Emma said, slamming down the receiver and
turning off the burner under the chokecherries. Marie already had a
jug of drinking water and was headed out the door. Emma ran to the
pickup, dialing the cell phone as she started the truck and threw it
into gear. Charlie answered on the fourth ring.

"It's racing toward Indian Creek. The Boss says to bring the horses,"
Emma yelled into the scratchy sounding phone.

"I'm across the river. I'll be there as soon as I can," Charlie screamed
into the static before the line went dead.

Emma and Marie rattled down the road, bouncing over washboards
and ignoring stop signs, but stopping when they reached the Indian
Creek property because a Forest Ranger stood in the middle of the road.

"The road is closed," he said calmly and politely.

"Not to me, it isn't," Emma snapped. "My husband runs this ranch."

"The Boss and Dee are up there. We haven't seen Charlie or S.R.,"
Fox called from behind the barricade set up by the Ranger.

"They're down on the river, they'll be here as soon as they can.
We've got to move the cows," Emma hollered back. Then she revved

the engine and threw the pickup into gear. The ranger wisely stepped out of her way.

"You'll be right back?" he remained polite.

"When we get done what needs to be done," she yelled into the cloud of dust the pickup threw behind itself.

The Boss had the tractor going as he scraped a firebreak around the hill house, dirt mixing with smoke to obscure his blue sweatshirt and faded jeans. Emma skidded the pickup to a stop in front and Marie beat her through the door by a whisker.

"What do you want us to do?" Marie called.

"Help me get this loaded in the Suburban," Dee said coughing and pulling boxes out of a closet.

"Let's back it up to the step," Emma said.

"You can't, it doesn't have reverse," Dee grunted with a heavy box.

"Typical damn ranch vehicle, no reverse, my hell, what next?" Emma muttered to herself as she fled the house and ran to her own pickup, dropping the tailgate then backing it up to the step. Marie had the first box ready to load as soon as Emma shut off the truck.

They worked furiously, throwing possessions into boxes and boxes into the truck and the Suburban, watching flames as they leaped and danced like a chorus line on the ridge a half mile from the house.

"What else?" Emma paused as the last box went in.

"Nothing I guess, the furniture is old, if the fire gets it I guess it doesn't matter. I just really wanted my antiques."

The Boss drove by on the tractor yelling, "Where's Charlie? He needs to get these cows out of here and move that log loader."

"He's on the river, he'll be here as soon as he can," Emma called back, twisting her long hair and poking it through the back of her cap like a ponytail.

"C'mon, let's move these tractors and vehicles out of here," Dee said.

Marie took the only pickup that was an automatic as Dee and Emma began shuttling equipment and vehicles away from the ranch and up to the barricade where the Forest Ranger patrolled. Every time they parked and jumped into the truck Marie drove in order to head back toward the ranch buildings, the Ranger scowled.

Charlie and S. R. arrived with the horses, and Ellis came with his old bay as well. He'd been watching the fire from the barricade when he heard Emma say Charlie was going to move the cows. Not waiting to be asked, he simply returned home, saddled up, loaded his horse in his trailer, and was headed toward the cows by the time Charlie, S.R. and Dee were on their own mounts.

"We'll get the rest of these vehicles," Emma called as the riders loped toward the cattle coming from the stock pond. Other neighbors had arrived to help, Butch and Frank rode their four-wheelers toward cattle bawling in the meadow.

"What can I do to help? You need another tractor to plow a line?" Don asked Emma as she and Marie took the last two vehicles toward the barricade. He'd cut across the foothills from his place, avoiding the road with the traffic-stopping Ranger.

"Check with the Boss, he'll tell you what needs to be done. We've got all the equipment and vehicles. We've taken what we can from the house. They're rounding up the cattle now to move them down to the river," Emma found a gear and took off after Marie, flames licking to within a quarter-mile of the house, ash coating her hair.

"Where the hell is the slurry bomber?" she muttered as she watched two six-by-six fire trucks make their way up the ridge to form a last line of defense.

Marie sat in the white truck in the middle of the road, blocking the access to the fire road and the cattle trail.

"Move that damn thing," Emma yelled as she jumped from her own pickup and ran toward her daughter's vehicle.

"I can't, it keeps dying," Marie called, tears welling in her grimy face.

"We gotta get it out of the way, the cows are headed this way and if we block the road your Dad will scream at both of us."

"I know, but I can't get it to run."

Don had followed them and unfolded his lanky frame from the seat of his old green pickup. "Here, let me try," he said, moving Marie from the seat and sliding in behind the wheel. No amount of coaxing started the engine. Even fiddling under the hood didn't help. The cows were nearly at the gate. Butch and Frank arrived on their four-wheelers and tried to push the truck, but they just spun their wheels in the sandy road.

"We'll hook a chain on and pull it out of the way," Don said, sliding long legs from beneath the steering wheel. "Just put 'er in neutral and steer," he told Marie as he hooked a new log chain from the dead truck to his old clunker.

"Remember whose chain that is, and get it back in the right truck when you're done," Emma called.

"Ah, you're no fun," Don grinned as he gunned his truck's engine.

It didn't take long to get the white truck out of the road and the path of the cattle, which bawled continuously. Calves kept turning back toward the meadow, forcing Ellis and Charlie to wear down their horses. Having been moved from Cottonwood only that morning, the herd hadn't had time to mother-up. Cows and calves cried for each other in the hot August sun as cinders and ash burned their eyes and those of the riders. Charlie rode up to Emma and the neighbors, taking the jug of water from Marie and gulping a pint before coming up for smoke-filled air and passing it to Ellis.

"Sure don't see any of those tree huggers around when there's work to do," Charlie said as he lifted his hat and wiped the sweat and grime from his forehead. Then he leaned forward in the saddle, signaling the horse to catch up to the cows that were kept moving by Dee and S.R., who whistled and slapped their ropes against their denim-covered legs.

"There he is," Marie cried pointing toward the sky, catching the Forest Ranger's attention, who looked relieved now that they were near the barricade and farther from the fire.

A slurry bomber swooped over the ranch buildings, dropping a load of retardant on the backside of the firebreak the Boss had been plowing and right before the wall of flame. All afternoon the wind had come from the southwest, driving the fire right toward the ranch buildings. But almost like he'd pushed a button, once the slurry bomber dropped his load, the wind shifted heading back toward the south. That spared the ranch buildings as the fire turned and marched up the drainage toward Frank's BLM allotment.

As the sun started going down in a red ball, and with the cows a mile from the Home Place, Ellis had to get off his old bay mare and lead her. She'd worn herself out in the heat and the effort of moving three hundred head of tired cows and calves.

Hours later Charlie and Emma stood outside their house, watching the fire as it topped the Big Hill, readying itself for a run down the east flank and possibly a race to their own front door.

"We can stop it on this side. We'll plow a firebreak from Pole Canyon down to Frank's reservoir. There's no way it can jump that," Charlie comforted.

"At least the cattle are out of the way," Emma replied, burrowing close under Charlie's arm.

"Ours are, but Frank has his on that allotment that's burning now. We may need to help him in the morning. I sure hope we got all the calves out of Cottonwood."

"Look, it's dying," Marie said, edging close to her mother.

"It's like somebody pulled the plug," Emma responded as the flames flickered and diminished on the hill two miles from their house. Apparently the fire had run out of fuel, at least for the time being. It had done this before, though, settled in the night, only to blow up when the temperature and wind rose with a new day.

"Let's get some sleep," Charlie said turning toward the log house he and Emma had built. They did it themselves years before with help from all her relatives and his two friends. Paying as they went, by the time they moved in and had S.R. sleeping in a decades-old family crib, it was finished and had no mortgage against it. That's what made it possible for them to make a living ranching, the fact that they had a place to live.

A blizzard of slurry bombers and two helicopters, along with more than three hundred firefighters attacked the blaze as it roared up Indian Creek in the days that followed, getting a break when the wind shifted and drove the fire back toward the north. Charlie still hadn't accounted for three cows and five calves. He'd lost his perfect hundred percent calf crop in the boiling, acrid smoke and flames that crept closer to his own house every time the wind twisted toward the south. The fire managers said the blaze exhibited "extreme behavior." Charlie just wanted it to quit threatening his livelihood and his home.

Daily for two weeks cloud banks built up in the afternoon, looking gray and ominous, and bringing the smell of moisture on the wind, but failing to let loose even a drop of rain, though Frank said he'd gotten six inches.

"Six inches between each of the sixteen drops," he told Charlie as they watched the smoke rage up the canyon behind their ranches, eating their fall pasture and moving ever closer to their own homes. They'd worked together days before to get the last of Frank's cattle out of the drainage where the fire burned. Now the cows bawled on the hay meadow, knowing they shouldn't be off the mountain this early in the year.

Three weeks of smoke and cinders, of stress and worry that the fire would burn the Indian Creek homestead cabin, the main ranch buildings, and now that it would reach Beaver Creek and then run down the drainage to their own place, the place she and Charlie had scrimped for years to build, left Emma wound tighter than a top. Walking alone up the road she felt the tears well and spill down sun-baked cheeks. "Lord, please? We need some rain. At least a little, please?"

Two nights later the clouds finally opened, pouring water straight down on the firefighters, the helicopters, and the ranchers. Emma stood outside, sucking in the clean smell and the moisture. It rained every evening for a week, dowsing the last embers, and clearing the air. But it didn't make a bit of difference in grazing conditions. Too much sun and too little rain for too long had left the range parched and brittle. It would take snow and winter followed by a warm, wet spring before recovery could begin there.

"Listen to this," Emma said, folding the newspaper so she could read the article. "The governor has declared Wyoming a disaster area. It says here that means ranchers can apply for low-interest loans, and maybe even get grants to replace water structures and fences that were burned in the fires."

"I don't even want to think about all the fence we're gonna have to build," Charlie said as he pulled his worn boots off and set them beside the chair.

"The paper says that the Kate's Basin fire burned more than 138,000 acres. And the Enos Complex up near Meeteetse charred another 28,000 acres."

"Did I see something from Katy and Mark?"

"A short note. They said the Blondie fire nearly got their house, but the earlier Grass Creek fire that burned their fall pasture served as a buffer zone so it didn't reach the buffalo or the main buildings. They said about 150 head of Arapaho Ranch horses died in Kate's Basin when they got caught in a canyon."

"We're gonna ship next week," Charlie replied.

It always bothered Emma how Charlie could switch from one subject to another almost in mid-sentence. She knew he did it when he wanted to avoid a topic. She put down the paper.

"Already?" she asked.

"Ya, there's a yearling sale down at Brush on the 23rd and I think we better get rid of ours so we can save the pasture for the cows and calves. We're only a little below a hundred percent. Besides, the market is still up."

"You think it'll drop then?"

"Guaranteed. With all the fires that have already burned, and those still raging in Montana and Idaho, plus the fact that the pasture is short and the hay crop is something like 50 percent of normal, a lot of people will cull their herds."

"You'll take a pounding on weight."

"That's true. But we just don't have the pasture to hold 'em."

"You still gonna keep the heifers?"

"We'll sell about half, keep the bigger ones and hope the hay holds out through the winter."

"You suppose this will be another open winter?"

"For the love of God, woman, don't even think that."

CANDY MOULTON lives, writes, and edits in a log house near Encampment, Wyoming. Reared on her grandparents' homestead, she found a cowboy at college and they have been married for twenty-five years. She spends her time writing and traveling the West, while he has his own herd of cattle and helps run the Fishhook Ranch, owned by Dr. Nicholas and Dorothy Jamison. Candy is the author of nine Western history books including *Steamboat: Legendary Bucking Horse* and *Wagon Wheels: A Contemporary Journey on the Oregon Trail.* She writes of agriculture, public land management, travel, and history for *American Cowboy, Persimmon Hill, The Fence Post, the Casper Star-Tribune, Western Horseman, Sunset,* and dozens of other magazines and newspapers. "Open Winter" is the first short fiction story she ever wrote; another short story, "Ribbons and Gee Strings," is included in *White Hats,* an anthology published by Berkley Books.

Junior

Dick Hyson

Whenever working cowboys got together over a cup of coffee or a cold beer or maybe waiting for cattle trucks, the conversation would sooner or later drift over to Junior. Somebody had seen something that Junior had done or heard something he'd said and wanted to pass it along. They were just paying their respects to a good man. He didn't do wild and reckless things to make a name for himself. He was just a top hand who was in the right place at the right time working cattle. He had confidence in his ability and he had the experience to know what to do in practically any situation. That's why the stories more or less built him into a legend.

These cowboys came from an area known as the Texas Panhandle. That includes the handle of Oklahoma and a pretty wide strip of New Mexico on the west, and runs fifty or so miles south of Amarillo, Texas. Most all the cowboys in this area that I'm talking about were kinda poured out of the same mold. When I say this I'm talking about the fact that the crease in their hat, their boots, their leggings, their saddle, their lingo, all were pretty much alike. Now Junior was one that had a little more shine than most. This was some forty years ago and at the time I had not had the privilege of actually knowing Junior. 'Course I'd seen him around at different functions: rodeos, auctions, county fairs, and what have you, though I never took the opportunity to just go up and introduce myself. He was some ten years older than I. But I felt like I knew the man because of the stories I'd heard.

Like the time a neighbor had a problem and was awful upset about it. He'd run into Junior in town and told him a story. He was in the

Hereford business and used good registered Hereford bulls of the Anxiety the Fourth breeding. Those bulls did not come cheap. But one of his prize bulls got his "business" broke. It wasn't unusual for this to happen, but the neighbor said he needed to go to town to auction because he couldn't breed any cows and he was just taking up space and wasting grass. But every time they started him toward the house and the pens he'd go a couple of hundred yards, but hurting like he was he got on the fight and you couldn't move him nowhere. The rancher and his hands had tried on several occasions to move him and the bull would just bow up and fight them terrible.

Now he was a big bull. In his showing clothes he'd weigh close to eighteen hundred, perhaps more. But in his working clothes, sixteen hundred pounds would probably catch him. But he'd had weights on his horns to bring them down like all registered bulls, so he wouldn't be high-horned.

Junior listened to his neighbor's plight. "You've got a bobtailed trailer, don't you?" The neighbor allowed he did.

"Call the wind miller and get his heaviest boom truck with those big old gin poles and winch on it and have him come over to your place. You bring the bobtail with the racks and have him come with ya and park a quarter of a mile from that bull. I'll be over there shortly after daylight in the morning. Tomorrow is sale day. He might as well go then."

The neighbor agreed, not knowing quite what was going to happen.

As an afterthought, Junior said, "Have that wind miller or yourself bring some heavy duty sling straps. You know, the kind that are six or eight inches wide and sure purty long. You know what I'm talkin' about."

His neighbor agreed, and the next morning he was in his bobtail truck with his wind miller with his winch truck when shortly after daylight they saw Junior coming at a trot from the north. He was riding a little horse he called "Poker." It was a gelding that didn't weigh much over a thousand pounds, if any. They saw Junior get his rope down and tie the end to the saddle, build a loop, and ride up to the bull, popping him and making him run. Now the bull wouldn't run too far before he'd turn and fight, but before he did Junior laced the rope around those horns, threw the slack over the right hip and rode off, the little horse digging into the ground. Junior tripped that big old bull, just like a light steer. The bull came off his feet and landed on his side. Junior was off his horse before the bull hit the ground. He didn't have a piggin' string. This bull was too big. He had a hoggin' line. He strung the bottom foot next to the ground, the front one, and gathered up the hind feet and tied him down, then waved for the bobtail and boom truck to come on in.

They worked the sling straps underneath the bull and had the boom truck hook on with a chain. With that they picked him up and laid him in the back of the bobtailed truck. Junior got in and took the rope off of him so he could stand up. And to town he went. Not many fellers would tie into a deal like that.

Another story frequently told was when some cowboys were driving two herds back off of Texas corn stalks in the early spring. They were all mother cows. Some of them had calved and some of them were fixing to. The riders were moving them back into New Mexico. The total distance of the drive was about forty-five miles and Junior was the ramrod of the deal. He was with the first group of about four hundred cows, had them strung out nicely, when he looked back and couldn't see the second herd.

He turned around and loped back to see where they were. Even though it appeared flat, evidently the curvature of the earth or a little rise on the ground made him unable to see where they were. He was riding a big dun horse called "Honker." When I say big, he'd weigh thirteen and a half, fourteen hundred pounds. And he rode into a patch of ground we called hollow ground. There wasn't any holes, but it looked like it'd been plowed. The gophers had undermined that little patch and Junior didn't notice it until his horse stepped off in it and started stumbling.

Junior said afterwards, "Hell, I thought he was goin' to get up anytime. I was pickin' him up," and smiled big. Cowboys'll do that when a horse stumbles, he picks up on the reins like he's gonna pull the horse up out of a hole. But he's sitting on him. He ain't a cherry picker. And the horse kept stumbling, his head getting lower to the ground, and finally he stuck his head on the ground and thankfully didn't go head over heels, but went head over the side. Junior never got his foot out of the left stirrup. The horse fell on his left side, hard. And when he hit, that oxbow stirrup flattened out and broke both bones right above the ankle on Junior's left leg.

He said later, "It hurt like hell, but it sure did feel good when that horse got up and my foot came out of that stirrup." Like any cowboy who will admit to it, he was afraid of being drug.

They were about fifteen miles from home and Junior had a little hell getting on the horse again. But he got back ahorseback, finished bringing the cattle to where they oughta be, loaded up his horse, went back home and told his wife, "I think we'd better go to town. My leg's broke." He wouldn't let them cut the boot off him, although he was in tremendous pain. He said he'd rather endure the pain than ruin a good pair of boots. Now that's a cowboy, and it's also the truth.

Everybody knows that a cowboy won't let the truth get in the way of a good story. But two incidents I recall stayed with me then and always will. One I had seen. The other, even after I got to know Junior and we were good friends, I couldn't bring upon myself to ask, because it was neither any of my business, nor any point to it.

The one I'd seen took place in Amarillo at a rodeo. They had eight bucking chutes, four on the right and four on the left with the gate in the middle. The gate in the middle was used for bulls and horses to exit the arena after their work was done. The opposite end of the arena was roping chutes. A young bull rider had got hung up in his rope and fell down inside of the spin, that we call the "well." The bull was spinning so hard, the cowboy lost his feet. Every time that bull would whip his head into the spin, he caught the young bull rider up beside the head and coldcocked him. Still being hung up to his bull rope, but completely out. The clowns, bullfighters, finally got his hand out of the bull rope and the cowboy lay there, right in front of the exit gate, and didn't move a muscle.

The bull was a big cross-bred, tiger-striped Brahma with drooped horns. The bull went down the arena to make a victory circle, but the cowboy was in need of assistance, bad. Several ran out to help the boy, but they didn't want to move him. To move him might have caused his death. Everybody's attention was on the cowboy.

The two arena pickup men tried to rope the bull, but missed. Junior came from the roping end of the arena, whupping and spurring, as the bull headed back toward the exit gate. The bull had to be stopped. Junior had his rope down and was tied on hard and fast, as always. Even with the horns in the position they were, low and down, he threw a loop that fit them like a bride's garter. I was watching him! If he'd roped him around the neck, he'd have ended up choking him. But Junior knew he had to hold the bull down on the far end of the arena 'til they got the cowboy out of the arena.

The doctor and medical people were working on him as quickly as they could, and they brought the ambulance into the arena. The other pickup man had thrown his loop four or five times before he got a loop over the horns and had the bull sidelined so they could hold him easier. They held him this way until the cowboy was in the ambulance and on his way to the hospital. Then they let the bull return through the gate where he knew he was supposed to go. Junior left the arena in the same way he'd come, and was gone.

I saw that.

But another man sitting around in this discussion of Junior's feat said he'd seen it, too, and asked Junior what if he had missed. He knew that bull would have gone down there and scattered everybody and probably hurt more people. And all Junior had to say, with a grin, was, "I couldn't afford to miss."

The other story was about an episode that happened over a fence and cattle, either getting in or getting out. No one was quite sure what took place, because the only ones there were Junior and a fellow from a neighboring ranch, who never got to tell his side of the story.

Now Junior was a big man for a cowboy. He stood about six two and weighed around one hundred eighty-five pounds. I'd never seen him without a smile on his face, but evidently something happened, either a water gap washed out or some cattle got in or out, nobody ever seemed to know for sure. Junior and this other cowboy, who was a big man himself and had a reputation of a hothead and scrapper, got into an argument over what happened, and it got so bad that they both got down off their horses and proceeded to have a fist fight. Some said there was bad blood between the two before the fight. I don't know.

Now it must have been one hell of a fight the way some talked, because there was grass mashed down, blood all over the place, and just one man walked away from it and that was Junior. He knew what had happened. He went to town immediately, and when the law got out there the man was still lying exactly where Junior had left him. But the man was dead. Junior was not in too good a shape himself; a broken nose, two black eyes, an ear practically ripped off, some ribs broke, and he ended up in the hospital.

They went to court, but I'm led to believe through all this gossip, and I'd heard this story many times, that Junior went to prison. Some said it was manslaughter, others say a different offense, and I don't even know if it's true. But I'll tell you what, if it is, there's an old saying, "You ride for the brand." I guess that's the ultimate of that saying. The fence, the land, the cattle didn't belong to Junior. But he thought enough of his job to go to war over it. If, indeed, that was what the fight was over, and I have a strong feeling it was.

The first time I saw Junior was around 1960, if I'm not mistaken. We pulled into the Coldwater camp just in time for the midday break. I was just along for the ride with a friend who had some business there. And before I even opened the door to the pickup, I noticed Junior standing out in the middle of a pen coiling up a rope and another fellow leading a horse off by the reins. If Junior was doing what I thought he was doing, I sure didn't want to miss it. I walked over to the corral and started watching through the slats in the fence. A young cowboy had entered the pen with a bridle and called out a horse's name as Junior shook out a big loop.

He swept the loop over to the left side of his body with his right hand. Then with a swift, smooth motion he quickly swung the loop from his left side to his right and back over the top of his head, turning the loop loose with his thumb pointing down. The loop turned over in the air and fell straight down. The horses in the corral stood with their ears up. They knew what was happening and they were close, close enough to touch one another. And they were all facing away from Junior. When the loop settled down over the head of a bay horse, Junior tugged on the rope slightly and the bay horse backed out, turned to face him and walked toward Junior as he coiled up the rope.

As he turned to hand the horse to the cowboy, I noticed a smile on his face. It was hard to miss because he had a gold tooth on the upper right side of his mouth and there was something else about his face. His right eye was white. I'd heard that it'd come from a rope breaking, and snapping back and hitting him in the eye. And I'd also heard that he'd got it during that fatal fight. He was mostly blind in that eye, but it didn't seem to bother him none.

I just stood there and watched him throw seven or eight more hoolihan loops and he never wasted a loop, not one. A hoolihan is strictly a horse catching loop and used only in the manner that Junior was using it. Every young cowboy wants to throw the hoolihan; they'd throw it at a high gatepost. It's not a loop that works good near the ground. I bet I've practiced it and thrown it a thousand times myself, even at a few horses. But this man had it down pat. It was beautiful to watch.

I saw that.

After he finally caught one for himself and led him out of the pen, I went over and introduced myself. He howdyed me like he knew me. I don't know whether that was just his way, or if he really did. That was a big country with few people. So it's entirely possible that he had heard of me.

But I wasn't bashful and I wanted him to know. So I told him, "God, I wish I could throw a hoolihan like that, Junior."

He smiled and shook his head. "Well, I was lucky today."

"Nah, I don't believe it. I was watchin' and I know. I can tell good from lucky."

He smiled. "You know, it's a shame. We don't use that loop much anymore. It's called for only on the bigger outfits that run a wagon or have enough hands that each'd have a string of his own. We only use it here when all the camps are in and we're in one place working cattle." And he winked at me. "I think you and I, Pard, were just born a little too late. Wouldn't it been somethin' to trail them cattle to Montana?"

I knew what he was talking about, deep in my heart. "I reckon."

"You know," he said, "I've always wanted to go to Montana ahorseback. But somebody told me there'd be an awful lot of gates to open. So, I believe I'll stay home." That gold tooth sure shined when the sun hit it.

"I saw Ab Blocker once," he said. "You know of him?"

"Sure," I said, "He designed the XIT brand but never worked for the XIT, that I know of."

"Right," Junior said. "He delivered some cattle up to the XIT and showed them a brand that would be hard to alter. They said he pointed more wagon tongues to the North Star than any man alive. I think it was 1946 he came to the XIT Reunion, he was sure pretty old, but had his pant legs stuck down his boot tops and had his spurs on. They said he never took them spurs off. It's like they grew to his boots. He led the parade ahorseback. He never learned to drive a car. Ain't that somethin'?"

"That evenin'," Junior continued, "he and some other old hands sat in the hotel lobby and told stories. I got in on that. It was good listenin', and I kept my mouth shut. I'll never forget it. He set the pattern, for us I mean."

Junior and I visited a little, while he was brushing off his horse's back with the palm of his hand. I noticed his saddle sitting on its fork, the blankets of course were wet. He'd spent all morning ahorseback and was just changing for the afternoon. I lifted his blankets off his saddle just to get a look at what kind of a rig he was riding, and boy was it a dandy! Fully tooled, over every inch of leather that was on the saddle except for the seat and it was hand ground and slick leather. That didn't surprise me. It would have surprised me to see a padded seat. The front rigging was tied together from the top by one piece of leather that was split, it went from the D ring on the left side about three inches wide over the fork, in front of the horn to the offside D ring. The other split was up to the horn and wrapped around it once and went down to the D ring. Much later in life I found out this was called a Sam Stagg rigging. A lot of cowboys had them, but they were all tooled to where if you didn't look good you'd miss it. Rounded, square skirts, a two-rope horn, and oxbow stirrups.

"Quite a kack," I told him.

"Thank you, Pard. You don't know what a dilemma we had buyin' that saddle. Me and Mary had just gotten married and, my God, that thing cost. Can you believe it? I gave over three hundred dollars for that thing. A whole year of living. But Mary was the one that convinced me to buy it, that we'd get by." All the time he was telling the story of the saddle, he was smiling and shaking his head, and saddling up.

"She said I might as well get what I wanted and get a good 'un and get it right, 'cause I spent more time in it than anything else; a bed, a chair at the house, or pickup seat."

But as he jerked his latigo and put it in its keeper, and pulled up his back cinch just tight enough to keep the hay from falling out, he took his reins in his left hand and held them lightly so his thumb would face toward the horse's head. He stuck his pointing finger between the reins, reached up and lightly laid his hand on the horse's mane, grabbed the horn, and just stepped up on him in one fluid motion.

"Pard, I've enjoyed visitin' with ya. Come by sometime. We'll sit and talk."

I allowed I would and watched him ride off at a trot. I knew there went a good 'un.

There was nothing different about Junior or offbeat. The hat he wore was an older silver belly with sweat stains showing on the outside, two or three inches above the brim, with a long cattleman's crease that went right down the middle, front to back and dented in on each side. The brim itself dipped low in the front and back from pulling it down because of the wind, the wind that blew incessantly in this country. It's something you lived with and never got used to.

His leggings were a cross between shotguns and batwings, belt in the back, whang string in the front, with a little batwing flare at the bottom. They had zippers that ran from the bottom up. It appeared like Blanchard spurs on his heels. I sure admired them. I'd always wanted a pair, but never had the money.

Junior always wore a wild rag, a silk bandanna looped loosely once around his neck and tied in a square knot, and wrapped double around his neck and tied in a square knot in the winter. Not a lot of silver, not a lot of flash, everything practical that helped him do the job that he did. But it was the air about him: an easy way of handling any situation without getting mad or flustered. Confidence!

As I watched him ride off it seemed like I'd known him forever. But you could bet that the next time we were all sitting around shooting the bull, the boys would hear about the hoolihan.

Whenever stories were told about Junior, every now and then there'd be a 'doubter' who'd say it never happened, or he could do the same thing or whatever. And occasionally he'd be challenged right there in the group that was talking, challenged to step outside and settle it with fists.

On one particular occasion, a fellow was telling about gathering wild and spoiled cattle off a ranch that had been leased by a friend years before. Before this friend could run his own cattle he had tried to gather the wild ones, having been told he could have them if he could get them. The original owner spoiled them because he wouldn't go get the cows that broke back, so, the next time more broke back and year after year they just let the cattle go back and it turned into a hell of a mess. So Junior was called on. He needed a number of cowboys and the requirement was, "Do you know how to forefoot cattle?" Everything that broke back had to be busted. Sometimes more than once, before they'd start hunting a hole.

Now, the fellow that was there said, "Everybody was swingin' heel loops at the forefeet of the cattle that broke back. They'd get 'em right up to the gate, then they'd start breakin' back, and god, they just scattered like sparrows." He allowed that Junior threw a Johnny Blocker loop. It was a fore footing loop that was a dandy. Johnny Blocker was Ab's brother. He tried to tell those that hadn't seen it how to throw it.

One feller said he knew how. So, they laid a chair on its back on the dance floor, and somebody got a rope, and the old boy that claimed he knew how to throw the Johnny Blocker swung his loop from the right side of the chair and stood it up in front of the legs of the chair, like a heel trap. That wasn't the Johnny Blocker at all. The feller that saw and had practiced it took the rope from him, got on the left side of the chair, swung the loop in a regular fashion, and when he went to throw it turned his thumb down at the last minute and spun the loop over hoolihan style, in front of the legs and pulled back and it fit on the front end of the chair.

"Hell, that ain't no Johnny Blocker loop," said the feller that had popped off. "Junior don't know every damn thing about everything, even though he thinks he does."

Right about there was where the fight started. Although we got them separated pretty quick and back to drinking beer, I thought, "It doesn't matter who you are, or what you do, there's always goin' to be jealousy." And that in itself is a kind of off-handed compliment to Junior.

It must have been five years or so before I ever got around Junior again. Not that I hadn't kept up with him. I knew where he'd been working and he'd changed jobs a couple of times in that period. Good hands like Junior sometimes just moved on so that they could see a little different country and maybe get a little better wage, move up a notch on the pay scale. But I'd never heard of Junior being fired. Everybody hated to see him leave and wished him the best.

In the meantime I had married. Me and my bride were just walking around meeting people, visiting, and waiting for the start of the local Labor Day rodeo, when I heard somebody call my name. I looked around and there was Junior and beside him a beautiful lady that I supposed was Mary.

Mary was one of those ladies whose hair turned silver early in her life. She wasn't that old, but her hair was almost completely silver. After introductions, my wife and Mary seemed like long-lost kinfolks and got to visiting a mile a minute so I had time to talk to Junior. I'd heard he was running an outfit less than fifty miles from where I was. Fifty miles is nothing in this country.

"Hear you've got a new job," I said. "How you like it?"

With that ever-present smile, "By golly, I think I may just stay awhile. The feller that owns the ranch lives at Amarillo and he comes up ever so often. But he's a good man and he knows that I know what I'm doin,' and leaves me alone. You know, this is a good ranch I'm on now and why a man who owns it would live somewhere else is just beyond me. I guess maybe it's the women folk, they want to be in the big towns. They want their society things. But when he comes to the ranch I try to get him to get ahorseback and ride out over it where he can see things. You know, horseback you can check and see so many things that you can't in a vehicle. But he always seems like he's in such a big hurry to get back that we'll make a run out over the feed roads for just a little while and he'll say that's enough. But he's a nice man to work for and I've got plenty of help. I just might set there a spell. This is just a pretty good job, Pard."

I knew the ranch that he was talking about, but I'd never been on it, so Junior described it to me. I believe he knew every blade of grass and weed that grew on it, and told me how it was set up for water. No pipelines, plenty of windmills, and when one of those windmills gets down, you call the wind miller and he comes out and fixes it. They keep a fence crew going pretty much year around.

I said, "Boy, it sounds like a good one."

"It's got a nice home and we're happy there. The kids only have to ride the school bus twenty-five miles. And that's it. I can't understand the boss. He owns it and lives in town. Me and Mary both would almost take a whippin' to have to go to town and get around all those people." Shaking his head, "I just can't imagine it. All those cars and traffic, not to mention people hustlin' around afoot like they was carryin' a bucket of fire. And the noise." Shaking his head, "Give me the high lonesome."

"Is it the perfect place? Would you give it up for another one? Or is this the one?"

"No. No. I believe that to be the cow boss on the Bells would probably be the ultimate in our business, wouldn't you?"

After thinking about it, I agreed with him. 'Course he was referring to the Bell Ranch north of Tucumcari, New Mexico, out on the Canadian

River. There was a big mound of mountain that looked like a bell that the name comes from. Junior and I both had known men that owned a pretty fair ranch themselves and leased it out in order to take the foreman's job on the Bells. It was owned by somebody that lived back east, and it sure was a cowboy's job. They had camps and they ran it the old way, and the old way is the way Junior liked it. We talked about it—all the calf tables, squeeze chutes, all the new modern things that had come up on ranches, but agreed if you had the help, you just couldn't beat the old ways.

As we sat there and visited, I can't guess how many other cowboys, some of them single, some of them with their families, stopped by and visited a little bit. It seemed like he knew everybody, and I knew quite a few. There's almost a fraternity, if you want to call it that, of cowboys in this region that either turned to cowboying as a way of making a living and didn't know anything else to do, or did it for the excitement or the freedom that the life allowed. They sure didn't do it for the money. There sure wasn't a great lot of money to be made working for the other fellow. Not cowboying.

But it's funny, and Junior agreed with me when we talked about it, how a fellow could go to town and go to work for a corporation, take some job that had a way that you could get ahead, move up the ladder, even become the boss, but who gave it up to live the life of a cowboy.

Junior just shook his head and smiled. "Pard, I don't know what it is about the life we lead. I've been around a lot of these boys. They're not dumb. They could make a livin' doin' somethin' else at the drop of a hat. A lot of 'em aren't born to it, either. I was. My Daddy worked for the Matadors for years. I grew up in a cow camp and out of seven kids, I'm the only one that took to it. And Daddy said I took to it like a duck to water, that every time he stopped I ran into the back of 'im because I was following him around."

"Have you ever been sorry that you chose this life?"

"Why, it never crossed my mind, Pard. I don't know. I knew I'd never own a ranch, so I did the next best thing. I run one. Early in the mornin' on a sure enough good horse, goin' out to do a job, or just prowlin', I can't imagine anything takin' the place of that. Maybe some of these fellers feel like they're the 'Knights of the Plains.' Some get plumb romantic about it. I've never really stopped and thought about that end of it. But there's a song, I know you've heard it, and somewhere in it, it says, 'I was foreman of a cow ranch, that's the callin' of a king.' I believe it. It's as honorable a way to make a livin' as I can think of."

I nodded my head. I knew the song he was talking about, *I'd Like To Be in Texas For the Roundup in the Spring.*

Texas is really just a state of mind. You can ride ahorseback and head west or north and you never know when you cross the state line. The country was about the same. The farther west you went, the less rain, and the more rough the country. Rolling plains, but cedar brakes and lots of rim rock. This was Junior's new country, as he described it to me.

"Everyday when you saddle up it's going to be a new adventure." He smiled. "A cowboy's country."

But Junior told me one time that back in 1941 when they were forming the American Quarter Horse Association, that they stated in there that they were not afraid of the coming of the automobile, and what it might take away from the horse. They weren't afraid because you can't work cattle with a car, or for that matter with a helicopter or an airplane. The only way you could really get down and get it done was ahorseback. And that's why they weren't afraid the quarter horse would become obsolete on ranches.

"But," he said, "I'll tell you what. Somebody's gotta ride those horses and as long as people are eatin' meat there'll be a job for fellers like you and me."

"There's a place in Oklahoma called the Cowboy Hall of Fame. Did you ever hear of it?" he asked.

"Yeah. I've been there."

"Well, I'd like to see that," Junior said. "I might know some of those guys. They've got a place for workin' cowboys. Now, a feller I worked for once, he might end up in there."

"You oughta be there," I said.

"Nah, I just do my job. Nothin' special." He smiled as always.

"No sir," he said. "Don't have any retirement. There's no medical insurance, there's no insurance of any kind. But I knew that when I come to work. It don't bother me now and it won't bother me later. I don't know how we'll get by, but, Pard, we'll get by. We always do."

I asked him what he thought the most important change in his job from when he started and up to now, not counting medicine. He got quiet for a minute, and while he was thinking, I told him my thoughts.

"The pot-bellied cattle trucks and the gooseneck trailers."

He laughed and nodded in agreement and told about the first ones he'd seen with eyes big as hubcaps. "But, I like to ride too much. Taking cattle to the railhead was fun."

Still thinking, he finally said, "I guess bulk cake bins and hoppers to put cake out to cattle in the winter was best. I hated those hundred pound sacks! Stackin' it in the fall and puttin' it out in the winter will give you a bad back and the piles. I'd just as soon pull on the lever and punch the buttons."

I agreed with him. But, I'll tell you what about Junior.

My God, that man could throw the hoolihan!!

I saw that!

———————

DICK HYSON is a voting member of the Pawnee Indian Nation and has been a cowboy and rancher his entire life. He spent nearly twenty years as a professional rodeo cowboy, and is a cowboy singer and entertainer. The University Press of Colorado published his first novel, *The Calling,* an authentic view of the Cowboy West. He lives in Durango, Colorado.

Spooky Cook

SALLY HARPER BATES

The sun was just breakin' in a new day for the cow-camp; Jody was mashin' biscuit dough around the counter fixin' a portion of breakfast for six hungry cowboys. Bacon was fryin' and she'd gathered eggs from the hen house out back, but they were gonna' have to be scrambled. The cow dogs between here and there had cold-nosed her and in her mad dash for the house she'd cracked a few. No big deal—the cowboys didn't much care how the eggs were cooked anyway.

Minutes later, she checked the biscuits and flipped the bacon again, then poured the eggs into a hot pan. She turned to pour coffee as black as mud-dobbers into mugs around the table. Three of the boys were knockin' the hay and muck off their boots and reachin' for the screen door. She made sure their cups were full before the boys hit the table.

About the time she was piling plates full of hot food, the rest of the boys came stompin' in. They seemed to be in unusually good humor ... maybe because they were on the downhill slide for gettin' the fall work done and things were going to slack off a bit before long.

Dave was "primed and cocked" with his usual sadistic humor being bantered about and nobody was above being his target. This morning, Jody was on the receiving end of more than her share. He dug her about the hardness of her biscuits and pointed out the fact that he'd found a shell in his scrambled eggs ... making a much bigger deal of it than necessary. As they were finishing breakfast he passed her the butter for her biscuit, and when she reached for it he quickly raised it just enough to be able to stick her thumb in it clear up to the first knuckle. She grinned a little cock-eyed and wiped the butter off with her apron. It didn't help soothe her put-on feelings when her husband joined in the laughter a little louder than she thought was appropriate.

They finished and headed for the corrals to saddle up horses that were just finishing grain from their morrals. It didn't take long for those capable boys to be leavin' the camp at a long trot headed for the big pasture behind the house. They'd be bringin' the stock down the fenceline in a bit, then start sorting bunches in the corrals. She stood and watched two of the young'uns tip their hats to the side and glance back at their shadow.

"Little twerps," she thought. "You need a lesson in humility, and it won't be long comin' I'm sure." She knew that Mother Nature had her ways of reminding a man just how insignificant he really is in the grand scheme of working cowboy ranching.

A couple hours later she went to pull her dish towels off the line when she saw the first of the cattle appear over the ridge where the road broke away from the fence line. One of the boys wasn't in the gap where he needed to be, and she could tell those cattle were going to head right down the road instead of the fence line.

"Probably watchin' his shadow again," she grinned as she slipped back into the kitchen and watched the show from her window. Sure enough, once they'd made the turn there were three cowboys tryin' to get 'em back against the fence so they'd come down the wire and into the big gate to the corrals.

She watched as four men finished the job and wondered where the other two were. Pulling out a loaf of homemade bread, she began to slice sandwich pieces for an early lunch. They'd be comin' in before they started the sorting and surely before they took the "keepers" back out to pasture. She sliced a big roast and stuck a pot of beans on the back burner.

She was wiping her hands with a big white dish towel when she glanced out the window and saw the two youngest cowboys come "packin' the mail" down the road . . . headed straight for the house. Couldn't be nothin' wrong . . . the other boys were at the corral loosening their cinches and airin' their horses' backs. She stepped to the door and watched as the two cock-sure boys did nothing more than show they were in a horse race . . . headed right for her back door. They probably thought they'd tie up to the hitchin' rail and march right in like they owned the place.

"Well boys," she thought, "It's time for your first lesson in camp manners." She stepped to the side of the door, leaving it open just enough to be able to slide through at the precise moment. Just as the boys slid to a stop in the yard, and Dave had his body standing out in his left stirrup to dismount, she opened the door, stepped out, and shook the flour out of her rollin' pin rag with a great deal more flourish than usual.

Both horses snorted and pawed the air as they spun out from under their riders, blowing snot and hot air clean to the moon, dumping them unceremoniously in the dirt near the hitchin' rail. Tails high, stirrups beating them in the ribcage, the pair galloped off with heads in the air, snorting all the way to the barn. There, they were gathered up by Jody's husband who was craning his neck to see what in the world had happened to set these two horses on the fly with no riders on board. He saw them both rising from the dirt like a couple of Phoenix birds, wings outstretched to beat the dirt off their pants, straightening themselves up like a couple of errant schoolboys leaving the principal's office. Her husband chuckled and headed for the house.

Jody simply moved back into her kitchen as though what had transpired was as unplanned and natural as it would have been any other time she'd stepped out to shake flour out of the towel. Once inside, she quickly went to the window and peeked around the curtain blowing in the cool mid-morning breeze that blew in from the snow-capped mountains beyond the borders of the ranch they worked for.

She watched as two sheepish young cowboys pulled themselves together and took the reins from her husband. He was laughing by now, poking fun at the joke and joshing the boys a little more than they were comfortable with. They glanced at the door and pulled their hats down over their eyes as they headed for the corral, still brushing dirt from the seat of their pants.

They didn't come to the house for lunch. She felt some sorry for them, and put together a couple of sandwiches wrapped in aluminum foil, sending them to the bunkhouse with her husband when lunch was finished.

They did come in for dinner. It had been a long, hard day and they were all tired out and dirty. It was sure quiet around the supper table. Extra big bowls of stew were dished out carefully with hot cornbread sliced. When she asked for the butter, it didn't get smeared on her thumb.

She had made hot apple pie for dessert.

SALLY HARPER BATES, who was born and raised in Yavapai County, Arizona, has been a part of the scenery and the lifestyle of the working cowboy as long as she can remember. She lived with her parents as a member of a working cowboy family and became a capable helper when it came to gathering cattle and working with horses. At age eighteen she married and continued to live on ranches where she rode and was a camp cook. She later worked with her husband in a saddle shop where they produced saddles and tack for the working cowboys in Arizona. She is a poet, musician, and has written for newspapers including, *Arizona Cowboy Connection*. She is working on a book about the Cowpunchers' Association.

Nightwatch

VIRGINIA BENNETT

Seeking the solitude right outside his door, Ben walked across the porch of the old cabin into the moonlight of a perfect Indian summer night. The wide boards creaked as he proceeded to the edge, where he stopped to gaze out over the meadow, where Rio Manuelito sidled down through a valley, which lay atop New Mexico's Continental Divide. Compared to its counterpart in Colorado or the Pacific Crest in the more westerly states, this part of the Divide seemed almost flat, with Oso Ridge keeping guard to the south, its Ponderosa pine–clad hillside home to deer, porcupine, and cougar. However, there was something coming Ben's way. Something unexpected out here in his big cowboy world.

Ben had worked at this cow camp every range season for the last seven years. He'd had a lifetime of experience at various cattle operations throughout the West, drifting from job to job, until he found his niche at the Richmond Cattle Company. Based out of San Rafael, a small Spanish settlement south of Grants, Ben enjoyed living with the cattle in the "sierra," the high country, in the summers, and then caring for them on the arid sections of the lower ranch in the winters. There was no irrigation and no haying, and that suited a man like Ben just fine.

Usually, several Mexican or Navajo cowboys joined Ben here at the Two Springs cow camp. He enjoyed hearing their laughter at night as they played cards in the bunkhouse next door to the old cookshack where he slept. Juan Gallegos was his favorite, with his quick, flashing smile of perfectly-aligned teeth, and his work attitude of "You like it, I love it," a phrase Juan was quick to use whenever Ben informed him that a job he was doing was done well enough.

Tonight, however, the bunkhouse was empty, and the October air hung like a heavy shroud of loneliness for the cowboy. This was the time for the Fall gather, time when he and his "hands" scoured the ridges and canyons, riding past ancient cliff dwellings unknown to archeologists anywhere, searching for the illusive cows and calves with the Rafter R brand. The uncharacteristically warm days caused the cattle to be quite content hiding out in PeaVine Canyon or on Lookout Mountain. Discovering these errant bovines was a game of great satisfaction for Ben, and one he felt certain all cowboys enjoyed. Whenever he rounded a trail or entered the edge of a meadow and spied a grazing cow or two, a grin would cross his face, even though there was no one within twenty miles to witness the lightness of his soul in this solitary sport.

He always knew Tom, Juan, Rafaelito, or Guillermo were on the next ridge, their presence often revealed by the bawling of rooted-out cows calling to their calves. The riders would converge in Cottonwood Canyon, each man herding his own small bunch of cattle. Coming down the trail, the cows would begin to hurry to join the others already in the lush bottomlands, as if it all suddenly made sense to them, this gathering off of range and eventual cattle drive to the rough, volcanic rock-strewn country of what is known in New Mexico as the "malpais" or "bad country." As soon as they arrived at the home ranch, their calves were taken from the cows, which were then preg-checked to be certain they'd have another calf come spring, and turned out to graze sparse, rich grasses near the Ice Caves. They settled down to the business of growing their next generation of calves. They required little attention.

Here at Two Springs, though, it was a lonesome night, but a night of unusual intensity. One night among the thousands he could not understand. Tom Yazzee had quit first, but that did not surprise Ben. He was a flighty young man, prone to superstition, unwilling to sleep outside after once hearing the plaintive hoot of an owl. He had been a good hand, though; talented with the handling of rough horses and fearless as he raced over boulders or down steep hillsides in an effort to turn a wild cow. When doctoring sick cattle, Tom was Ben's first choice of "header" and the old cowboss would miss counting on him whenever dangerous situations called for quick decisions and reflexes.

As Tom drove his rusty, '78 Chevy four-wheel drive pickup off of the ranch two weeks before, Ben had no inkling of the reason for his hasty departure. He chalked it up to the usual cowboy-drifter syndrome, something which he himself had suffered from in his younger days. Ben just took up the slack, and carried on with his three competent Mexican punchers. They would be all the help he needed to finish the Fall roundup.

Yet, four days ago, the unexpected had happened. Juan, carrying his beat-up Stetson in his hand, had walked shame-facedly to the door of the cookshack before breakfast. Ben had been awake for two hours, having brought the saddle horses in from the meadow, pouring coffee cans of oats into pans scattered throughout the corral, preparing for the day's activities of gathering.

"Amigo, I am sorry to tell you that I and the others are leaving today. We can take it no longer. We like you, it's not that. You are a good *patrón,* but last night, well, last night was too much." Juan stood with his head low, as if counting the nails in the tacked-down linoleum on the cabin floor.

Ben invited Rafaelito and Guillermo to join him and Juan inside, pouring them each a cup of strong coffee that had just finished boiling on the wood-cookstove, the grounds having been tossed generously into the water of the dented coffeepot. He motioned for them to sit at the picnic table around which they had shared all of their meals on the vinyl tablecloth of vibrant colors pulled tight and stapled underneath by Ben that spring when he had arrived early to sweep out the place and prepare for three seasons of work and companionship.

"What is it, boys?" he asked, looking each in the eye.

Juan, obviously the spokesman for the group, explained. "Last night, we were playing cards in the bunkhouse. We'd heard things before, you know, and Tom Yazzee, he heard more than we did, but we didn't believe him. We joked with him, you know? We might have been too hard, but we didn't believe what he said he saw." Juan paused to sip his coffee, and Ben looked out the small, paned window over the table, uncomfortable with this man's obvious admission of fear.

"As I said, we were playing cards, and I had a good hand, too, you know? Then, we heard them again. We'd heard them before, many times before, but somehow, this was different. The sound of walking on that old boardwalk that runs between your cabin and the bunkhouse. Those steps kept right on walking, coming closer and closer until they stopped right outside of our door. Then, Madre de Dios! Something shook the doorknob!"

Ben looked into the faces of the other two men, and saw that they were also reliving their night of terror. Whatever it was that happened, it was real enough in the minds of these men he knew and respected.

Juan continued. "We jumped up, each of us. The table fell and the chairs, too. Cards everywhere. We ran to the door, and we all three leaned against it, to hold it shut, you know? We are not weak, you know that, Ben, yet we pushed as hard as we could against that door, and even still, it was hard to hold shut! It kept opening against us and we would somehow get it closed again. Then, then! Guillermo, tell Señor what you saw!"

Ben turned to the weathered cowboy, a man he had ridden with for five years. Guillermo had grown up near Pie Town, and he reflected generations of brave vaqueros who had made their living riding fancy-trained horses and swinging the wide riata. In spite of his encroaching years, Guillermo was the strongest man Ben knew.

This morning, his wrinkled face seemed apologetic. "Ben, you will not believe it. I hardly believe it myself. I was closest to the door as we were trying to hold it shut, and as it came open a few inches, I looked out and saw . . . well, that thing out there, pushing against the door? It had EYES! Of green!"

Ben sat back from the table and looked at his old friends. Something had occurred last night; there was no doubt of that. He would not dishonor them with disbelief or teasing. There was nothing he could do but accept their story, which they finished by saying that the "soul" had left as suddenly as it had arrived. Footsteps retreating up the boardwalk. The men had remained at the door for what seemed like an hour, then had turned and each silently began packing his bedroll and possessions. They kept a fire going in the small stove all night, and kept each other awake with stories, stories from other villages on topics that were far distant from ghosts or untimely footsteps.

They drove away after Ben promised to tell headquarters to send their paychecks to their home addresses. The silence in the cow camp seemed interminable, as Ben strode immediately to the bunkhouse. He gingerly pushed open the low door, bent slightly and walked inside. The men had left the place cleaner than when they had arrived. The old table that had been cast aside swiftly the night before in a moment of terror had been pushed against the wall, the three chairs placed around it. The beds were straightened; the stove even cleaned out. One thing remained out of place: one solitary card on the floor. Ben knelt beside it and turned it over. A dog-eared queen of hearts. He left it where it lay and walked out, closing the door behind him. Hearing his own footsteps on the boardwalk, he imagined their fright.

He had, himself, experienced strange events over the last two months. He was a man who always slept with his pistol and wallet beneath his pillow, a habit born of sleeping so many years in bunkhouses with sometimes less-than-trustworthy characters. But then, one morning, after a sound sleep that had been filled with dreams of the woman he almost married ten years before, he awoke to find his pistol, broken down and in pieces as if for cleaning purposes, along with his wallet, lying on the picnic table. Ben knew in his heart that he would never do such a thing, but then, with no other explanation, he thought nothing more of it and called himself a fool for forgetting to perform his lifelong, nightly ritual.

He'd heard many screams in the middle of other nights, high-pitched screams of a terrified woman, but reason told him that mountain lions lurked in the old root cellar at times, hunting rodents, and surely that accounted for such frightening sounds.

Ben also recalled the times he'd seen the four men, whispering together as they sat ahorseback, allowing their mounts to rest after a hard morning's work. It all added up now. And now, he was alone.

He shrugged off the uneasy chill that ran up his spine, and walked out to the corral. He had a lot of work to do if he was going to single-handedly gather Richmond's cattle. And he knew with certainty that once Juan, Tom, Guillermo, and Rafaelito hit the town of Gallup and visited a few bars there with their tales of strange spirits in the Zuni Mountains, each drink adding a flavorful embellishment to the story, there would not remain a skilled cowboy in the county who would come to work at this cow camp. Ever.

Ben spent the next few weeks scouring the surrounding rincons and ridges for Hereford cattle. His horse picked his way sure-footedly up the old railway bed to the deserted gold mine at the head of a rugged canyon, where Ben stopped to eat his lunch and haphazardly look at the ore and tailings lying about. Later, he found several head of cattle lounging in the shade of alligator-juniper trees near a red rock outcropping. Each day, he pushed more and more cattle into the sheltered valley of Cottonwood Creek, and each mile, as he rode, he was haunted by the story of the green eyes that had tormented his ranch hands.

He knew much of the history of the old homestead that was comprised of a three-room log house, a barn fashioned from square, hand-hewn timbers, and the bunkhouse that originally had been built up on Oso Ridge but whose logs had been numbered, dismantled, and reassembled next to the trapper's cabin that now served as a kitchen and meeting place for cowhands. Rumor had it that the old building serving as a bunkhouse had been an outlaws' hideout.

Also on the ranch was a weathered, board-sided building, which he was told once housed a rural post office for the many families who lived in the surrounding valleys. Mostly, they were of Polish stock, hardy folks who wouldn't quit the land until it became too evident that survival in those harsh mountains demanded too high a sacrifice with too little return. The homesteaders moved on, and much of their land reverted to public domain and became the property of the U.S. Forest Service.

Ben reached back into his memory to find a story of a killing or some other tale that might explain the haunting of Two Springs, but he had heard nothing that he could recall. It seemed to be a puzzle destined to remain unsolved, in spite of the fact that the questions themselves hounded him constantly in the daylight hours.

Alone at night now, Ben placed his wallet and pistol firmly beneath his pillow, and locked a door he'd never locked before. Objects within the camp were never out of place again, though often he heard the familiar footsteps on the boardwalk outside, and twice, he'd heard his own doorknob rattle in a demanding fashion. Such activity would normally rob a man of his night's shuteye, yet this cowboy, weary from doing the work of five men, found some way of sleeping, for the most part, soundly.

One crisp day found Ben near the old ghost town of Carson, once a thriving community of loggers and sawmill workers, but now just a scene of empty foundations, cabins now only two logs high, and piles of rusty tin cans, predominantly of the Prince Albert tobacco type. As he rode his dun gelding into the clearing, he saw at least a hundred head of cattle grazing near the shallow lake south of the old community. A ready grin came to his face, as such a find would put him almost ready to head all of the cattle he'd gathered in the last two weeks down off the mountain toward winter range. He knew how many he'd been missing, and this discovery put him pretty close to being done with the roundup.

He began pushing cows, calves, and the occasional bull toward the end of the lake and in the direction of the trail that would lead them down to Cottonwood Canyon. However, they did not want to leave the lush grasses by the waterside, and old Dunnie had to work hard to convince them of the way they should go. Finally, the first cow headed down the trail, and then another, and soon they all followed, and behind them all, Ben rode Dunnie at a walk, oblivious to the dust raised by the trailing cattle.

"Boy, what I'd give for a good hand right now," Ben thought. "One that could help me get all five hundred of these brutes down off this hill next week." His musings strayed to the four ranch hands he'd lost, and he missed their help. It was then he thought nostalgically of Jennie.

Ah, Jennie! She was the teenage daughter of the ranch owner, John Richmond. She loved to come to the cow camp each year and help with the gather, and she'd often told Ben that Two Springs was her "favorite place on Earth!" Ben thought of her as the daughter he'd never had, and taught her to ride young horses and to rope. Each year, he had looked forward to the day Jennie would arrive, all coltish laughter and bouncy ponytail, bringing brilliance to his days like the sun peeking through the dark pines.

The last time he'd seen her was at her funeral. It was such a sad day, the day she and her date drove to her prom dance. He a young man so filled with excitement to think that a joyful Jennie sat at his side that he failed to notice his speed as he went into a corner too fast.

Ben missed her terribly, especially at times like these, when her expertise could be counted upon, and her youthful exuberance made the most dreary job seem light. He missed her constant teenage chatter and her dancing green eyes.

Green eyes! It couldn't be! Or could it? Ben began to wonder if he was just a foolish old man, prone to fanciful thoughts, alone too long, in need of companionship other than that of an old, horned Hereford. He pushed the idea to the back of his mind, and continued with the task at hand, driving the cattle down the trail toward Cottonwood Creek.

Three nights later, the moon was again rising in the East. It was a glorious harvest moon, large and yellow and it lit up the entire meadow surrounding the old homestead. Inside the cookshack, Ben lay in peaceful sleep. Soon, he would be packing up his own bedroll and heading down to civilization and something more of a social life. This grazing season would be far behind, and the events something to tell someone else's grandchildren. In a week or two, he'd be in the headquarters bunkhouse, and able to run for coffee into the little village of San Rafael, a town complete with a life-sized crucifix painted in vivid colors standing in the middle of the main street.

Suddenly, he was jolted awake by the familiar footsteps upon the boards of the old walkway outside. He listened as they tramped a step at a time, with an insistence that seemed designed to wake him. He sat up in bed and grabbed the pistol from beneath his pillow. He cocked the hammer, and quietly, taking no breaths, strained his ears to hear the footsteps come across the porch floor and stop at the door that he faced ten feet away.

Ben stood up and aimed the gun at the door. As before, the doorknob rattled firmly, not in the way someone wanting to gain entry might do, but in a disturbing manner, as if entry was not the desired result, but the gaining of his attention was. This told Ben something very clearly: what was at the door was not human. A prowler would have approached in a much more secretive manner. An unexpected guest would have knocked upon the door. This was the same visitor he'd been dealing with all summer, since last May, since Jennie had died.

Ben dropped the hand holding the pistol to his side. He released the hammer carefully, and placed the .44 back under his pillow. Then, clearing his throat, he summoned up his courage and called out.

"Jennie, I know it's you! You can't keep coming here. You need to go where you can rest. I'll take care of Two Springs for you if you leave. I know you loved it so. But if you refuse to leave, I'll burn every building here to the ground, and I mean it. You know I do. Jennie, please, goodbye!"

The footsteps retreated down the boardwalk. The aging foreman took a deep breath, and went to the stove to light a fire. In a couple of hours, it would be time to arise anyway, time to wrangle in the horses, feed them their morning grain, time to begin the routine of a lifetime. He might as well get started with the business of it. At any rate, he suspected he would not be able to go back to sleep that night.

Ben stayed at the cow camp for another ten days. Each night, he listened for more evidence of his nightly guest, and each night brought him more peace, more understanding, more assurance that she would never return. And to his knowledge, she never did.

Today, Two Springs is haunted only by the mountain lions that find no resistance to their presence there. The cabins lie empty and still, baked by the heat of the summer suns and surrounded by swirling, high country snows in the winter months. The Richmond Cattle Company, having no one of any savvy to inherit the family business, has gone defunct, and their grazing allotments have not been picked up by any of the smaller, nearby ranches. Though the grass is rich and plentiful, the country is just too big, and good cowboys too hard to find.

The winds sweep down off of Oso Ridge as they always have and always will. Panes of glass are broken from the cabin windows, and squirrels have made their homes within. Occasionally, a hunter or firewood gatherer stops by and curiously investigates each of the old buildings. Hardly noticeable to any visitor, however, on the floor of the old bunkhouse, amidst the litter of rodent droppings, leaves, and pine cones, is a playing card: the faded queen of hearts.

VIRGINIA BENNETT, born and raised in an agricultural family in rural New Hampshire, moved West in 1970. She first settled in Arizona, where she professionally ran barrel horses at local rodeos for three years before meeting her husband, Pete. In their twenty-eight years of marriage, they have lived and worked on Western ranches in New Mexico, Colorado, Wyoming, Idaho, Oregon, Washington, and now California. Virginia broke colts for twenty years, and worked alongside Pete on ranches where he was employed, helping in every capacity, from haying to calving, from fencing and building to all aspects of cattle and horse management. She first drew cowboy wages ($25 a day) on the Quarter Circle Five Ranch near Daniel, Wyoming, a ranch that ran five thousand head of yearlings. She has since been employed as a range allotment rider, a dude wrangler, a hunter/jumper trainer and competitor, a draft team driver, and freelance agricultural journalist. Virginia is also a cowboy poet, having performed at the Elko Gathering for ten years, and presented her work at the Smithsonian Institution, and on PBS and NPR. She is the editor of *Cowgirl Poetry: 100 years of writin' and rhymin'* (Gibbs Smith Publishers, 2001). She and her husband, Pete, currently co-manage a ranch in California.

Wreck

CURT BRUMMETT

Friends—and even my one or two enemies—we have all been told since a horse first kicked us that life is a series of ups and downs. We've been told this by preachers, teachers, kinfolks, and bartenders. I even had a falling-down wino advise me once that there was good times and bad times. He just failed to explain that most cowboys seem to have an abundance of just one of these. You guess which.

People, sometime when you think things has gone down hill as far as they can go, think again.

Here in the last couple of months, I have managed to total out a brand new (3,900 miles on it) four wheel drive, four door, three-quarter ton pickup.

Broke three ribs, cracked two, busted my collarbone on the right side, and screwed up my shoulder joint pretty bad.

Crippled two of three horses, neither of which was the sorry one. Pert-near destroyed my horse trailer, and got a letter from the I.R.S.

The rib situation came with the pickup wreck; the rest are all separate events.

But when you think you are so far down, you can't go any further, (like I said) think again.

When you are in such bad shape you can't even get up out of a chair without someone helping you, you find out who your true friends are.

As a result of my misfortune, I couldn't lay down to sleep. I had to sit up in a recliner. I was bruised from my ankles to the top of my ears. To say I was stove up would be an understatement to end all understatements.

The first week was pure dee hell. I was so swelled up from the wreck, I couldn't wear my regular Levis. I had to wear sweat pants. I was wrapped up in about eighty yards of elastic wrap for my ribs, another forty yards of brace for my collarbone, a sling for my shoulder, and I had the scours.

This will not only let you know who your friends are, it will also prove your friends are mentally degenerate perverts with a sense of humor that only truly sick people can acquire.

For example . . .

I was sitting in this stupid low slung recliner, trying to keep from coughing, when the urge (and I don't mean to cough) hit me pretty hard.

I asked Jeremy to help me up so I could hobble to the bathroom. He looked at me, grinned, and said, "Ya sure, soon as the next commercial comes on."

We were watching a P.B.R. bull riding session.

I was building pressure.

I said, "Man, I really need some help."

He grinned and said, "Ya, I know. Don't you just hate it when there's something good on TV?"

I started trying to work my way out of the recliner. Now I was really under pressure. I did not want to cough for two reasons now. One, because when I did cough it hurt so much I would nearly pass out, and two, I didn't need any extra strain to break my concentration concerning muscle control.

I finally told 'im that if he didn't get me out of that damn chair, he'd be the one that had to clean up the mess.

He got me up out of the chair, and I got my business taken care of. As I was hobbling back to the chair, I got pretty dizzy and was fixing to pass out.

Old Jeremy come to the rescue.

He had just poured us some iced tea. He couldn't get me in time to keep me from falling as I was trying to pass out, so he did the next best thing.

He threw that cold tea on me from across the living room.

I didn't pass out from being dizzy, fact is, I didn't pass out at all.

You can't pass out when you've sucked in enough air to stretch eighty yards of elastic wrap to a hundred and twenty yards.

You don't want to pass out—you want to kill. But you can't kill because the sudden intake of extra air and the chilling effect of sudden cold put you back in the "URGE" mode.

Jeremy said he did it for two reasons. One, it kept me up. Two, it was sort of a unique way to get me some exercise.

Damn but that tea was cold.

After about two or three weeks, my wife Deb and me figured we would go to see a couple of friends of ours in Mountainair, New Mexico.

It's four hours from Canyon, Texas, to Mountainair and another seven hours from Mountainair to Leon and Darla's. (They live a way off the highway on a road that is not quite smooth.)

I'm not saying old Deb can't see, but I feel reasonably sure a bat could've seen most of the boulders she ran over. By the time we got there, I had used up about half of a three week supply of pain pills, ripped the dash out with my good hand, and held my breath so long that I had shrunk the eighty yards of elastic wrap to forty yards.

Leon and Darla live on a ranch that is remote to say the least. They had been working on their house and sort of remodeling things. Darla had just purchased a new refrigerator and they had a new roof.

Yep, old Leon sure takes care of Darla.

They are not used to having a lot of company.

After supper and some visiting, it was bedtime. I found a chair I could sleep in and everyone else went to bed. Somewhere along about midnight, Leon got up either to get a drink of water or to go to the bathroom. (By the time this story is over you will know why he couldn't remember the reason he got up.)

I was sitting in a chair in the living room in a state of semi-awake. Leon walked past me headed towards the kitchen. I was relaxed and enjoying the cool night air when it happened.

There was a scream that came from the kitchen. I had never heard anything like it. (Well, I did once, but that was a long time ago.)

It scared me so bad I jumped, rebroke one rib, started coughing, and the urge was upon me.

Darla came stampeding out of their bedroom, Deb came stampeding out of her bedroom, I was trying to control my coughing, and Leon was hollering for someone to bring him a shotgun.

All three of us got to the kitchen door about the same time. Darla turned the light on and, folks, what we saw was not a pretty sight.

There in the corner was old Leon in his drawers. He was about three inches off the floor and pale. And there by Darla's new icebox was a rattlesnake. The snake was somewhat upset, but not near as upset as old Leon.

Now folks, old Leon is not what I would call the Charles Atlas type. His legs are somewhat bowed, a way yonder pale, and skinny. And, I might add, them boxer shorts with the little hearts all over 'em just didn't do old Leon justice.

Leon demanded a shotgun.

Darla said she would get 'im a hoe or a shovel. She didn't want to take a chance on killing the only new icebox she had ever had.

Deb mowed me down trying to get as far away from the snake as possible and I was laughing my fool head off.

I was laughing so hard I could hardly stand the pain. But the tall, skinny cowboy in the heart-covered drawers was worth it.

Darla finally got the shotgun, came in from the other side of the kitchen, and handed it to the Don Knotts look-alike. Old Leon did the deed. Only took 'im three blasts. He didn't kill the icebox, but he scattered that snake all over hell and half of New Mexico.

By the time we got the mess cleaned up, the holes patched in the wall and floor, we still had enough time to get some sleep before sunup.

I guess Darla and Deb got some rest, I didn't.

I mean, it's hard to sleep in a chair with your ribs hurting from laughing at a man who has taken it upon hisself to keep watch the rest of the night for more snakes.

I wasn't laughing at his motive, I was laughing at his anti-snake security uniform.

Yep, seems as though he was still upset from stepping on that snake in the first place. He was wearing his high top boots, his hat, and had his shotgun laid across his lap. And them drawers with all the little hearts on 'em was all he had on in the way of uniform pants.

If it hadn't 'ave been for the state of mind the man in the drawers was in, I would've laughed out loud.

Friends can be so sympathetic.

The way it was, all I did was grin and fart. Even that hurt, no matter—it was my turn for the good times. They'd been a long while acoming.

———————

CURT BRUMMETT has lived a story-creating existence, and now he's a professional storyteller. He has worked as a cowboy, a roper, a roughneck, and a firefighter. "As I see it," Brummett says, "caution is the main reason a lot of things don't get done." His work has appeared in *Team Roper's Times, DeBaca County News, Livestock Weekly,* and *Horse and Rider.* Among his books are *Roping Can Be Hazardous to Your Health, My Dog's a Democrat,* and *A Snake in the Bathtub and Other Stories.* He frequently performs at storytelling festivals and cowboy poetry gatherings across the Southwest. Brummett lives with his wife, Sheila, in Canyon, Texas.

The Old Man

JIMBO BREWER

"Did you really never know, Hijo?" Those words . . . that question . . . were to change my life and my way of thinking. They couldn't rub out the hurts of the past nor put my family back together again, but they did give me a closer look at the Old Man.

About all I knew of him up until then was that he was my blood and that his heart was so hard as to leave no tracks that would lead you to his soul . . . if he had one. He lived by the credo that "you have to ride your own horses." It took me a while to understand that it meant a hell of a lot more that just bucking out some old bronc.

And, it still galls me that had it not been for one old Mexican man, who, though blind, could see more than anyone I ever knew . . . had it not been for him, I would have never really known the Old Man . . . my grandfather.

But all of what I learned and know now came years after my story began.

Let me tell it to you.

The thing I remember most about the Old Man was the sound of those big rowelled spurs just ajinglin' along as he moved afoot or ahorseback. That, and the fact that I never really knew him 'til it was too late.

He was a hard man to get to know. I don't think I ever met anybody who said they really liked him. Oh, there was old Homero and my mother and while they said they loved him, I don't remember them saying they "liked" him . . . and both said they damned sure didn't like his roughhide ways. He was my dad's father and he ranched up in the tough lands of the Texas Panhandle. The land up there sort of matched his disposition. It's rough and rocky and the growth will scratch you and stick you.

My dad was the youngest of five. The two oldest were girls, then his two brothers and then himself. When my grandmother died . . . long before I was ever around . . . the Old Man just got to be more miserable-dispositioned as each season passed. Finally it got to be too much and the two girls up and left. The oldest, Fannie, was a brilliant student and was high-educated. She was the only one, other than my dad, who went to college.

Anyway, Fannie and her sister took off for Georgia where she went to work at the university and ultimately married a professor there. Then the boys, as they came of age and mind enough, took off for parts unknown. They finally ended up in Georgia too, as did my dad, who one night just took his hotroll and lit a shuck east.

Mother said he never talked about how he got to Aunt Fannie's, but for a boy as young as he was it would have been a scary journey.

So, Fannie educated Dad through high school and then he went to college to become a lawyer. And a good one he did become, they say. You see, I never knew my father. He died when I was three and I guess that's where this story really begins.

For some reason, my mother had a special feeling for her father-in-law. She said while my dad and his brothers and sisters never spoke to the Old Man again, she would call him and write to him often. She never let my father know that, though.

As I grew up, my uncles told me stories about their own growing up out there. One uncle, Lent, would get a funny look on his face when he talked about life up there along Kiowah Creek. I would turn away and find something to fiddle with when he got that misty look and then he'd come around and tell me some more stories. It was Uncle Lent who bought me my first horse and taught me to care for him and to ride. He also taught me to rope and I admit I did take to it all. But there ain't much demand out east for a man who can throw the hoolihan and ride like a Comanche. Little did I know how much I would need it later on. It was the summer I was fourteen when mother came to me and said that she wanted to ask a special favor.

She'd been alone eleven years then, except for me and my little brother and I knew how hard she had worked for us. So it was without thinking that I said yes and she asked me to do something that would change my life forever . . . she asked me to go to Texas to spend the summer with my granddad.

The Old Man was as unreal to me as my own father. I knew them both only by stories and some faded old black-and-white photographs mother had put away in a shoebox in her dresser. I instantly wanted to take it back, but something in Mama's eyes told me to do what I said I would do.

"But," I asked, "how will I get out there?" I figured our old car wouldn't make it much past the county line, much less out there. Wherever the hell "out there" was. She said she had talked to him and he said to put me on a train. There was a crossing near his place and he'd have the train stop there and he'd get me.

Well, it sure sounded like an adventure to me, but from what my uncles had told me, I'd probably as soon a' gone straight to hell as to the Old Man's ranch.

That night, this fourteen-year-old, big-for-his-age Georgia boy went to sleep crying . . . scared to go and scared not to. Come morning, we packed an old leather suitcase and Mama tried to make it better by telling me I could wear my ridin' boots and big-brimmed hat on the train. It didn't.

The trip out there's still a blur even today. Maybe it was fear. Maybe it was like the Indians say and I had medicine that told me this was the beginning of a way of life. Whatever, the first thing I really remember was the conductor coming to get me and telling me I was "home in Texas." Godalmighty, I sure didn't feel like I was home. I felt like I was one of those Israelites who was cast to wander in the wilderness.

I stepped down to a new world. The land was yellow-red and most if it seemed to be airborne and gettin' in my mouth and under my collar. I squinted through the dust as I moved a bit while the train chugged off. There was a fellow there beside a truck, but he didn't look like the pictures of my granddad. And it wasn't him. It was Homero Calderon, maybe the Old Man's only friend and a hand on the ranch.

While I can't remember the train trip, I'll never forget the strong, brown, rough hand that shook mine that day. His voice was soft and had music in it and his smile was as real as anything I'd seen before or since. And as much as I liked him, I thought it was sure a hell of a note to come halfway across the country and my grandfather sent somebody else to pick me up.

Everybody, he said, called him by the Anglo version of his name . . . Homer. He told me to do the same, but "Homero" seemed the right way for me. In fact, I'da probably called him Mr. Calderon but that seemed, someway, to be almost impolite.

He loaded up what little I had in the truck and said we'd go on to the ranch. We just drove across one little road and Homero announced that we were on Granddad's place. He asked me about my home and my family and about the things I did back there. When he seemed satisfied that he knew a little about me, he started telling me about the ranch.

The ranch wasn't really big, he told me, at least not by Texas standards. And, he added, with some sadness, each year it was getting smaller because of taxes and droughts and . . . well . . . because of my grandfather's refusal to sell mineral rights to oil companies.

"But, your grandpa is just who he is and no more can be said. Does no good to discuss matters." I found this to be a real understatement.

When we got to headquarters, the Mexican took me right to the bunkhouse and set my plunder down on a bed in the far back corner of a long room full of identical bunks. He looked right sheepish when he told me that Grandfather had decided I should stay with the hands so as to get to know the real cowboy life. It was almost an apology the way he said it and I was quick to say I liked the idea. Really, I didn't want this man, who I felt to be a friend, to be embarrassed by the situation.

In my mind, though, I felt slighted again by a man I didn't even know and had no feelings for, one way or the other.

"The hands will be in soon," Homero said. "We're working the headquarters pasture and they're close by." He said we'd all get together in the cookhouse for some supper after the boys had time to clean up a little. "They all know you're comin'" he said, "and they're right friendly. You'll make friends easy with them."

Then he was gone and I was left alone to survey my new home away from home. I didn't really have any expectations about this summer deal, but I thought, at least, that I would stay in the house with the Old Man. But, in a way, I was right relieved that I didn't have to.

I didn't like it, though, that I was gettin' to where I disliked my Grandfather when I wouldn't have even known him if he came up and kicked me in the butt. Uncle Lent had said that was a distinct possibility, too.

So, I sat down on the threadbare army blanket–covered bed and leaned against the rough board wall that butted up against the bunk. Up above my head was an old yellowed photograph of somebody riding a bucking horse. There was some writing on the photo, but it too, had faded and I couldn't tell what it said. One thing for sure . . . it was a hell of a ride on a "sunfishin'" bronc.

On other walls were calendars with pictures of shiny horses and cattle. They were pretty, but I knew they didn't belong in this country. There were more photographs of riding and roping men. All were identified in the same scrawly hand as the one over my bed. And on all, like the one over my bed, the writing was faded into a ghost script that could not be ciphered by the sharpest eye.

Hanging over and near the other bedding places was an assortment of cowboy truck. A pair of old leggins, needin' repair. A half-finished braided horsehair headstall. Ancient rusty bits with tarnished silver. Worn canvas coats waiting for winter. In the middle of the room was a common table with cards strewn about. Next to it was an almost completed saddle. It was plain there was a saddle maker . . . and a good one . . . in the midst of the ranch workers.

The place smelled of leather and tobacco and old wool. And, I thought, it smelled of a kind of life I was becoming anxious to know and to experience. The first man through the door that framed that West Texas sundown was Dutch Johnny Van Horn. Dutch Johnny didn't live in the bunkhouse with the men as he and his wife had a little house up the main ranch road. Homero had the same and there were a couple more for any married hands who were good enough in the Old Man's eyes to merit ranch-provided housing.

Dutch smiled at me and thrust out his hand. Like Homero, his hand was rough and callused and I noticed he was missing a finger from the big joint. Later that summer, he would use the stump as a visual reminder of what would happen to me if I didn't mind my rope as I took my dallies.

"We're glad to have you here, Bubba," he said and I knew he meant it. Now Dutch called everybody and lots of the animals on the place Bubba. He even called a young hand, whose name was Bubba, Bubba. 'Course, Dutch didn't even think about it being his real name.

As he turned to pull a chair from the table, I noticed his spurs. They were brown steel with leggin guards and inch-and-a-half rowels. He had had them made with some engraved silver on them and there was a brand. It was the reverse SB connected. It was done in sort of a loose script with the S backward and the B sort of tilted to the right. It was the Old Man's brand. And while it has taken a heap of blood, sweat, and tears, as the poets say, it is mine today.

Dutch was the wagon boss and worked as the go-between with the cowboys. He told me a bit about the crew and said that while I was the button at fourteen, there was a sixteen-year-old named Charlie Gibson who was riding for the outfit. 'Bout the time he told me about Charlie, here through the door he came. He was slim and cotton-topped. His near-white hair stood in bold contrast to his sun-browned face.

Charlie was another one who acted mighty happy that I had come to Texas. He told me later he figured my being the youngest now . . . even if I was the boss's grandpup . . . would make me the brunt of all the cowboy jokes. I probably wouldn't have cared if he had told me. I needed a young friend right about then.

Well, I met them all as they came in. Dutch stayed to introduce me. Some were outgoing and friendly and some just shook hands and went on. I know now, it's most always that way in any crew.

I followed the crew to the chuckhouse a bit later and met the

cocinero, Buck. He was a stove-up old cowboy who took to cookin'
when he couldn't do the hard work anymore. He didn't look right
clean, but his food was 'bout as good as Mama's and one of the cowboys
called Bronc said his grub had never killed nobody. He added a few
eaters had wished they'd died but they didn't. Buck cussed him out . . .
another thing the cook was good at.

We was scrapin' our plates and puttin' them in the old washtub
when Homero came in. "How was it, son?" the old vaquero asked and
he smiled right big when I told him I compared it to Mama's table.
Buck was standing close by and turned plumb red at my comments.

"Aw, hell, boy," he grumbled. "You was just half starved is all." But
from then on Buck made sure my plate was always filled.

Homero said we needed to get on up to the big house 'cause himself was on the way in from Amarillo and he would want to see me. It
was about time, I thought.

The big house wasn't really big at all. Just an old Texas-type two
story house with a big front porch. We went in to the cool dimness of
what was, at once, a living room and an office and from the looks of an
Indian blanket–covered bunk on one wall, it was also a sometimes
bedroom. You could tell from the clutter of papers on the rolltop
desk and the magazines and books stacked here and there, that what
time my grandfather spent under this roof, most of it was right here
in this room.

Homero took a seat in an ancient stuffed leather chair that had
hills and valleys where the stuffing had piled up here and spread
out there. I went to a bookcase where, in addition to books that
looked to be almost new, were photographs of a family that seemed
to be more fiction than fact. There were pictures of my dad, uncles,
and aunts as children. Then the youngsters with their mother, my
grandmother, and the Old Man.

They looked right strange to me because they were all smiling as if
their lives were perfect. The photographs didn't match the stories I
had heard, but, then again, Mama had said the Old Man had changed
for the worst when Grandmother died.

I was deep in thought when the sound pushed its way into my

musing. It was the sound that I will always remember and will always be the identifying memory mark when I think on my grandpa. His spurs rang loud and musical-like as he mounted the porch. The maker of those spurs, I've always thought, must have been a musician to put such sound into the metallurgy of those rowels.

When he came into the room, my eyes were instantly drawn down to the iron and silver on his boot heels. And when I finally did look up into the white-blue eyes of old E. C. He was studying me like I was daft. "What is it boy?" Those were his first words and delivered a bit more abruptly than I thought necessary.

"I was just lookin' at your spurs."

"I see," he said, but I knew he didn't have a notion. Now, I know it was like a calf's first smell of its mother. That defining sensation that locks in the brain and remains with you 'til you're dust. But that day I just knew the spurs . . . and the man . . . were special.

Hooked to those spurs were tall-shafted boots with lots of bright thread stitching. The bottoms were just plain old tan roughout leather, but the deep scalloped tops were rich, shiny brown calf hide. His pants were tucked into those boots, and he never wore them any other way. He was taller than I had pictured, pushing six two. Right heavy-chested and a bit of stomach pushing his belt out. His hair and mustache were light brown once . . . more gray the day I met him. And, like every West Texas cowboy I had met, his face and hands were burned a deep chestnut.

"How's your mama doing?" he asked as he stuck out his hand to shake mine.

"Fine, sir. Least she was when I left her." It had only been a few days but it seemed like forever and I guess my resentment of being sent out there must have shown in my voice.

"Well, you can go back to her anytime you feel like you need to. I told her you might be young to come out here, now."

Well, there it was. I felt like that Old Man had already started looking down on me, just like Uncle Lent said he did with all his own boys.

I bowed up my back right fast. "No sir, mama sent me here 'cause she figured it'd be good for me to see where Daddy came from. So, I'm here for ... for ... well, however long it takes." I didn't know what I was saying, I just knew I was reacting to a lot of hard talk I had heard about the Old Man. I also knew I didn't like him, even though I didn't even really know him.

"Mama said it'd be good for you, too."

His old eyes sorta squinted at me and he chewed on the edge of his mustache. He never in his life ever said ... in words ... that she was anywhere near's right.

Homero had been silent to that point but under his breath, and plain as daylight, he answered it himself. "Damn right," he muttered and locked hard eyes with the Old Man, who looked back at me right fast. I knew he figured I was easier to deal with.

"Your mama tells me you can ride some and she wants you to learn a trade, so we'll see if you can be a cowboy. Best thing is just do what Homer says and don't get in the way 'til you savvy what's needed. You got a rig with you?"

He saw I didn't know what he was talking about. "Don't matter. Homer, give 'im those leggins Salty left here and, hell, let him ride my old Hamley." Homer smiled a bit at the reference to the saddle but it took me a lot of years to know why.

"I see you got boots and a lid. We'll find you some spurs."

"I have some spurs for him," Homero said. Grandpa looked at him right puzzled-like. "They were for Lucero," was all he said.

"Why, hell, you don't have to give him those," the Old Man said but Homero ended the talk with the same statement ... "I have some spurs for him."

"Be best if you stay with the boys in the bunkhouse, so's you can learn from them." He said this in a way that even me, knowing him as little as I did, could tell he was a bit embarrassed. "Homer will help you get your gear together and I'll see you in the mornin'. Oh, and let Homer pick your horses, ain't no need for you to take anything but gentle stock ... let the hands ride the broncs."

Uncle Lent had told me enough so's I knew that every string had at least one rank-like mount and each hand was expected to call for the rough ones as regular as his good stock and what he said rubbed me wrong. I, sure as God, knew I couldn't ride like those other fellows, but I damn sure wasn't going to shirk that part of the job.

I sort of spun on my heels and faced the man.

"No sir!" and I said it hard. "Mama said I was to learn. She said I was to do whatever had to be done. I'll take a regular draw and try to ride what I get. I guess that's what your own boys would have done."

Now, I shouldn't have said that, but I was mad. I had hurt him and like anything that's hurt, he come back at me.

"All right, by God, cut him a string and give him one of those from Tongue River."

Homero started to object but the look on Grandpa's face said it all and it was final. "Sí, patron," was all he said but I knew there was a special meaning, something like, "I'll do it, but only because you're lord and master of the land."

I dang sure found out about those Tongue River horses in the days to come. Seems they were the boot . . . bad boot at that . . . in a cow deal that went sour with a failing rancher down on the Tongue River. They were all old spoiled working horses—made that way because that rancher had a crew of tinhorns working for him and they had let the remuda do pretty much however they wanted to. Anyhow, they would all buck and do their best to get out of work. Some just crow-hopped around and some would sure enough swaller their heads.

Well, it's sure enough took me a good while to get to the meat of my story, but they were words that needed to be said, so's you would know about how the Old Man was and about old Homero, who sort of adopted me, and about me . . . a green kid from the East who was sent West to try to cowboy and, really, to try to sort of build a bridge between grandpa and my dad's memory. I wished it had all gone different.

It was well before even a rim of light in the east when we gathered in the horse trap to get our mounts. Homero called out a horse for me to start the day's work and as a bit of daylight came, I saw it was a

well-made yellow gelding with the reverse SB connected on his left
shoulder. I put my headstall on him and he stood obedient to the
dropped reins while I saddled him with Grandpa's well-used Hamley.
I couldn't help but run my hands over the deep basket stamping and
think that I probably would never ride a better rig.

The crew rode out with Dutch Johnny but Homero told me to
hold back 'cause we had to pick one of the Tongue River horses. They
were all in a big pen and honestly looked to be some good horses.
Looks, I found, can be right deceiving.

Homero started in telling me about the horses. Which ones were
bad and which ones were plumb sorry. I could tell he was pointin' me
towards one of the lesser of the evils, so to speak. He grouped four
of the cayuses in the "rank" category and in those was a mighty
fine-looking gray. Fifteen hands, big hips, and a long neck. His little
ol' head was just plain pretty but his eyes were hard and cold. Lord,
how I wished he had been gentle.

"Just take one of those ol' crow-hoppin' horses," Homero told me.
"I picked you some real good mounts and ain't no need to get yourself
all stove up on one of those rank sons of bitches."

"That's good advice, son." It was the Old Man. He had led his horse
up behind us and we were so intent on looking at the Tongue River
remuda that we hadn't heard him. "Nobody'll expect you to have a
rank horse, so just get you one of those easier ones."

You know, I think I knew even then that he didn't mean nothing
by what he said. He really did want me to take one that wouldn't
be likely to hurt me. But, damn it all, the way he said it just got me
boilin'.

"I'll take the gray, Homero." Both of them went sort of cold in the
eyes. The Mexican shook his head like he knew I was just a damn fool
kid tryin' to show out. Grandpa, well, he just kinda looked out over
the flat, brushy land and real quiet-like finalized my crazy move.

"Homer, rope out the gray." Then, light as you can believe, he stepped
onto his horse and headed to the work grounds at a long trot.

"I'll do it later, boy. Let's go to work." I could tell Homero was
right mad at me and, truth be told, I was mad at myself and scared,

too. I knew I'd have to call for that gray way too soon. I couldn't spit if I'd had to.

Thinking back on those first days, I don't know how I made it. Ten hours a day in the saddle. Swappin' horses two . . . sometimes three . . . times a day. Rope burns on my hands. Legs so stiff I couldn't walk good and seems like hardly any sleep . . . although I was gettin' more than I ever did back in Georgia. But each day got better and somehow I knew I was born to this work and to the whole ranchin' deal. I listened to everything that was being said. Even when the cowboys was just spinnin' windys, there was something in them that I figured I needed to know. Oh, and I'll admit I got right puffed up from time to time. I sure couldn't rope nor ride like the hands, but Uncle Lent had taught me good enough to where I surprised that crew and Grandpa and, well hell, I surprised myself, too.

I loved the smell of the land at dawn and the sound of the old bell mare out there in the horse trap. And, I loved the sound of the spurs Homero gave me. I traded a pretty good wristwatch to Charlie Gibson for a canvas bedroll and a pair of binoculars to another hand for a nice broke mouth bit with some silver on it. I figured I was gettin' right punchy—that is 'til the morning I had to call for that rank gray.

I didn't sleep one wink the night before. The boys all knew I had used up my good string and I had to call him out and they sure gave me a good ribbin' about it. Charlie sorta sidled over to me and quiet-like said the boys couldn't understand why the boss's grandboy had to have a bad horse.

"He don't treat me no different from any of you," I said in defense of the situation and Charlie took off his hat and scratched that cotton top and said, "Yeah, that's just what we was thinkin' and it don't seem right. It's like he don't even . . ." He let it trail off knowing he had said too much already.

And there it was again. I was the son of his son and he didn't even act like I was no more than a hired hand. Oh, he had had me up to the big house a time or two to eat supper. Homero was always there and they just talked away about the shape of the grass and beef prices and the lack of rain . . . always the lack of rain. And Homero would try to include me, but the Old Man just sorta ignored me. Never said no more than did I want another biscuit or such.

Truth was, over the days I had watched him and saw he was a real top hand. He could roll a hoolihan over an old "hidey head" horse quick as you ever saw. Even as old as he was . . . at least old to me . . . he could and would top out as bad a bronc as he had on the place. He'd just float up there in the saddle and I couldn't help but be proud that I was his blood.

But, it didn't make no difference how I felt, he damn sure didn't seem to feel the same. Every now and then, he'd catch himself trying to tell me something about the land or the cattle and it would seem to startle him, and when I'd make a pretty good loop in the branding pen, I'd sometimes see a right funny look on his face. It was like it softened or something. But he never . . . not once . . . said just the least thing to make me feel like . . . well, his grandson.

So when the dawn came and I had to call for the gray, I figured whatever happened, it wouldn't matter much to him one way or the other. The boys had started calling the horse "Badger." Said he was mean as an ol' badger. It sure didn't help me none. Dutch Johnny and Homero were ropin' out the stock and when we pushed the remuda into the corner of the mesquite post pen and started calling out the names of the horses, I just yelled it out loud as I could. Might as well get it over with. Johnny snagged him and brought him to me. I slipped my loop under his and stood 'til everybody had their mounts.

He was ground gentle enough. No pullin' or jumpin' and when I eased my saddle up on him, he acted like a lady's horse. I knew they was all watchin' and I didn't waste time. To this day I'm that way— when I got to do something I don't want to, I rush it to get it over with. I slipped the bit in his mouth and tightened the girth. I decided to cheek him just in case he fired while I was swinging on.

Charlie was nearby and sort of whispered. "Take a deep seat on him. I've seen him go and he's strong and he bucks hard. See if you can pull his head around, it'll help some."

I stepped into the wood and he just stood there. I pulled my lid down near over my eyes and squeezed him. They were all lookin' and for a minute, I thought maybe God had decided to just let me slip by without gettin' hurt or embarrassed . . . or both. I looked at Charlie and he looked more scared than me. Then old Badger went.

Even though I had been thinking about this ride for a bunch of days, I was still surprised. The gray jumped like an oversized jack rabbit, clearing the ground with all four feet. When we landed, it 'bout split me in two. Then it was hell to pay. He bawled and swallered his head. But something wasn't quite kosher with the deal. My pony at home had bucked me harder at times. Don't get me wrong, the Tongue River horse was turnin' the crank, but it didn't seem as bad as I thought it would be.

I might have rode him but he lost his footin' and went down and I got thrown clear. While he was scramblin' to get up, I just plumb lost my mind and stepped into the saddle while he was down. Back on his feet, he jumped a time or two more and then threw his pretty head up and went to lopin'.

The boys was lookin' like they'd never seen nothing like it and Homero and Johnny was slappin' each other on the back. I, myself, didn't know what to do. I didn't know if he was going to fire again or if he had done his do.

Charlie loped up beside me grinnin' like a chessie cat. "By God, I never seen him give up that soon. Hell, looked like you wore him out. How 'bout that slick?" I said he might just do some more when he got his wind, but my friend said the few times they had rode him down, he never bucked the rest of the day. "In fact, he's a pretty savvy cow horse," he added.

Through the day, the rest of the crew, one by one, said something to me about the ride. And while they all kidded me about it saying I was lucky or such, they all added that I had done good. Needless to say, I was swole up like a courtin' turkey. It was one of the best days I ever remember . . . except that the Ol' Man never said one word even when me and him was cuttin' out some drys together . . . he never said one damn word.

Every time I called for that gray, every time all summer long, he bucked. And he certain enough dumped the wagon a time or two.

But, I swear, it seemed I could ride him a bit better that the others in the crew . . . at least that's what they said.

Red Sartain told me one night he'd never seen the like. "I had him in my string for awhile and godalmighty he seemed to get me every time. Boy, maybe you'd better go on the rodeo road. You seem to have a way with bad horses."

I just said my uncle had taught me to ride pretty good, but truth was, I was right perplexed myself. I asked Homero, one day, if he thought the horse might just be givin' up and might make a usin' horse.

"I don't believe so Hijo. Some just get along better with some horses, but I don't believe he'll ever stop buckin' and I don't believe he'll ever gentle."

But for whatever reason, he never bucked like his reputation.

So the earth kept turnin' and fall was on the way. Mama called me and said she had sent a train ticket in the mail . . . a ticket for home. I sure was mixed up about that time. In one way, I couldn't wait to get home and in another, I wasn't sure where home was anymore. I'd growed a bunch that summer in both my body and in other ways. I was on my way toward bein' a man and right then, it wasn't too much fun.

That last night sure didn't help things any. Grandpa had me and Homero and Johnny up to the house. Johnny's wife, Cille, cooked for us and when we was through, we went out on the porch to watch the last of day fightin' with the oncoming night.

We'd hardly set down when Johnny pulled out a brown-paper-wrapped package and told me to open it. Inside was a pair of shotgun leggins like Dutch Johnny, himself, wore.

"Bubba, you'll need those next summer when you come back," he said with a grin.

It was the first anybody had said about next summer, but I knew he was right . . . I'd be back, at least if the Old Man would let me.

Dutch told me he and Homero had took a pair of my pants and had the maker measure from them.

"They'll be a bit loose, Hijo," the Mexican said. "But you'll grow to them fast enough."

All the while, Granddad just sat in the swing going back and forth and he never said pea turkey about the leggins . . . or . . . about comin' back. At least, not for a minute, he didn't.

"Well, boy, if you're set on comin' back, you best just keep that old Hamley. Spud's 'bout got my new kack ready." That was the saddle I had seen in the bunkhouse. "I won't be needin' that old riggin' anymore."

Damn, he got me up, then knocked me down. Why couldn't he have just said he wanted me to have it? Well, he, by God, just didn't say it. That was it.

And that was my story for right at twelve years. I came back in the summers and went back home to school in the fall. The ranch got smaller each year because himself wouldn't let nobody drill for oil or gas on the reverse SB.

He'd sell off a piece to pay taxes and cut down on his stock so as to not overgraze.

Dutch Johnny went to work for the county extension agency but Homero stayed 'til the end. He and Grandpa would have before dawn coffee together each morning and talk about the work to be done that day . . . even when the work got less and less. Me and what few hands stayed would get our orders and do the work and along the way, I'm proud to say, I made a hand.

The Old Man passed away in his sleep eleven years after I first laid eyes on him. No sickness. No nothing. He just died. We buried him by the grandmother I had never known and a few days later, the lawyer read the will. Even in death, he never said what I so wanted to hear.

The will read something like, "being of sound mind and body and having but one living blood relative . . . that being me (he didn't know him so forgot all about my little brother) . . . and one friend . . . that being Homero . . . I leave what's left of my land and stock to them equal." That was about what it said. And that was all.

Homero was too old, he said, to do any more cowboyin' so he went to live with his daughter down in Houston. He told me to do whatever I wanted with the ranch and just send his share to his daughter.

I thought about sellin' out, but it was almost like I was born, maybe reborn to that land, so I stayed on and, well, I'm doin' all right with it now. Even bought back some of the land he had to sell. Every fall after I ship, I take a trip down to Houston to give Homero his cut.

And after all this rememberin' and all these words, it was down there sittin' with old Homero . . . *abuelo viejo* was how I thought of him . . . that the story finally got told.

He was near blind by then . . . cataracts . . . but his milky eyes still smiled when he heard me comin'. That day he was out back of his daughter's house sittin' under a big tree. It was warm, but he had a wool shirt on and his thin old shoulders stuck out 'neath the fabric.

As I always did, I gave him a report on how we had done and asked his advice on matters for the coming year. He seemed to appreciate that and he never gave me advice that didn't make us money.

That day, though, he seemed to want to talk more about the old times. Someway he knew he was near the end of his string. We laughed about the good times and we whispered about the bad and the sad.

"*Todo en todo,* Hijo. It was a grand time. I wouldn't have changed it."

Something just boiled up in me. I took one of his old rope gnarled hands and said, "It gave me you *abuelo.* And Dutch Johnny. And the best life a man could have, but damn, I'da changed it."

He seemed right puzzled. "How could it have been better for you, boy?"

Tears was in my eyes and years of hurt was comin' out. Out toward the Big Bend the sun was on the horizon and the evening was cooling.

"If he could have just said he loved me one time . . . hell, if he had loved me like I did him."

How strange was the look that came over the *anciano's* face. "Did you really never know, Hijo? Were you as blind then as I am now?"

I didn't know what the hell he was talking about. He didn't give me time to answer before he had another question. "Did you really think you were such a bronc rider as to be able to hang with that gray . . . you know, the first year."

"I . . . I don't know what you mean" was all I could say, but my mind was spinning.

"Boy that gray was *muy malo.* There wasn't but one man on that place that could ride out that horse." He waited a minute then added. "It wasn't you, Hijo."

Then it all came. "Every morning you had to draw that horse, your Grandpa would get me up about three o'clock and we'd go rope him out and take him down to the pen behind that far back shed. He figured that was far enough away, so's nobody would find us out. He'd buck him out, out there in the dark, and, by God, that animal would throw a wall-eyed fit. Bucked your grandpa down a bunch of times, but he'd get back on and ride him 'til he was wore out. Then we'd kinda wipe him down to get the sweat off and turn him back in the remuda."

"He loved you boy. He couldn't say it. It just wasn't his way."

I couldn't believe what I was hearing.

"Too many years and too much hurt took the words out of him, but he did love you and he was just so proud of you."

I was confused and I was more than a little angry.

"Well, why in hell didn't he tell me or you tell me about the horse. It woulda been something, Homero. Something for me to hold onto."

"I thought about tellin' you, but he said 'no' and he said it so's I knew he was dead serious about it. He said it would kill your pride and kill your spirit to know what he had done. Remember how he always said 'a man has to ride his own horses.' He loved you enough to break his own rule . . . that once."

"But, if he had just once put his hand on my shoulder or told me I was doin' good . . . just one time."

"I know son," the old Mexican's eyes filled. "But that was what I was there for. We both loved you, mi Hijo. And we were both proud."

I never saw his kind old face again. At least not alive. He died two weeks after we sat there and watched the dark come to Texas. I asked his daughter to let me bury him with my grandparents and she knew it was right. I go see the three of them right regular now.

I bought me a gray bronc last spring. Oh, he don't really look like the Tongue River gray, but every now and again I take him down to that far pen and try to twist him out. I haven't done a real good job with it yet, but when I pull Granddaddy's saddle off him, I sure do get a funny feeling.

It's sorta like I feel a hand on my shoulder

———————

JIMBO BREWER of Gainesville, Georgia, kept the "wolf away from the door" by catching wild cattle and breaking horses when he was in college. He has worked on ranches in Texas, Wyoming, New Mexico, and Florida. As a teenager he worked on the VS Ranch owned by his grandfather on Kiowa Creek in Texas. He has also worked on other cow-calf operations, including the Snake River Ranch in Jackson Hole, Wyoming, for the Wyoming Stockman's Association in Jackson Hole packing salt to range cattle, the Mockingbird Hill Ranch near Radium Springs, Georgia, as a Forest Service packer for Lloyd Jones of Elk City, Idaho, the Knox Ranch near Crockett, Texas, the Jake Hughes Quarter Horse Ranch near Roswell, Georgia, and White Farms, in Chiefland, Florida. He spent many years working on his wife's family ranch in Florida with holdings near Hastings and Okeechobee. He has managed the Britt Martin Santa Gertrudis Ranch near Gainesville, Georgia, and a one hundred–horse commercial operation for Brenan College in Georgia. He's done additional day work on ranches near Llano, Eagle Pass, Denton, and Paducah, Texas. He's done a lot more cowboying than writing, but has had his work published in *Cowboy Magazine,* various newspapers, and shared as short radio commentaries called "Ramblins."

Divine Intervention

PAULA PAUL

The wind came in a steady rush from the southwest, like a giant wave moving across the short pale grass of the prairie. Mesquite brush, stunted by harsh winters and low moisture, made small formal bows in its wake.

The wind had given up all its moisture swooping across the Sonoran Desert on its way to the panhandle of Texas where it had come for its mission of drying out the grass and the skin of the women and of turning the blades of the windmill on the Chapman ranch.

Anna Clara, who sat on the front stoop of the ramshackle old ranch house, stared out across the pasture, wondering what was out there beyond the wind and the treeless flatness. She was only partly aware of the swoosh of the air or of the hollow, haunting minor-key melody of the sucker rod dipping deep into the hidden underground caverns of water or of the one-note song of the blades making deep, bloodless slashes in the wind. The trio of wind, sucker rod, and windmill blades was an almost constant serenade, so that Anna Clara had become used to it, yet she could shut it out only partly because the refrain was so melancholy.

The preacher would be here soon, and that meant she should go inside right now and make the gravy to go with the chicken and shove the biscuits into the oven. Pastor Baker was bringing another preacher with him, a man he called Brother Sanders, who was visiting for two weeks, so he could preach at the revival meetings.

It was Dawson's idea to have the preachers come for dinner. He was supposed to be back in time to eat with them. He'd gone to Muleshoe to get a tire fixed for the pickup. He'd gotten a cactus thorn in that tire when he was driving the pickup out across the north pasture to look for that cow who got herself snake bit. Why he took the pickup instead of one of the horses, Anna Clara didn't know, and she was afraid if she asked, his answer would be something incomprehensible about the Lord's will.

Dawson was a strong believer in the Lord's will, and he was a strong believer in revival meetings. He said it was good to give sinners a chance to be Saved from the fires of eternal damnation and to give backsliders a chance to rededicate their lives to Jesus. His getting religion a couple of years ago had come as a surprise to Anna Clara. When she'd married him three years ago, he'd just come back from Korea with the determination to raise as much hell as he could, and some people had said he was in danger of burning in the fires of hell himself. But Anna Clara had liked his laugh and his cocky, carefree ways, and being with him had made her feel carefree herself. Being in love with him had also served to heighten another feeling that had, since her childhood, lain germinating in her soul. It was an unnamable feeling of delicious Anticipation.

But two years ago, Dawson had found Jesus and lost his laugh and his cocky, carefree ways. Somewhere along the way, Anna Clara had misplaced hers, too. All that was left was the Anticipation. In the middle of the night, when Dawson was snoring beside her, she could still get that old feeling that something wonderful and life-changing was about to happen to her, and she would hold her breath waiting for it, trembling with excitement.

Dawson said it was the Lord speaking to her. Jesus calling her into his fold, wanting her to accept him as her personal savior. But Anna Clara had never done it. Never walked up the aisle of the Baptist church that sat on the rocky northeast corner of old man Hicks's place and given her life to Christ. She knew what a disappointment she was to Dawson, knew how he prayed for her soul to be Saved every night. But it seemed the more he prayed, the less she felt like getting herself Saved.

It upset Dawson, made him downright mad, in fact. He was as intent now on saving her soul as he had been on having a good time three years ago, and he just wouldn't let up. He'd called her a non-believer and told her that non-believers would burn in hell. She told him that she wasn't a non-believer; that there were, in fact, a lot of things she believed in.

Sometimes he'd leave off being mad and try to sweet-talk her into it and tell her how wonderful her life would be if she would just get herself Saved. But it hardly seemed worth the trouble, since she could see for herself that the Saved Dawson's life wasn't really all that much different from her own unSaved life.

The wind shifted more to the south, evoking a screech from the windmill as it turned its face into the wind. The sound brought Anna Clara out of her reverie and back to the realization that she had to get those biscuits in the oven and the gravy made.

The chicken was already fried and keeping warm on a cloth-covered platter on the stove. Within a few minutes the biscuits were in the oven, and Anna Clara was stirring milk and flour into the skillet where she had fried the chicken.

Outside, the wind, hot and insistent, made the windmill bring up sweet water from underground, and Anna Clara believed in that. She believed in water and in the endless stretch of grass and cactus. And she believed in the wind.

She believed it would turn malevolent in the fall and lash across the prairie bringing a coolness that made the mesquite leaves look like rusty nails, and that it would change course in the winter and sweep down out of the north with the materials it needed to build snow drifts so high she couldn't open the back door, and Dawson would have to take hay and cottonseed cake out to the cattle in the pickup.

She believed in the way the wind would get feisty again in the spring and spit at them with rain and with the sand it would pick up from the southern part of the county where all the cotton fields were.

She believed, too, that if you turned a bull out with the cows in the summer, the cows would be calving by spring, and that if you cut the calves in the wrong phase of the moon, they wouldn't make good steers, just like potatoes wouldn't grow in the garden unless they were planted in the dark of the moon.

Most of all she believed in the great Anticipation. Although it did depress her and maybe frighten her a little to think that Dawson might be right—that it was nothing more than a need to be Saved.

When the dogs raised themselves from their eternal siesta in the shade of the catfish tank and started barking, Anna Clara knew her company had topped the hill down by the mailbox. It would be the preachers, because the dogs had a different bark when it was Dawson approaching. She took a quick peek at the biscuits, which were just beginning to rise in the oven, untied her apron, smoothed her dress over her hips, and was waiting at the front door, ready to open it when Pastor Baker knocked.

He took off his funny little narrow-brimmed hat and pressed it to his chest. He was a big ruddy man, grown soft around the middle. "Hello, Sister Anna Clara!" His smile reminded her of a peddler's too-eager smile.

"Come in, Pastor Baker." Anna Clara spoke without looking at him. Her eyes were on the small dark man behind him. She thought at first he might have been Mexican, but his skin was more olive than brown, and he had a foreign unMexican look to him.

Pastor Baker went on talking as he stepped into the living room, smoothing his thinning blond hair, now charged with electricity from the wind and flickering about his head. "Sister Anna Clara, this is Brother Sanders from up at Pampa. He's preachin' our revival this year."

"How do you do, Brother Sanders," Anna Clara said, giving him the smile she reserved for peddlers and preachers. "I'm afraid my husband's not home yet, but he'll be here just any minute now, I'm sure." There was a hint of panic in her voice that she hoped the two preachers didn't hear.

The dark-skinned man nodded and said, "Pleased to meet you." His voice had a slightly foreign sound. But then Pampa was awfully close to Oklahoma, so maybe that accounted for it.

"Her husband is Brother Dawson," Pastor Baker said, settling himself on the couch and pulling loose the broadcloth slipcover

Anna Clara had ordered from Monkey Ward's six months ago during their up-to-fifty-percent-off-after-Christmas sale. "You met him," Pastor Baker said. "Good man. Been comin' to preachin' nearly every night during the revival. Rededicated his life to Christ Tuesday."

"Sure, I remember," Brother Sanders said. Anna Clara decided that maybe he didn't have a foreign accent after all. It was just that his voice was surprisingly deep and rich for such a small man.

"We haven't seen you there yet." Pastor Baker made no attempt to keep the accusing tone out of his voice.

"Well, no, but I keep meaning to go," Anna Clara said, hating the way it came out sounding so defensive. It was true, though, she had kept meaning to go, just as she kept meaning to get herself Saved. It was just that both seemed like an awful lot of bother. The way it feels when you know you ought to clean out the closets.

"It's the devil that's keeping you away," Pastor Baker said. "I don't know whether you realize that or not, but I believe it with all my heart, and I know Jesus believes it, too."

Brother Sanders didn't say anything. He just looked at her with his odd yellow-flecked eyes.

"Your husband prays for you without ceasing," Pastor Baker said. "He knows you're a good woman, and I know that Jesus knows you're a good woman, but good works won't save you, sister. You must accept the Lord Jesus Christ as your personal savior and turn your life over to him and then be baptized in his name, just as Jesus himself was baptized in the River Jordan."

Pastor Baker, Anna Clara realized, wouldn't make a very good peddler. The good ones knew how to soften you up before they got to the hard sell. Like the Watkins man. He always started off talking about things like how nice the slipcovers looked, and how you couldn't tell them from a high-priced upholstery job, and what was that good smell coming from the kitchen, and how you could just about tell who was a good cook by the way things smelled. Then she would always end up buying an extra bottle of vanilla extract, even though she might have one in the pantry that never had been opened. She would know that it was all just sweet talk and flattery, but it was as soothing as a summer rain and it had gotten them both something they needed.

If Pastor Baker wanted to add one more notch to his liturgical pistol handle by claiming her soul for Jesus, then he was just going to have to improve his technique, because Anna Clara was growing restless now. She said she thought she smelled the biscuits burning, but Pastor Baker had opened the Bible he carried under his arm and was reading from the book of John.

Verily, verily, I say unto thee, except a man be born again, he cannot see the kingdom of God.

And Anna Clara was struck by the fact that he was talking about men and not about her.

For God so loved the world that he gave his only begotten Son that whosoever believeth in him should not perish, but have everlasting life.

That always made Anna Clara shiver. Not the part about perishing, but the idea of anyone letting their son die nailed to a cross when he had the power to save him. If she ever had a son, she knew she'd never be so foolish. It was impossible for her to think of it as generous.

He that believeth on him is not condemned: but he that believeth not is condemned already, because he hath not believed in the name of the only begotten Son of God.

Now that was downright ungenerous in Anna Clara's mind. Why would anybody who claimed to love everybody offer just one way to salvation? He ought to make it easier for people if he really loved them. When she told Pastor Baker that, he responded with another Bible verse. This one from Matthew.

. . . straight is the gate and narrow is the way which leadeth unto life, and few there be that find it.

Which seemed to Anna Clara only to prove her point, and she was trying to decide whether to tell him that and risk him reading another verse or just to keep her mouth shut when Brother Sanders interrupted.

"There's something wrong with that windmill."

Both Anna Clara and Pastor Baker turned to look at him. Pastor Baker looked annoyed, but Anna Clara was puzzled.

"The windmill?" she asked. "Let us pray," said Pastor Baker at the same time.

"I think it's about to quit."

"How can you tell?"

"Our heavenly father, open this sinner's eyes and lead her from the darkness into . . ."

"The way it sounds. I think you need new leathers."

"Lord, I hope it doesn't just quit on us. We need the water for the house and the cattle as well. Dry as it's been there's nothing left out in the tanks."

"Open her eyes, Lord, that she will see her wicked ways and see that . . ."

"It's not a very good well anyway."

He was right, of course. It wasn't a very good well, but how did he know that? A person couldn't see from this distance that the water it pumped was just a slender stream.

"I can tell by the way it sounds," he said, as if she had asked the question out loud.

" . . . just lay it upon her heart, Lord, that she who was born of water must be baptized by the Holy . . ."

"Windmills is my specialty." Brother Sanders stood up from Dawson's chair and was on his way out the door. Anna Clara got up and followed him outside.

The wind tangled the skirt of her dress around her legs and blew strands of her ginger-colored hair into her mouth as she walked behind Brother Sanders to the windmill. They walked across a stretch of hard-packed earth that had been denuded of grass by Anna Clara's own footsteps, until they reached the tower. Brother Sanders put his hand on one of the posts and stood very still.

"It's the leathers all right," he said. His eyes seemed to be fixed on something in another dimension, out beyond the barbed wire fence and beyond the spot where the land sloped down to the south tank.

"Are you sure?"

"I been a windmill man for ten years. My daddy was a windmill man, too."

"I thought you were a preacher."

He looked at her with his yellow-flecked eyes. "I got The Call last year. Been preachin' off and on ever since."

"Leading folks to Salvation in between fixing windmills," she said.

He nodded. "That way I'm never out of work." His smile and the yellow flecks in his eyes made her think of the devil.

"I can see how that would be true." She spoke to his back, because he was walking away from her now, toward a mesquite bush.

"Way I look at it, folks need something to believe in about as bad as they need water." He had taken out his pocket knife and was whittling away at one of the slender gnarled branches of the mesquite. "What's bad, though, is when you go out looking and you get your hopes up and it turns out to be a dry hole."

Anna Clara watched as, with one more cut, he separated a Y-shaped branch from the mesquite and stripped it of its slender pale leaves. The wind blew the wood's spicy scent to her and tangled itself in her hair. She watched him, mesmerized. Finally she asked, "What are you doing?"

Brother Sanders held the forked stick up to give her a better look. "This here's what you call a divining rod."

"A divining rod? You a water witch, too, along with everything else?"

"I prefer to say I'm a diviner. Them words 'water witch' don't sound too good for a preacher. You see, what you do, is you take and hold it by these two forks and you let the other part stick out, parallel with the ground, and you walk along until—"

"I know how it works. I seen it done before. If there's water under the ground, then the witching stick will—"

"Divining rod."

"—turn itself down toward the water that's underground without you doing anything. It's kind of magic."

Brother Sanders began walking along at a ninety-degree angle from the water barrel, holding the forked stick so that the base of the Y was parallel with the ground. "I don't know if it's magic or not. Fact is, I don't know much about it at all. My daddy was a diviner and a good one to boot, but I ain't never been worth a damn at it." He was concentrating so hard on his divining that he didn't seem to notice he had sworn. "You see, I'm basically a windmill man."

Anna Clara brushed at a strand of hair that had blown into her mouth. "Then why are you doing it if you're not any good at it?"

He gave her a puzzled look. "Why it's just force of habit, I guess. When my daddy come upon a well that wasn't no good, he'd walk around divining for some place where you could drill a good one, just as a favor to his customers. I guess I thought that was the way you was supposed to do it. Even though I ain't worth a d . . . ain't any good at it. Don't have the touch. I ought to just stick to fixin' windmills."

Anna Clara was walking along beside him now, her eyes on the divining rod. "How do you know when you *do* have the touch?"

Brother Sanders shook his head. "Well I don't know if I can answer that, since I ain't got it, but I figure it's just like anything else that you know you can do or that you know you got to do. You just feel it pulling at you, and you just cain't help yourself because you are anticipating something good. . . . Well, what I mean is, it just pulls at you. Like me and them windmills. I just kind of feel 'em pulling at me."

"Like people feel the Lord pulling at them when he's calling 'em to get Saved?"

"I don't know. Maybe."

"Maybe? Don't you know about people gettin' Saved, Brother Sanders?"

"Well . . ." His yellow-flecked eyes moved up to the top of the windmill where the fan was singing its monotonous tune.

"Haven't you ever been Saved, Brother Sanders?"

"What?" He seemed distracted. "Oh, yeah. Sure I have."

"What's it like?"

"Kind of like being on top of a windmill."

"Is that all you can talk about? Windmills?" Anna Clara couldn't keep the anger and frustration from her voice.

Brother Sanders's eyes looked sad and troubled now. "Look, I'm new at this, and like I told you, I'm basically just a windmill man, so all I can tell you is how it feels to be a windmill man."

"That doesn't make sense."

"It does to me. I'm a damned good windmill man, and that makes me feel good. Hell, I guess it makes me feel Saved."

Anna Clara looked at him dumb-struck for a few seconds. She might have finally figured out what to say or ask, but she was suddenly interrupted.

"Anna Clara, Brother Sanders!" She shifted her eyes to see Pastor Baker running toward them waving his hands. "Lord have mercy! We got to do something!"

"What is it, Pastor?" Anna Clara asked, suddenly frightened.

"They's a fire! They's something burning in there!"

"Oh my lord, the biscuits!" Anna Clara ran toward the back door of the house. Behind her, Brother Sanders hooked the divining rod over a cross tie on the windmill and ran, too.

When she opened the door, a gauzy length of smoke wrapped itself around her. She made a few futile attempts at pushing it away with her hands as she made her way to the oven.

"Go on back to the living room," she said over her shoulder to the men. "I'll take care of this."

She turned the oven off quickly, then opened the oven door. A shroud of gray, sticky smoke engulfed her. She coughed twice and ran to the window above the sink and shoved it open, then grabbed a dishtowel to pull the pan out of the oven. The biscuits looked like lumps of coal hissing steam. When she plopped the pan down on top of the stove, one of the biscuits bounced off and shattered into a million black shards at her feet.

Another time she might have felt like crying, but this time she merely stepped over the biscuit, crunching some of the fragments with the soles of her shoes. She was eager to ask Brother Sanders more about things that pull at you.

Before she got to the living room she could hear the two men talking, and in the background, the dogs barking.

Pastor Baker's words came out of his mouth in round, sonorous tones, the way they did when he was in the pulpit. "I left you alone with her, Brother Sanders, because she is a simple woman, and I thought your unschooled ways might be God's choice for leading her to Christ and Salvation, and now you're telling me you didn't?

"Well, we got to talking about that windmill, and—"

"The windmill . . ." Pastor Baker's face was turning red with passion. ". . . is nothing more than God's instrument, which he put in your hands to lead that woman to Jesus."

Anna Clara could see from the doorway where she was now standing that Brother Sanders had a shocked look on his face. "Oh no, Pastor, it's more than that. A windmill is—"

"I'm concerned about you, Sanders." Pastor Baker's voice had grown gravelly and menacing. "We are now three days into the revival, and not one new soul has walked the aisles to surrender to Jesus. Just a few routine rededications."

Anna Clara could see the look on Brother Sanders's face, and it made her feel sorry for him. Made her think for a second that maybe she ought to go to church tonight so she could walk up and get Saved just to make him feel good. She thought better of it, though, and she was just about to join the two preachers in the living room when the front door opened and Dawson walked in.

She knew then she'd never get a word in edgewise, so she went back to the kitchen and set the table with the cold chicken, the congealed gravy, and three-quarters of a loaf of store-bought bread she pulled out of the bread box. It wasn't until they were almost finished with the meal that she remembered she had forgotten to get the Jell-O salad out of the refrigerator.

A pious conversation went on around her, and she wasn't sure whether she had taken part or not. She did remember that Brother Sanders looked decidedly unhappy (but that could have been because he didn't like congealed gravy or store-bought bread), except when he was telling Dawson about the windmill.

"You probably got two, maybe four weeks with them leathers, but you're going to have to pull that sucker rod, I'll tell you that. I'd fix 'er for you right now, but I don't have my—"

He was interrupted by Pastor Baker who turned the conversation back to the glories of redemption. Anna Clara stood up quietly and began to clean the kitchen and after a while, the men went back to the living room. She was only vaguely aware of the two preachers leaving later and of Dawson coming into the kitchen, angry because she hadn't come out to see them off and because the meal was a disaster. She was too distracted to think about what he was saying, though, and he must have decided that his anger wasn't paying off, because he started sweet-talking her. He was trying to get her to go to the revival meeting with him that night.

"You go on Dawson, I'm just too tired," she said. She had to say it over and over again before he'd stop trying to persuade her. He left, finally, acting wounded and pious. He said he had to go fix the fence over by the sand hills. He came back in time to eat supper and to change his clothes before leaving for the revival meeting, but he hardly said a word except to warn her one more time about her immortal soul.

Later, when the windmill had stopped singing, and the coyotes had begun their performance, Anna Clara walked outside in the red-streaked twilight. She saw the forked stick, hanging there on the cross tie of the windmill, and she picked it up and studied it. Then, holding one branch of the Y with each hand, she began to walk. She walked across grass that was too tough and close to the earth to humble itself by bowing to the wind. She walked around cactus with defensive spears always ready and passed scrubby mesquite with roots that penetrated a hundred feet looking for survival. She walked until the sky was becoming pricked with stars, until at last she felt a tug, and the base of the wooden Y quivered. She gripped the branch tighter, and the stick almost turned out of her hand as the end pulled itself down toward the warm center of the earth.

And then Anna Clara felt it, water rushing in torrents beneath her and coming up through the soles of her feet to mingle with her blood, to engulf her and baptize her from the inside.

Then the great Anticipation returned to her, and she knew what it was. It was Anna Clara herself, and the world was waiting for her.

She left the next morning before Dawson awoke, but she left him a note she hoped would comfort him:

I am Saved!

Paula Paul grew up in west Texas near the New Mexico border on the VVN Ranch, one of the few ranches remaining today that was carved out of the legendary XIT Ranch. She began her writing career as a journalist and for several years worked as a reporter for the *Albuquerque Tribune* and as a freelance writer for the *Albuquerque Journal*. She is the author of sixteen novels, several of which have won awards including the New Mexico Zia award, the Texas Institute of Letters Award, and a National Press Women's award for fiction.

Dry Bogged

HELEN C. AVERY

She was alone. The big house echoed around her. It did not yet feel like hers. It was a great rambling agglomeration of rooms—full of shadows, unfamiliar furniture, and photographs of strangers. When they'd married, they had moved into the old homestead that he had known all his life. Even now, eighteen months later, there were just little sacred bits that were hers—theirs together. The bed. She'd insisted on the bed—theirs, and when the dark night settled around them they could plunge into the joy of each other, floating in their own space, surrounded by the great dark ocean of other peoples' memories, other peoples' arguments and leftover passions.

It had been difficult, very difficult, to make the transition from her family's three generation Colorado ranch to the Australian one. The green wetness of the lush Colorado pastures below the snow peaks melting to creek water that coursed down the massive bones of rocks called the Rockies pulled at her. It was her blood, her family's blood, imbedded in that green land.

The man's Aussie blood also pulled at her so strongly she felt she would simply split in half. Then, like a stretched barbwire snapping, she gave up the soft greenness to go with him to a landscape as harsh as a sandpaper highway. She couldn't do otherwise.

Now, though, she felt more at ease in the landscape than she did in this house that was not yet hers, and the landscape was a vast and aching emptiness—loud and mocking in its intensity. Coming from a country of hills and cows full-uddered on lucerne flats where creeks actually had water in them, and patches of fern, she still missed the softness of moisture in the atmosphere, so much so that when they crossed the last shrunken pool of water on the road out from the station, the sudden rush of freshness on the air clung to her senses with the sweetness of an old, old melody. This country—there was something in the vastness, the spareness—an essential essence of something that caught her.

There were moments when she nursed a tiny flutter of fear that maybe it was going to be too much—this marriage to so much more than the man—the land; the house too full of his past; his joyous expectation that she could accept all this. Maybe she couldn't make it. Maybe it was too much. At those moments, she would fling herself into his arms with an intensity that surprised and gratified him, and he thought her whimpers spilled from passion.

He was out now, on the other block, a full day's run in a vehicle laden with dogs and wire, and stinking of hot metal and burnt oil. Early in the morning she had packed him a lunch, slicing thick meat from Tuesday's roast—cold meat and pickle sandwiches—it was always cold meat and pickles, and the thermos of black tea. She had packed it with love, knowing that by 2 P.M. it would taste of hot metal and burnt oil, and he wouldn't notice. At the moment he was doing this daily—a mindless routine of windmills, troughs, bog holes, and death. They had been too long without rain.

The baby woke, its cry filling the house. She lifted and nuzzled the child. Changing the nappy was routine now, but she could never take for granted the intensity of the naked beauty of this, her child. She bent and nuzzled again; nose and lips against the innocence of skin and sweet animal smells of birth and babyhood 'til the child gurgled in delight and clutched her hair. In the comfort of the old lounge chair, she nursed the child; her breast curved and full beneath the curve of the child's face, the greedy tugging at the nipple. This was her sweet-as-honey magic moment. Her loins ached with joy.

She packed the baby, the water bottle, and the dog into the back seat of the old car, thrust the gears into reverse, and backed out of the shed. There was another water run to do—a two-hour round of watering points in each paddock. On the days that he did the mountain block, she did the home block. The vehicle rattled along the tracks gusting hot air and dust, radio blaring Hits of Yesterday. She sang along, creating her own words when she'd forgotten the original. At each gate, she'd wrestle with the tangle of wire and wood she'd readily come to call a "bloody gate . . . ," talk, and play with the child, wrestle the "bloody thing" shut, and move on through the next paddock.

Another trough, a ribbon of lukewarm, milky water set in an apron of stone—check the float, the flow, getting slimy—bring a broom to clean it next time. A windmill—check it's turning, pumping. Check head, rods, buckets, turkeys' nest—a complete language she'd known nothing about previously. A dam . . . the dying bog hole in Sandy Creek. . . . After months and months of drought, a web of stock pads deep with talc fanned out from each trough or dam or waterhole, and each place stank of death. Morning and evening everything came to drink—not just the stock that were their livelihood, but a wonderful diversity of all creatures. Water had never meant that much 'til she came here.

She changed gears down again to cross a dry gully that wound its meager way through a dense patch of gidyea scrub. The sand was as clean and fine as beach sand. The irony made her smile! Beach sand! The engine ground down. Feeling the surly response to the wheel, she thrust her foot on the accelerator to climb out the far side of the gully. The engine roared in answer, and—nothing happened. They sat exactly where they were. She thrust the gears into reverse and roared the engine again. Forward, reverse, forward . . .

She flung the door open and climbed out. The back wheels were sunk to the axle in fine "beach" sand! She twisted branches from nearby bushes, pushed them under the wheels and revved and roared again and again until the light on the console glowed savage red, and she felt the heat of anger and frustration rise up the back of her neck . . . Shit!

The baby gurgled. The dog, freed from the car, loped after his nose along the edges of the gully. A walleroo blundered through the scrub in astonishment. She heaved a sigh heavy with resignation and gathered them all together—baby, dog, water bottle . . . and they walked. Even she began to enjoy the delight of the dog and the baby. It was less than an hour 'til sundown. The heat of the day had eased and it was that mystical time before the descent of night.

It was a five-kilometer walk in to the dam. On the scalded clay beside the dam wall sat the tractor. They'd been fencing last week. Job unfinished, they'd parked the tractor in the thin shade of a boree tree. There would be no one past to disturb it. If she couldn't start it, they'd have to sit and wait until he returned from the mountain block around midnight—throw a panic at finding no one at home . . .

Mechanics was not her strong suit and tractor driving pure theory. She'd never driven one before, only watched him swear and curse and swing on the crank handle til the sweat flowed. The cursing seemed to be an integral part of the process. She circled the machine looking for familiar landmarks and found few. Not too many dials and knobs and things to confuse the issue. This reconnoitering was done in serious collaboration with the dog and the child, both assuming vast interest, but dismal lack of knowledge.

"Okay, Baby, this is it!" She stood tall, straightened her shoulders, glanced at the sky. "God, I'm depending on you," and to the tractor, "C'mon Ferg . . . do your thing!" She bent, gripped the crank handle firmly, then swung mightily. The momentum nearly dislocated her arm. The old Ferguson gasped, shook, trembled, then to her utter astonishment, roared into life with a great gout of smoke. "Yee-haa! Thank you, God!"—a twinge of guilt because she never went to church, and she seemed to call on God an awful lot these days.

Clinging together like castaways, she, baby, dog, and water bottle piled aboard the roaring tractor seat built for one. Gears and throttle sorted themselves out with grinds and bellows, and they chugged into the gloom—no headlights that she could find.

The night was soft as velvet as she finally turned with a rattle over the grid into the house paddock. Her arm ached with clutching the basket heavy with sleeping child. She was exhausted. She still had chores to do—tea to prepare; bathe the baby, feed the animals . . . But tonight! Tonight, her heart sang! She'd done it! By herself, she'd done it! The faintly helpless, infinitely ignorant, brand new bride . . . by herself she'd done it!

The Fergie lurched and farted to a halt beside the back gate. She swung down, and despite legs buckling with weariness and relief, floated inside the old homestead like a Queen.

HELEN C. AVERY grew up on a small farm in the hinterland of coastal Queensland in Australia. She came to the outback as a governess teaching three children living on a sheep station out of Longreach. Here she met and married her husband who had spent his life on "Nogo" and had taken over management on the death of his father. They now have four children and run a sheep and cattle grazing enterprise on sixty thousand acres of wide, dry grasslands typical of this part of Australia. Helen is a poet as well as a writer and performed as a guest poet at the Elko Gathering in Nevada in 1998, finding a wonderful rapport with the American cowboy lifestyle and culture.

The Present

GWEN PETERSEN

At noon, her husband, Ernest, and the hired hands, hot and sweaty from the morning in the hayfields, tramped into her white and yellow kitchen to fill their stomachs. Hungry men, they cared only that the food was plentiful, the coffee hot. They ate rapidly, with passionate concentration, sprinkled now and then with brief requests: more potatoes or pass the salt. As usual, she had brightened the table with a bowl of flowers and colorful paper napkins. None of the men bothered with the napkins and the flowers were set aside to make room for the bowl of gravy.

Bellies full, the men pushed away from the table, each plucking a toothpick from the hollowed-out deer-antler holder and as they filed out, they thanked her for the meal. Some, too shy to look at her, spoke to their boots. Others grinned and told her what a great cook she was. They shuffled outside to shade up on the lawn and have a smoke. Ernest went with them, not even glancing at her as he moseyed out.

She could hear the men joshing one another, their rumbling male voices drifting through the open kitchen window while she did the dishes. As she finished scrubbing the last pot, she heard Ernest's husky voice urging the men back to work. "Don't s'pose that hay'll bale itself," he drawled.

"Yuh never know, maybe if we set here long enough, them machines'll bale and stack all by themselves," one of the men offered, and she could picture him, lying stretched out, hands behind his head, toothpick angled from the corner of his mouth.

"Could happen, Wade," said Ernest with a throaty chuckle, "but watch that baler, it's been missing a tie about every third one. I tinkered with it. Think it's fixed for awhile. Jones, you can start swathing the creekside pasture."

They drifted away and Ernest went with them without stopping to say a word or two to her. She knew her husband had his mind on the haying. She knew he worked nonstop to harvest the crop between bouts of rainy weather. A cold dry spring had been devastating. Grass, the bedrock of ranching, was thin and short. Now the heavens decided to drop too much moisture just when ranchers needed to harvest every blade. She knew how Ernest worried. She had no real reason to feel so lonely, she told herself. Getting used to ranch life—that was it. Four months of marriage, why that was no time at all. She knew Ernest loved her. She simply needed to adapt, fit in, make herself useful, and wait for the demanding summer work to slacken. Thankfully, today the sun shone hot with the next several days predicted to be dry. Maybe Ernest could finish up the haying and then they could take time just for the two of them.

She flipped the dishcloth over the towel rack above the sink and went out to gather the eggs, feed the chickens, and make sure the milk cow hadn't broken through the south gate. In a few short hours it would be time to cook and serve supper to Ernest and the hands. Relaxing at workday's end, they would banter about how much hay they'd cut, baled, and stacked. They always spoke with shared pride and respect for each other's ability, for a job well done. She liked listening to their talk, though no one spoke directly to her except, sometimes, to murmur thanks when she served the pie.

On most afternoons, she took a snack to the men in the fields. Today, she called to Ernest as he started to climb into his pickup. He trudged back to the kitchen door and she handed him a box containing jugs of water, coffee, and lemonade along with half a sheet cake, forks, and cups.

"Ernest, I'm not coming to the field this afternoon. Take this with you for afternoon break."

Her husband's serious blue eyes reflected surprise. "Okay," was all he said. She watched him stride to the pickup and place the box of food in the back and gazed after the truck as he drove away. Then she stuck a book in her pocket and took the path toward the river. Sometimes she thought Ernest disapproved of her constant reading, but he never said anything.

A half mile from the house, the riverbank curved around a small peninsula, dense with underbrush, cottonwoods, and willows. Pushing through the growth, she stepped into a tiny, grassy clearing, no bigger than her vegetable garden. Sunbeams filtered through cathedral-tall trees, illuminating the glade with shimmering fairy-tale light. The rushing sound of the river deepened the velvety stillness within the tiny glade. She took two steps and stopped, surprised. A single dandelion, as tall as herself, basked in a shaft of sunlight.

"Well, hello, there." She spoke the words with delight and the flower appeared to sway an answering greeting. Once or twice before, she'd come across a hip-high dandelion growing sturdy as a tree in a shady moist spot, usually near the river. This one, its yellow petals still hidden within its green calyx, promised near-Goliath maturity.

"Mind if I join you?" she asked as she settled down facing the river, her back to a tree. The beauty and cozy peace of the little meadow seeped into her bones. *How wonderful,* she thought, *if I could share this place with Ernest.*

Next day, she hurried through chores and visited the glade again. The dandelion greeted her proudly. Overnight it had reached full bloom, its golden head lifted, reaching for the sun. The yellow-topped weed listened attentively to everything she had to say.

Walking back to the house, she decided Ernest really must see this unusual plant. The men had nearly finished haying the south pastures, which meant tomorrow they would move the equipment to another field. Tomorrow, she would urge Ernest to take a break and come with her on a picnic.

After supper, when the hands had left, she started to tell her husband about her private woodland bower. He smiled absently.

"Lot of daylight left," he said, interrupting her. "Baler broke down this afternoon and I just got it fixed. I think I'll go back and finish that last little bit of baling. If we're going to move equipment tomorrow, best I get that done while there's still daylight."

Oh, well, she thought, as she finished the evening dishes, *he has a lot on his mind right now, but tomorrow, I'll get him to take some time off. He can come with me to admire my flowery friend.*

Later, in bed, she said, "Ernest, you ought to relax more. You deserve some time for yourself and—for us. Tomorrow I'm going to pack a lunch and we'll go on a picnic."

He laughed softly and ruffled her hair. "This is a ranch, honey. A man can't go waltzing off in the middle of haying. It's as simple as first grade, we've got cows to feed this winter and need to get the hay up now while the weather's good. I sure don't want to have to buy hay. The price'll be higher than a cat's back. Probably have to go all the way to Dakota to find any. We're walkin' a tightrope this year, honey. Don't need any more debt. As it is, the bank's gonna take a dim view when it comes to next year's operating loan."

"I know that, of course I know that, but can't you take an hour at noon? I'll put the meal on and the men can eat by themselves, surely. I want you to see something special." Annoyed at the pleading she could hear in her voice, she said sharply, "Ernest, please. You'll enjoy it. I know you will." She hid her face against his chest, trying not to cry.

"Hey, c'mon now. Don't cry. You want a picnic that bad, why sure, we'll go for an hour or so." He patted her shoulder.

"Oh, Ernest, she mumbled, clinging to him, "it's—just that I want to show you—there's this flower, a dandelion, it sounds silly, but, just wait . . . tomorrow, on our picnic, you'll see what I mean. It's the most unusual . . ."

A throaty snore cut across her murmured words. She sighed. Oh well, the poor man was exhausted.

Next day, she prepared noon dinner as usual, but when Ernest and the hired hands trooped in, she said to her husband, "Remember our picnic."

"What picnic?"

"Ernest! The one we talked about last night!" She hated the wail in her voice.

"Oh, yeah. Did you mean that for today?"

With relief, she realized he was teasing. They held hands as they walked to the grove of trees shielding the clearing. Ernest carried the small picnic basket she'd packed.

"What's this special thing you want to show me?" he asked as they strolled. But she wouldn't tell him.

She stepped into the little meadow first and turned to watch her husband's expression. Sunlight showered golden mist into the small space and leaf shadows patterned the grass. The freakish dandelion, by now so tall she had to look up to see its fluffy head, bowed in welcome.

"Well, say, look at that, would you!" exclaimed Ernest. "That blamed thing must be six feet. Is that what you wanted to show me?"

She could only smile and nod happily, pleased with her surprise. As they ate, she told him how she'd been confiding in the giant weed, even reading to it.

"Probably why it grew so tall," said Ernest as he ruffled her hair. Finished with his meal, he sat with his back against a tree trunk and drew her within the circle of his arms. She snuggled against him. "This is nice, Ernest. We haven't talked about things in a long time."

"We talk all the time," he said, hugging her.

"Not the way we used to, you know—books and plans, what we want to . . ."

"Hon," he said, glancing at his watch, "that was a good meal you fixed up." He shoved her out of his arms. "But right now, I've gotta get back. Work to be done. Can't laze around here all day." He stood up, slapping bits of grass and bread crumbs off his jeans.

She stared up at this man who was her husband. The tips of her fingers tingled. Wordlessly she began clearing up the picnic, packing away utensils, folding the tablecloth. Ernest helped her, then strode off to admire her dandelion friend and she felt a little comforted. At least he could understand her amazement and pleasure in that remarkable and glorious weed.

Closing the picnic basket, she straightened and turned just as Ernest, pocketknife in hand, bent and sliced through the dandelion's stem. He came toward her carrying the severed flower like a banner. "Here, honey," he said, "present for you."

GWEN PETERSEN, a Montana ranch woman, is a published author of humor, history, plays and poetry, and a weekly humor column, "In a Sow's Ear," that appears in several publications. After the death of her husband in 1999, Gwen sold their ranch and downsized to a small place where she still owns horses, dogs and cats, a handful of cows, and a computer where she continues writing about the Working West. In 1985, Gwen was one of the representatives from Montana at the first National Cowboy Poetry Gathering in Elko, Nevada. That experience led her to start the first Montana Cowboy Poetry Gathering in Big Timber, Montana, which she directed and co-directed for five years. She is the author of *The Ranch Woman's Manual, The Greenhorn's Guide to the Woolly West, Menus for the Cooking Impaired,* an audio novel, *The Whole Shebang,* as well as numerous books of cowboy poetry. She is co-editor of *Ten Years' Gatherings, Montana Poems & Stories* and is a contributor of limericks to the BBC. Her essays and poetry have been published in *Persimmon Hill, Roundup, Montana Magazine, Writing Montana: Literature Under the Big Sky, Leaning Into the Wind, Cowgirls Writing the Range, Graining the Mare,* and others. She has appeared on the *Tonight* show reciting her poems. She is currently working on two novels and her attitude.

Once A Cowboy

MAX EVANS

You never quite get to know anyone—anyone at all. Most especially how they'll end up. Even if you've been through decades of bar, car, and horse wrecks, like I had with ol' Rusty Carver.

I see him now as I ride this damn forest line fence that's been kicked down in places by newcomers. They drive their gas-greedy SUVs up as far as possible, then walk the fence line on the U.S. Forest side, kicking weak posts loose so the boss's cows can get out and cause weeks of hard riding to gather. Some we never find.

My mind's image of ol' Rusty was clear as spring water. He was mounting a green horse. He could just barely reach the stirrup. But he cheeked the bridle and swung his body in the saddle, smooth and easy, riding out circling the round pole corral, getting the feel of how the horse moved, how he reined, ready for him to buck if he thought he had to.

As I dream-watched ol' Rusty, I thought of how different we looked. He was about five-eight and had so much hard, round muscle that he didn't seem to have—or need—any bones in his body. Well, except for his hands. The bones sure showed big there.

Everyone in our country dreaded shaking hands with him. He didn't know it, but he was a hand-crusher.

His nose was broken from tree limbs that horses had run him into—and other things, such as rocks, fists, and a skillet his longtime girlfriend Shirley Mae had swatted him with.

He had a round scar on one side of his belly and one on his back where a Nazi sniper had shot him during World War II. I reckon he'd healed up fine because he never said a word about it in all the years

I knew him. Not one damned word.

Now me, Roy Barrett, I was six-foot-two of bones tied together with beef jerky. My nose had never been broken, but it did bend over about a half-inch to the south from the cartilage being torn loose. I can't recall how it happened, except I was having fun getting drunk.

It wasn't hard to remember most things we'd shared, but some I couldn't call up any closer than a coyote howling in the next county.

I sure remember, and my spine still feels the time I roped the seven-year-old outlawed steer around the neck and he jumped off in an arroyo, jerking me and my horse over the side, where we all fell in a pile. The horse got up before I did, and the steer as well. They both tried to run in different directions. Ordinarily, that would have been natural, except I was in between them with the rope wound around my middle. I felt like I was one of those poor people that magicians put in a box and then drop the blade down, cutting them smack dab in half. Luckily, I was still in one piece, except my waist was pulled down to about thirteen inches.

Now, I reached out and grabbed the rope on each side of me. No matter how hard I pulled, I couldn't get any slack in the rope with a thousand-pound horse tied hard and fast to one end and a thousand-pound steer on the other.

That makes an even ton.

Ol' Rusty had been following on a good bay cow horse, his rope down to heel up the steer if I was unlucky enough to catch the wild shit-splattering son of a bitch.

Well, my eyeballs were being pushed out of my head by all my insides that had been shoved upward from the rope around my middle. I saw things in a blur, but here's how it went when I double-checked it later. Ol' Rusty's double eagle eyes—and brains faster than a war room computer—saw my entire problem in a glance. He spurred right along the bank of the arroyo and threw his loop over the steer's head, jerking him down hard. He bailed off the bay and flew through the air like a red-tailed hawk, landing rolling in the bottom of the arroyo not unlike a big round rock, and got up pulling his pocket knife out, opening the blade, and cutting the ropes in two, right where they were tightened against the addled steer's neck as he stumbled up to his feet.

Rusty yelled, "Hold the rope that holds your horse," being an efficient cowboy and rescue squad all at once.

I had been doing this with one hand all along, but now I could use two. The well-trained cow horse turned, looking down from the rope where it was tied to the horn like he was supposed to do.

The world was flat full of blurs. One went by me going south.

The steer had charged my savior with his head down some. Our luck just kept on running, and so did the big steer. One horn had gone on one side of Rusty and one on the other. He was trying to shove my best friend toward—and possibly through—the far side of the arroyo bank, but Rusty was knocked down, and all the steer did was step on him with two of his four feet, ripping the back of his shirt for about a foot and removing only a six-inch strip of hide— Rusty's hide, not the steer's.

I want everything clear here.

I also found out later—as we so often do in this puzzling life— that I had a wide belt all the way around my waist that was also missing hide—my hide, not the steer's.

It's a good thing we'd been working in a sandy part of the arroyo or we might have gotten hurt.

When old Rusty got up and looked things over, he said with a good deal of seriousness, "We're gonna have to ride back to headquarters and get some more ropes."

He was twenty years older than me and had been a mentor for longer than that, so I just nodded my head yes, thinking the fifteen-mile ride back over rocky hills, one rocky mountain and four rocky canyons would be good exercise for both men and beasts. It surely was.

Rusty Carver had saved my life and other little particles so many times I pretty near cried as I looked back on the long years with him. I would have wept a keg-full all right, except the smiling and the giggling got in the way. As a fair example, the long weekend trip we made to the wonderful little hamlet of Hillsboro, New Mexico, and then on over to El Paso would do.

Now, Hillsboro is in the eastern foothills of the Black Range, where the great Apache warriors Victorio, Nana, and Lozen fought to a standstill two thousand U.S. cavalrymen and infantry as well as about six hundred civilian militia. Me and ol' Rusty have worked cattle over every damn battlefield in their wild history. There was big gold and silver booms there and all sorts of other history, too wonderful for me to remember right now.

A feller just naturally favors a place where he has a good time. I would have liked it if I'd spent half my time in jail. You see . . . Hillsboro is a one-bar, two-church town. My favorite kind. You can get in a lot of sinning and saving all in one little place. These little wonderful havens were the foundation, the cement, and glue of the entire West at one time. Now the *New* West has made them scarce as picnics in a dust storm.

Hillsboro's one great bar, the S-Bar-X, is named after a cow brand. They hardly ever ran out of whiskey, even though I can honestly say that a couple of times the miners, cowboys, artists, and other wastrels have had them down to less than three bottles. I actually witnessed the time they ran plumb out of beer. Some people got real cranky and had little nervous fits.

Hillsboro has two good restaurants most of the time, one gas station, one motel and a museum or two, art galleries, and antique stores. It was a good place to drink and dance, you see. Ol' Hoss Hogan had a little band that played weekends at the S-Bar-X. He tried to dress like a cowboy, but you could still tell he was a fix-it-upper repairman on the side. However, by nine o'clock at night, he sounded like Guy Lombardo, Patsy Cline, and Hank Thompson all at once.

Shirley Mae taught first grade over at the county seat—Hot Springs. And she was there waiting for us. She was built a little like Rusty, except for her milk glands. They were a half-gallon apiece. But she had a kind and pretty face framed in thick brown, curly hair that made her big brown eyes seem to shine like little headlights.

My girl, Cindi, tended bar right here where the fun-havin' people were gathering. She was kinda tall and skinny like me, except for her butt. It was wider than her shoulders. Before I ever dated her, a local miner showed his appreciation for beauty by saying a sort of dumb thing: "When Cindi walks, her butt looks like two corn-fed pigs in a gunny sack." Even so, it was enough of a compliment to make me take notice. Careful notice.

Well, we got us a table and got down to drinking. I hope some of the young will also remember how valuable it is to have a girlfriend for a bartender. The drinks seem to heavy up a bit. The band was playing, most everybody was dancing and things got louder and louder. Friday night in the high desert makes more than the coyotes howl. It smelled real good—full of spilled drinks, lung-killing smoke, sweaty citizens, and other noisy-scented things.

Now Rusty dances slow with his shoulders all bunched up as if he was afraid his head was gonna fall off, and he looked down at his and Shirley Mae's feet like he was afraid they were gonna cripple one another. Suddenly he stopped, raised his head up and howled, trying to really get the sound through the ceiling to the moon outside.

It must have worked because every one in the S-Bar-X caught the howling disease. Hoss Hogan and his Good Boys—that's the name of the band—played louder to be sure they were heard, and the place turned into a yelling, drinking, dancing heaven. There wasn't but one fight that night, and it was outside. People were having so much fun, they didn't even bother to go watch. Now, that's having fun in anybody's town.

Cindi started trying to get everybody out by closing time, which is two o'clock in the morning in New Mexico. By three, there wasn't anybody left but the four of us.

Since it was too near sunup to go to sleep, I said, "Cindi, you got tomorrow off. Hellsfire, let's head down to El Paso."

Rusty jumped in, his little tiny eyes opening wide enough so you could see they were dishwater blue: "That's the best thing I've heard since cattle was a dollar a pound." I couldn't recall when that was, but the girls seemed willing. Cindi had a purse full of tips and got us a bottle of bourbon to keep us awake till we got to the great Del Norte Hotel in El Paso, Texas.

Shirley Mae drove her Ford until we rolled into Las Cruces, where she got sleepy. Rusty took a drink out of the bottle—big one—and decided he'd drive so we'd all be safe for the upcoming adventures in the great Del Norte.

We were on the outskirts of El Paso at daylight when a siren caused me to take both my hands off Cindi and quiver like I'd been shot in the butt with a flaming arrow. Rusty pulled over after the cop drove alongside for about a mile, making mad pull-over signs. He got out seeming somewhat irritated and asked Rusty for his driver's license.

He didn't have one that he could find. He said, "Shirley's got one. Let me have it, hon."

The cop said, "That won't quite work, sir."

"Oh," said Rusty.

"What is your name, sir?"

"All I can remember right now is Rusty."

"OK, uh-huh, OK. Mister Rusty, did you know you were speeding?"

"Speedin'?"

"Yes, sir, ninety miles an hour in a fifty-five-mile zone."

Rusty grinned real appealing-like and bragged: "Sure, I knew it. I was trying to get home before I got drunk."

The cop didn't know what to say for a minute. I didn't know what to say for a minute, but Shirley Mae evidently did. She got out of the car, moved around the back, smiling so sweet you'd think she'd just swallowed a chocolate bar, and motioned the red-faced cop to her. They talked, and they talked some more.

The cop got back in his patrol car. Shirley Mae got back in her car on the driver's side. As ol' Rusty scooted over, he asked, "What did you tell him?"

"Just what I told you the first night we met."

Rusty damn near wrinkled all the hide off his forehead trying to remember what it was she'd said.

Sure enough, we made it through the city of El Paso to the great

Del Norte Hotel right at full service, sunup. I emptied Cindi's bottle so it wouldn't evaporate in the upcoming heat of the Mexican border.

We slept until midafternoon and had a good breakfast of *huevos rancheros* in the coffee shop along with a couple of nice bloody Marys with our coffee.

By eight that night, the great round bar was full of visitors mostly enjoying themselves. There were local businessmen, gold and mercury smugglers, ranchers, oil lease men from farther east in West Texas, and even a few plain old working cowboys like me and Rusty.

The tables and booths in the large lounge were mostly full, and a mariachi band was tuning up. So were we four. The air was full of fun and action. Nobody noticed the deadly cigarette smoke in those days. Just goes to show you how easy even the brightest of people are to brainwash. Course, in our own bunch, we only had one genius, and that was Shirley Mae.

I know it's hard to believe, but things got better. The mariachis were strolling and playing. Some people left the famous circular bar, so big that you had to have a hunter's eye to see all around it, but others filled their empty places as fast as popcorn farts. The table next to the bar emptied, and that sharp-eyed Shirley Mae moved and claimed it for us. Now we were set comfortable with a good view of the whole wonderful place.

We had no more than got our second wonderful drink than that crazy Rusty Carver said to me, "Hey, Roy, let's go over to Juarez, where things are really wide open." The rest of us were silent, staring at him like he was a rabid skunk. That ain't a pretty sight to stare at.

Then Shirley Mae broke the crushing silence, sweetly: "Now, Rusty, dear, Juarez is certainly a freewheeling place, a place to let loose, especially for men. However, I don't feel we should crowd our luck driving any more while drinking."

Rusty meekly said: "It ain't but a half a mile. We could walk."

Since Rusty realized there wasn't a single certainty in what he'd just said, he got up and danced with Shirley Mae. I did the same with Cindi. We were snuggling while we moved, and I couldn't see a single hard rock anywhere on the dance floor. Everything was sure keen. We just got mellow as cherry Jell-o, and everything we said broke us up laughing. Everybody at our table was a goddamned comic and had an audience sitting there who knew how to appreciate those flint-edged quips and showed it. Fun. *Fun.* I tell the cockeyed world.

I said something like, "You know, if we got up in the morning and there wasn't a single chicken left in the world, there would be panic in the streets."

Of course, I was simply observing, seriously, how everybody was going crazy over the fried chicken joints just beginning to sprout up all over the country. Well, not all over. Hillsboro doesn't have one. Anyway, this just rocked everybody back. Cindi was laughing so dang hard she had to put her head down on the table. Shirley Mae was so full of mirth, she was holding her stomach with both hands and had her eyes closed so tight they were squirting out tears. Ol' Rusty was leaning over, slapping at his knees, about to fall out of the saddle. These two big ol' college football players came over to get our girls to dance. That was fine, but the girls didn't want to. And the young men were so impolite as to insist before the girls could stop laughing. After the third "no thank you," one of them pulled Cindi half up, spouting off, "Ah, come on, Slim. It'll do you good."

I don't know what it was that caused me to stand up. Maybe it was him calling Cindi "Slim" before he'd had a chance to see that wonderful big butt. Maybe it was the crude, macho way he butted in. I don't know. Hell, I just stood up in resentment and was knocked down before I could say more than, "Didn't you hear the . . ."

I was a little dizzy, but I rolled away fast to escape the kicks I expected to follow, and even that was too slow.

Ol' Rusty took a shortcut right across the table, spilling a few drinks and breaking a few glasses. That wasn't nothing compared to what he did to the invaders. Rusty was very limited as a bar fighter. He just had two punches. That great big bony hand-crushing left to the belly or ribs and then a sort of overhand right to the cheekbone.

Down the big kid went, flat as a penny on the pavement, and still as a mummy's ass.

There was no way his companion wanted to enter this sudden competition. But being good at competition was how he was getting through Texas Western University. Besides, what was worse, people were watching to see what he would do.

Whup. Whap. And he joined his friend on the ballroom floor. However, he moved a little bit, and Rusty went down and whapped him on the side of the jaw. Rusty was always a true gentleman, and this last proved it. He could have kicked him instead.

There were evidently folks present who didn't understand loyalty and protecting the hearth and all that.

The El Paso jail for drunks and derelicts was underground in those days. That's where we all spent the night—safe from atomic bomb attacks. Since I had only received and not delivered a punch, this detention was puzzling. Also, when the law arrived we were all trying to explain that we were the pickees, not the pick*ers*. If Cindi and I had shut up and let Shirley Mae do her trick talking, all the trouble to follow could have been avoided. There's no use saying more about the jail. Hell, most everyone who experiences it once decides not to let it happen again. Ever.

The courtroom was full of hangovers. There were other kinds of criminals, of course, but we were with the majority for one of the few times in our lives.

Our turn came. Cindi, Shirley Mae, and me, ol' Roy Barrett, were fined for resisting arrest, drunkenness in a public place and three hundred dollars in broken glass. We paid up. Even so, I was puzzled by how four whiskey glasses and a cheap little ash tray could mount up to three hundred dollars. Maybe they were imported crystal and I'd been having too much fun to notice.

Then there stood Rusty before the judge, his hat held in front of his chest with his head down like he was praying. I knew better. He was being tried for assault. He was straining his brain matter trying to keep straight all the things Shirley Mae had told him, such as: "Now, dear, don't be afraid. I know this judge. My uncle helped him get appointed, and he's an art lover."

Rusty's little pig eyes opened up so you could tell he heard. "An art lover?" he said.

"That's right, he collects from Tom Lea, José Cisneros, and all kinds of fine artists. He even thinks he's an artist himself. Half the basements and closets in El Paso hide at least one of his paintings." She went on to close the deal out: "Now, you have no doubt noticed how he asked every defendant what their occupation was. Well, when he does that, you tell him you're an artist and he'll be easier on you."

Rusty stared and stared. This was asking a bit much for a hard-rock cowboy and efficient bar-room brawler to actually admit in public that he was an artist.

It was finally Rusty's turn to be questioned.

"And Mister Rusty Carver, what is your occupation?"

Rusty choked. He turned his hat in his hands. I thought the tough old son of a bitch was gonna fall dead as year-old dung right there.

"Well?" Judge Chavez asked.

"Your honor, sir, I'm an artist."

The judge relaxed back in his chair, his hands locked together across his chest, and beamed kindly down on our dear desperate friend.

"I'm a portrait artist, your honor, sir."

"Oh, a portrait artist, huh. Are you good?"

"Well, I s'pose I am."

"Modesty in an artist is very rare, my son. I'd bet you are very good."

"I sure hope you win your bet, your honor, sir."

Cindi and I were hopeful. Shirley Mae was just swelling with pride.

Judge Chavez paused, his nostrils flaring. "Do you think you'd have time to paint me?"

Political machinery was running through the judge's head. I could see it. The thought of a free portrait was perhaps turning the wheels of justice.

"Well, your honor, sir, I'm out of art supplies right now."

The judge leaned forward with serious intent, his pen poised above a blank paper and said, "Well, son, give me a list and we'll see what we can do about that."

My God. We all breathed. It looked like it had worked. Then, *then*, my dearest friend and Shirley Mae's closest loving friend said, "Well, let's see, your honor, sir. If I had a broom and a bucket of fresh shit I believe I could get an exact likeness."

The entire courtroom gasped and stared up and down and even sideways as the judge turned that shade of purple you see in mountain crevices as the sun sets in the peaceful West. There was no doubt in my mind that my very best friend was going to be sentenced to hang until he was that same shade of purple.

Shirley Mae became a heroine of the first order as she charged past the guard and the judge's all-around man and pulled the judge's head next to her whispering mouth.

He shook his head at first, still dangerously purple. Then he lessened to red and then to his natural, nice olive. Now he was healthy again and occasionally shook his head in agreement to whatever in the hell Shirley Mae was saying. Then she smilingly glared at us with kind assurance and I for one felt safe and warm.

The judge, amidst slight confusion, calmly dismissed Rusty's case for lack of evidence. There were a few protestations, but simply lifting his manicured hand, palm out, was enough to bring a welcome silence.

We finally followed Rusty's wishes and went to Juarez, and Rusty asked Shirley Mae to marry him. Like the feller said, "In those days you could do anything in Juarez you were big enough to do and still pay for." Nowadays, of course, you've got the dope smugglers instead of the gold smugglers. But there's a big difference here. It takes many mean and greedy bastards to get the dope for the dopers. It takes good miners to get the gold for the smugglers. Yeah, I miss the miners. Miners ain't nothing but cowboys who can't ride.

We had one hell of a fun time in Juarez, Mexico, before heading back to the Hillsboro country. As I think back on ol' Rusty now, he wasn't near as dumb as some people might think. The first thing he did when he escaped hanging was marry Shirley Mae. That's what I call plumb wise and wonderful.

It was about impossible to figure how a man that smart could suffer such a terrible blow later. You can't build any final forts against the future no matter what the experts tell you.

Shirley Mae and Rusty pitched in their savings, mostly hers, and made a good down payment on a little white-painted, five-room frame house in Hillsboro. He went on working with me on the Ladder Ranch and she continued teaching first grade in Hot Springs. They soon had one cute little daughter, Mary Anne, and another in the chute. A family had been cemented. On weekends in the spring and summer he helped her patch up the place real good and make a good garden of tomatoes, corn, green beans, and most important of all, chile. And every winter he killed a deer to round out the bounty.

The best I'd done was finally get engaged to the new bartender at the S-Bar-X. Cindi had run off to Tucson, Arizona, with a used car dealer. She'd been fun.

However, my new—and I hoped forever—love had been raised on a ranch until her father lost the place when she was eighteen years old. She was still pissed about that, blaming the U.S. Forest Service, the Bureau of Land Management, and above all the "Do-Gooders." She just said it once so as not to be a whiner. "Five generations of us fighting droughts, blizzards, cow disease, low prices and now, where bear, cows, and antelope roamed there's a bunch of trashy trailer houses and the water's turned sour as cat shit."

I never did know all of it. What I did know was Susie Lou was a strange but good looker. She had auburn hair worn in a pony tail and oddly enough, considering the red showing in her hair, eyes as black as Geronimo's. She walked back and forth around that S-Bar-X bar like she owned it. She had everything that makes up a young woman a man would want to spend his old age with, moving smooth as water in an irrigation ditch. The mother ditch.

She laughed at all the silly things us humans do and at the same time she could get tough and mean as a badger if you got out of line smart-assing. She also got along great with Rusty and Shirley Mae. That just about cinched it.

I didn't have anywhere to put her on the Ladder, and I hadn't got up the guts to mention it. So when I heard about those forty-eight horses a feller wanted to get rid of over near Hatch, I got ol' Rusty to go with me and take a look.

The man had a combination farm and cow ranch most commonly called a stock farm. The man who owned the horses was over northeast, a ways from Mountainair, and said his name was Tom Nothing, but most everyone called him Nothing Tom. Well, we walked around the corral and looked over Nothing's forty-eight horses. They were every color from bays to paints and every shape and condition from bony to fat.

"What do you want for 'em?" I asked.

"Hell," he said, "I don't know. A couple of 'em ate a little loco weed. The effects ain't shown up yet, but who knows? Huh."

I couldn't give him an answer.

"Some of them is a little green and some of them has been rode hard with a lot of living with dried sweat," he added.

"What do you want for 'em?"

"Some of them has been kid ponies and one or two has been bucked out in rodeos."

I was beginning to show signs of irritation. Even Rusty had taken his five-inch-brim greasy old Stetson off and was scratching his thick-haired gray head.

"For the last time, how much do you want?"

"What you got to trade?"

"Well, let's see, we got ten bred heifers between us that the Ladder lets us run for free."

I looked at Rusty and he looked at me. Then we both looked way off across the desert mesa only a half mile to the west waiting the fatal answer.

"They in good shape?" Tom Nothing asked.

"Yeah," I said.

"Yeah. It's a trade if you deliver them right here," he said.

It was done.

Then we did what all cowboys have to do on their own at least once in their lives. We quit the Ladder, where we had hard but good jobs, and went in business for ourselves.

We owned one good cowhorse apiece and the rigging that goes with 'em. Rusty's cousin over at Hot Springs had two pack mules we borrowed. We used most of the little savings we had and with the hesitant blessings of Shirley Mae and Suzie Lou, headed out across country. We were now cowboy entrepreneurs and aimed to come home in a few weeks with lots of money and other goods to make our women happy and secure. I aimed dead on to ask Suzie Lou for her hand and everything else tied to it.

We headed north along the Rio Grande at first, then angled off northeast later. We had decided to ride a different horse each day and that way we could be testing while we were trading. It didn't take long to realize these horses had spent more time on loco weed than it first appeared. If a tree limb touched them on the head, some of the horses would just fall down and wrap around the tree. We couldn't get them up. So we'd have to tie a rope on their feet and drag them away and then tail them up like a dying cow. It was turning into the damnedest mess a feller ever saw.

I was riding a good-looking sorrel, plumb shiny, and every time he'd see a shadow from a fence post or a tree, it didn't matter, he'd drop his head down and examine it carefully, then jump just as high and far as he could. That sure slowed things down. It wasn't quite so bad if you weren't riding them. Some of them would suddenly see a cow trail and just jump straight up and fall down on it. Sometimes more than once. But the ones that got my total attention were the ones that would lift their heads to a sudden breeze that had blown across a waterhole way off somewhere. They'd run around in circles, their heads down, until they found a sink place or a bare patch and just stop and drink. That invisible water must have tasted pretty good cause they'd switch their tails and walk away acting satisfied with all that dusty air they'd swallowed. One really did smell water at a farmer's water trough and just fell into it. He must have got water in his lungs. He died. One mare went up to an arroyo bluff and just walked off it, hitting her head and breaking her neck. She didn't hardly kick before she was still forever.

We lost four head before we sort of got the know-how to sort of handle them.

We made our first trade on the fifth day out. A small rancher needed a gentle horse for his kids. Rusty really surprised me. He was a genuinely good liar.

"That little sorrel mare there was ridden by my brothers' kids over at Las Cruces all the time," he said. "Hell, his three-year-old rode her in a Fourth of July parade."

"Well, I'm gonna take your word for it, but this little bay here is a mite too spooky for my kids."

We made the trade and the man had told the truth, mostly. Spooky was not the right word, however. That sucker bucked so hard, Rusty had to run into him three different times with his own good horse to keep me from being thrown hard.

When the new horse finally stopped, I told Rusty: "We made a hell of a good trade there. We'll swap this bastard to a rodeo stock contractor. This is the kind of buckin' stock they're prayin' to find."

"Yeah," the great liar said.

The very next ranchhouse we came upon was about five miles westerly. The feller took a liking to another sorrel mare we had.

"How old is she?"

Rusty ran up right quick, pushed her lip back, and said: "She shows to be a coming five." Rusty had always been good at teething a horse's age, but now he was also fast, and all those natural muscles stopped folks from doubting his word.

Rusty went on and said: "Why, three of my little nieces and nephews rode this horse to school at the same time down at Nutt." Now, Nutt, New Mexico, is famous for being nothing but a bar between Hatch and Deming. There sure as hell ain't no school there.

We traded that fourteen-year-old sorrel mare for a bull with one nut. That was fine with me. We might have to eat the half-loaded critter to keep going on our trail of riches.

After a trade was done and the handshake made, we'd hear bragging through their laughter such as, "That ol' horse is spavined."

"That ol' horse has been foundered and has a bad ankle to boot."

We heard our victims spout such things as: "That milk cow ain't had a calf in three years. You couldn't get a drop of milk out of her with an oilfield suction pump. Ha ha ha."

We got to having a lot of fun out of this. It's always a good thing because the joke was just as much on us as them. Oh, it went on and on for weeks. 'Course, what these gloating local traders didn't know was this: as soon as we were out of hearing, we nearly fell off our own crazy horses laughing about the shadow-jumping, air-drinking trick horse they now owned.

We weren't gaining much yet, but we knew now we didn't have much to lose, if anything. In the fun department, we were many rocky miles ahead. All this fun puzzles and pains even more when you know what happened to old Rusty later on.

We tried to camp out one night and count up. We had a hundred and seven-dollar gain in the cash department. Some few cattle, bulls, cows and heifers of various colors and conditions. Sixteen new horses—some lame one way or another and four or five that were working real good. We had about half our loco'ed stock left to trade. 'Course, they were the craziest of the forty-eight.

When we were trading after three o'clock in the afternoon, we stalled by teething, checking out every joint on the horse, cow or whatever was on the docket. Rusty and I held endless sidebar conferences and then about sundown we'd make the trade. We'd shake hands in the old-fashioned way that used to hold water better than the tightest contracts you can get now.

Invariably, the traders would ask us to stay for supper and the night. The feed was always better than the crackers and sardines we'd gotten down to.

We had trouble every night, though, when people were so generous. You see, we had so many trading tales to discuss that it was impolite to just bust a gut laughing at midnight or after. Not only that, it would wake up and scare hell out of our host and hostess thinking they had a couple of real nuts in their place. Well?

We spent a lot of evenings planning what we were going to get our women with our profits. Rusty wanted to buy the lot next door so Shirley Mae could have room to raise the flowers she loved so much as well as the vegetable garden they both cultivated. I was heavy on getting a little house like Rusty's and a diamond ring for that special finger on Suzie Lou's hand.

"Hellsfire," I told Rusty. "I may just buy the S-Bar-X for her."

"Well, by damn," he said. "That's what I call a wedding present."

Over by Mountainair in the rolling hill and mesa country, we accidentally ran onto a bootlegger. He was friendly from the start, knowing that if we were any form of the law, we would not have the sad mixture of stock we had.

He was holding a really good thirty-thirty Winchester. I could tell Rusty really wanted it for a deer rifle. His old .30-.40 Krag was about done in.

So we settled for a little tradin' talk over some of the best corn-made white lightning I ever tasted. Damn, we sure had fun. We stayed three days. Old Jake finally got drunk enough on his own concoction that we traded him a beautiful pinto mare that didn't go crazy but every other day—this was her day off—for the Winchester and three crock jugs of homemade whiskey.

Then we got the hell out of there.

Old Jake would have a hangover next day—the day that paint mare was scheduled to go crazy and kick at shadows, sunlight, cedar trees, barn doors or humans.

When we got to Mountainair we traded another kid horse for a good-looking cow and calf to a feller just west of town. Damned if it wasn't a good old pony. He had six kids, and they all took turns riding him, happy as a fried chicken dinner with biscuits and gravy.

And that's exactly what we had for lunch. Mister Hawkins insisted on us dining so luxuriously on his wife's cooking. We tried to appear reluctant but damn near knocked one another down getting to the table. We did give him a couple of drinks from ol' Jake's jugs.

And we all ate. With the kids and his wife and a visiting sister and her two kids, there were too many to count.

After three cups of coffee and some killer tobacco, Mister Hawkins said, "I can tell you fellers been tradin' loco'ed horses and I counted 'em perty close in your"—he hesitated before he said it—"remuda. I was a horse trader for thirty years. That's how I traded for this fine place here. There's a twenty-acre pasture right out there. I suggest you put all the locos in there, and we'll turn the rest of your stuff"— yeah, he called our walking goods "stuff"—"and I'll pass the word around and we'll see what happens. If you get rid of them, you can just give me whatever you like. Loco'ed horses sometimes get over it in a few years, sometimes minutes. But there's a little shortage of *using* horses right now."

Rusty pitched right in at this: "They've all been rode several times. We did it ourselves."

"Well, well, well," he said, increasing the volume each time. "That means they'll show better than I thought."

Mister Hawkins's trading blood was beginning to fire. It took about two weeks, and that was fine with us. Mrs. Hawkins seemed to have an unlimited amount of chickens to fry, and she could cook biscuits and gravy that would make a heroin addict quit cold for just one serving. And that ain't much of an exaggeration.

The horses behaved and reined out pretty good most of the time. There was one day when a skinny ol' gray stud tried to mount the hood of a man's new pickup, and another time a little chestnut mare we'd traded for lit out in a dead run. She did a full circle in the pasture, slid to a stop and turned around and retraced the whole thing, her ears laid back and her beautiful chocolate mane and tail streaming out in the sunlight.

Now this would have been a beautiful sight to a circus horse trainer, but to a bunch of ranchers, cowboys and part-time farmers, this was a puzzle. It didn't puzzle me. We'd traded one loco'ed horse for another. However, when she slid to a stop and looked around, spotting the little gathering, she stood right in front of Rusty.

He smiled as if he knew everything in the world, reached out and patted her on the forehead, saying softly, sickeningly, "My little darling, just like I trained you. Thank you for the fine show." He eased a loop over her head, and a bean farmer bought her for his wife for an astounding forty dollars.

It was time to go home. We were traded out. We had to settle up with Hawkins. He was smarter half asleep than both of us at our best, so we had to cheat a little to even the odds. We took the last gallon of ol' Jake's whiskey and just kept toasting such things as "to the hospitality of the Hawkins family . . . to the beautiful Hawkins children . . . to the best fried chicken in the world . . . to new friends and old memories." If we hadn't had to put Hawkins to bed, we'd have gone on all day and far into the night. As it was, we watched while Mrs. Hawkins threw a cover over him. Rusty asked her if she had an envelope. She did. He stuffed some bills in it, licked and sealed it and placed it on the fireplace mantle. Mrs. Hawkins smiled knowingly. We saddled our own horses—the two we'd left home with—and got the pack mules ready. We gathered our new horses, cows, bulls, and heifers up and headed out across country as far off any trail as we could. We were aiming in the general direction of Hillsboro, way off southwesterly.

A few days later, tired, hungry, and with the sardine diarrhea, we stopped, looking down from a hill above our town. We were on the far eastern edge of the Sterling Roberts ranch, I think. We counted up our money. We had six hundred twelve dollars and seventeen cents to split up.

There were twenty-six horses, none of them loco'ed where you could tell by looking, but a lot of them limping. There were nine milk cows, from Holsteins to Jerseys and a couple of brindles. Some of them had even given milk at one time. We had four cold bulls, one hot one and another with one nut, three burros, two mules and a Rolf collie dog who was about to have pups. Of course, Rusty had his Winchester.

The only thing we could figure out was the split on the money and we had figured hard. Before even facing our beautiful women, we gathered the little courage and energy we had left and pushed this bunch of livestrock up the road north past Jimmy Bason's F-Cross Ranch and way on up into the U.S. Forest land of the Black Range, opened a gate and drove them scattered out in the vast Gila Wilderness. We'd lied so long on the trading trail that we now lied to ourselves about how all our livestock would heal and fatten up and then we'd gather them and hold a big sale. What few the lions, bears, and coyotes would miss couldn't be penned in that huge and wild country with a dozen top cowboys and that was about all there was left in the whole of Sierra County. The Rolf collie bitch would turn into a fair cowdog. Shirley Mae fell in love with her, though, and we never got to use her much.

We mounted up, leading the two pack mules. After having spent two days near Hillsboro, we finally headed straight for the S-Bar-X bar. It was all downhill right to the front porch. Then two steps up and four more to the door. We'd made it.

It was a Thursday. Shirley Mae would be home from Hot Springs for the weekend on Friday night. So we had time to sip a few drinks and talk over our next move. Suzie Lou evidently had a day off, so we sat at a table and relaxed.

No matter how we figured, that three hundred odd dollars we each had pocketed wasn't going to last long, and it sure as hell wasn't going to put us in business for ourselves. Before we could admit we were going to have to go back to cowboying, Ginger, the relief bartender came over and handed me an envelope. She turned around and whipped up to get away from our table before I could ask her about it. I unfolded the letter. It was from Suzie Lou. My eyes blurred over as I read it. The gist of it was that she loved me but didn't see any future for her in Hillsboro, and she didn't see any for me anywhere else.

I wanted to yell out about the lonely beauty of the whole damn surrounding country and the fun a fella could have if he worked it right, but all I did was say to my best friend, "Suzie Lou left the country."

Rusty just said, "Awww, shit. What did she do that for?" with disappointment showing on his old broad, busted face.

I don't care what people say, when this happens you get shook up. There was a rock in my throat I couldn't have washed away with a barrel of beer.

Ol' Rusty and ol' Roy were sure surprised when Art Evans, the foreman of the Ladder, told us the boss knew we'd be back and had just hired a couple of gunzels (phony cowboys) to help out until we returned.

Art was a hell of a good cowboy and a fine feller, but he had to issue the orders the big owner gave. Our first punishment was building a mile and a half of fence in solid rock. We got blisters bigger than silver dollars digging those post holes with regular hand diggers and a heavy steel bar. We finally had to use dynamite on most of the post holes.

Then we were exiled to Farber Camp, a powerful forty miles from nowhere. There were a hell of a lot of cows in the Farber pasture to be checked out and a count made.

We pulled six good horses over with the Ford pickup and a six-horse trailer the boss had bought from a broke racetrack runner.

Farber Camp held a pretty fair three-room shack that had actually been painted twenty years back, and it had recently been left vacant by a cowboy and his wife who took off for Montana. Art Evans told us that they had left some grub there, as was customary. He said there was enough for a month.

There was plenty of pinto beans and sowbelly and a starter of sourdough bread. There was also a rare luxury—three boxes of Post Toasties.

The next morning for breakfast I poured us out a big bowl each of the corn flakes. Rusty had our thick bacon ready, but I was still scrounging around looking for some canned milk to eat them with. I looked everywhere but the outhouse. There was no cockeyed canned milk. Rusty seemed a little disappointed, but I was half mad.

"Rusty," I said with much conviction. "We are surrounded by big pastures. These pastures are grazing over seven hundred head of mother cows. All those mamas who have calves have milk."

"Let's saddle our horses," he wisely added.

We rode a long way. It was a nice feeling, though. All we wanted was one cow to give us enough milk for the breakfast of delicious Post Toasties. We'd eaten the sowbelly before we left. A good thing.

The Ladder had over two hundred thousand acres of mostly rough rocky land, but good grass for the cows and brush of all kinds to feed the numberless deer, elk, bear, mountain lions, coyotes, foxes, wild turkeys, and even quail in the lower flatlands. As we rode along side by side, our heads down looking for cow sign, as cowboys do their entire lives, we saw the tracks of most of these wild critters. Then I pulled up and stared a minute across mesas, breast-shaped foothills, and smaller rolling hills where you could find great meadows. I looked all the way across the Black Range, dark bluing the lighter blue of the sky, and into the mighty Gila Wilderness. No, I didn't feel small in this vastness. I *knew* that. I just felt at home. Just like old Nana and his little tiny surviving tribe had felt and fought so damn well to save what I so easily viewed.

We saw a lot of cows, but in widely scattered bunches. Most of them had been sucked dry by their calves. Finally we found the cow we were looking for. She and about ten more head of mothers were returning from a drink at a spring down below. She was the only one that had a full bag. The other cows were flabby-bagged, and the reason why was their calves were with them. It was obvious this big old cow had a late calf, and she'd hid it while she went for water.

We were taking down our ropes, angling off so she wouldn't booger, waiting till they hit the open meadow just up ahead.

Now, me and ol' Rusty had made a lot of little punkin' roller rodeos around the country, trying out bull-dogging,' bronc riding, and calf roping, but about the only thing we'd ever won much at was wild cow milking. Whichever one of us got position first roped the horns. If you caught the neck, it choked them and made a cow mad and harder to mug. Rusty usually mugged because he was a lot stronger than me.

I had brought along an oversize Coke bottle to get our breakfast milk in.

We pulled our hats down over our eyes.

The little bunch of cows hit the opening. We spurred after them. Damned if that old sorrel horse didn't put me just right to fit a loop around her neck just as she hit the brush. Rusty bailed off his horse and was fighting tree limbs and brushy entanglements to get to her head and mug her, so I could squeeze a teat or two and get us a Coke bottle full of milk.

Now several things had already gone to hell and back twice. Not only had I caught her around the neck instead of the horns, but deep next to her chest. Now she could get mad without hardly choking. She did that. She was bellering and bawling in bass. And she ran through the thickest skin-plowing bushes she could find. There were millions of them bushes. Old Rusty was hanging onto her horns with a hand on each, but she was flinging him up and then down. She was dragging him a spell, then turning back and stepping all over his legs with hard, sharp, fast-moving hoofs. Skin ripped off, but Rusty held. I was running after them through that same hide-loving brush. Every now and then I'd stick my head in her flank, grab a teat with one hand and try to squeeze milk in the small opening of the big Coke bottle.

I mostly missed it because of the thrashing about. My cowhorse was trying his best to hold the rope tight, but she twisted and turned so many different ways it was impossible. I must have had about an inch of cloudy milk in the bottle when she got loose bowels. Of course, she was swinging her tail all the time, hitting me all over, but especially in the face. So now, with the added weight on her tail she whopped me across both eyes and I damn near went blind. I was forced to wipe the brown-green stuff out of my eyes, and it made the bottle slick and harder to hold, and some of it was getting into the milk. Course, I was too busy at the time to know it. Then, too, there was a little blood from my scratched face mixed with the cow shit and then into our breakfast milk.

The second time she whopped me across the face with that dirty old tail, I not only went blind; I got mad.

I was calling her names I usually reserved for child molesters, wife beaters, crooked politicians, and road ragers. I used all these expert names and more when I fell down under her and she kicked me in the side of the head. I was thinking maybe she'd kicked my left ear off, but I knew damn well she'd ripped at least half my hat brim loose because it was flopping in my face.

After several years passed in about fifteen minutes, I had the bottle three-quarters full of dark-colored milk.

I yelled, "We got the milk, we got the milk! Rusty, hang on till I get my horse."

He yelled back, "There ain't nothing left to hang on with but my arms. The rest of me is in pieces in the bushes."

I sympathized as I got on my horse with my thumb over the bottle top to save every drop of the precious liquid. It was difficult to believe, but it happened: We hit a little opening, Rusty plowed his worn-out heels in the ground and stopped the old cow. She was getting kind of worn out, herself. I spurred my horse up, loosening the rope. Rusty jerked the loop wide and off over the cow's head. By God, we'd done it!

The cow took off bellering in the direction of her calf. Rusty was standing in the way. One horn grazed a trail on the outside of his rib cage and several hundred pounds of cow knocked him rolling.

He lay still. The cow tore more brush apart vanishing in broad daylight. I got down carefully, so as not to spill our milk, and went over to see if Rusty was dead. My knees buckled and I sat right down by him. With my free hand I tried to roll him over face up. It worked. He sat straight up.

"You got milk?" he said.

I proudly held the bottle out where he could see.

"That there looks like chocolate milk," he said.

"Now ain't that something," I said. "A cow that gives chocolate milk."

He stared at me so hard I got scared.

"Something is wrong with your hat," he said.

Before I could move, he reached out and jerked my hat brim. It all came off. I was wearing a little cap with no bill. What a feeling of inadequacy for a working cowboy. Terrible. By gollies, I got home with the funny-colored milk. The sun had been coming mostly straight down on my face. I didn't know it until about sundown, but I was burned red as a woodpecker's head. My cap that had once been a hat didn't do the job.

And I'm ashamed to admit that my best friend Rusty refused to let me pour the milk on his Post Toasties. I had strained it several times through a dish towel into a little pitcher, but he kept saying there was cow shit in it and always would be. He poured water and a spoon of sugar on his cornflakes and ate them with no expression of appreciation on his face at all.

Of course, one has to make allowances in special situations. Rusty's face looked like it had been pounded for an hour with a steak softener and had barb-wire dragged across it until the barbs wore off. His shirt and even his Levis were ripped and skinned from the cow's front feet and the strangling brush. There was just no way you could foresee the tough old bastard's futile future.

Anyway, I had strained that milk over and over through clean dishtowels until the chocolate had turned plain gray. That was the best I was ever going to do for my Post Toasties milk. And by doggies, I want the world to know that I poured half that little pitcher of semi-chocolate milk on my cereal and ate every damn flake and spooned what was left out of the bowl, making the most gluttonous sounds. As everyone says, a man has got to do what has to be done, and I'm still here to tell about it.

The second day of actually working cattle for the benefit of the Ladder outfit, we were riding along with our heads down looking for fresh cow sign. Without even looking up, Rusty said, "You look just like a rabbi on horseback with that little skull cap."

I didn't hesitate. I reined my horse around, rode to camp and drove all the way to Hot Springs to buy me a new hat. I couldn't go to headquarters for the spare hat I had there. I'd have to explain to the other cowboys forever. My face was red as a monkey's ass in every way.

The owner finally let us go back working under Art Evans, and the Hillsboro world moved on and on with cattle prices going up and way down like always. A few miners grubbed enough gold from the hard hills to keep their bodies and dreams barely alive. Some of the artists who had drifted here stayed, but most, like the world around, moved on to other little colonies, then still others. But there was an amalgamated core community here that was both solid and bizarre.

A big movie star bought a half-serious, half-play ranch over across the state border in southeastern Arizona and Rusty got the job as foreman with Art Evans's recommendation. It seemed far away, but actually it was only a half-day's drive. So Rusty got back to Hillsboro to be with Shirley Mae about twice a month. This raise in pay, combined with his mate's teaching wages, allowed them to raise their two daughters perty good. The girls were just one year apart and were both running straight A's in high school. That meant college scholarships would come if the grades held up, and they did.

I kept looking for another Suzie Lou, wondering how many chances at such a woman a cowboy's God would grant. I hated to quit the Ladder outfit, but I had the itch to hunt for something I hadn't found, whatever the hell that was.

I worked up near Hi Lo in the northeastern part of the state for a few years. Here I was catty-cornered completely at the other end of the state from where I'd come. It's really good cattle country, but old Jim Ed Love, who owned the J L outfit, was so cockeyed unpredictable I finally had to pull out of there to keep from throwing a rock or something at him. One minute he was sweet-talking you into doing twice the amount of justified work and the next second he was sweet-talking you and meant it. Course, that was his way of keeping us dumb-ass cowboys confused and doing what he wanted.

I worked up there for several years—on three different outfits—

and still had the same saddle and maybe a hundred fifty dollars more money than I'd had the day I left the Hillsboro country. I told ol' Wrangler Lewis and Dusty Jones who had worked for Jim Ed most of their lives, "This cowboyin' has got me stiffened up all over, but the one place that counts."

Dusty said, "Me, too."

Then he looked way off at the sky for bird migrations and sadly went on, "However, I sometimes wish my dinger was as stiff as my neck."

That was too much truth for me to handle. A week later I quit the Hi Lo Country and started working dude ranches in Wyoming and Colorado. The dudes were only there in the summertime, and these dude outfits kept their play cattle in the barns in the winter. I didn't have to go out in sixty-mile-an-hour blizzards and feed freezing cattle with a freezing cowboy riding a freezing hay wagon. Why in hell hadn't I figured this out before my temples turned gray?

It was easier work for sure. There was more women available, as well as more whiskey. Some of these women, even rich women, seemed to like me, but even if I could have put up with holding my hand out behind me with my palm up, I never seemed to be able to hook up with one that suited. I sure fought my head to do it, though, but the money didn't make them anywhere near Suzie Lou.

Cowboys, unfortunately, aren't much on writing letters. Me and ol' Rusty mailed about one a year for awhile, then none. Shirley Mae wrote me three or four times a year, no matter what. The girls were going to graduate from New Mexico State University on the same day this year. Time flies faster than falcons. Before Art Evans and his wife retired, he got ol' Rusty a sort of easy horse wrangling job on the Ladder. I went back and thought I'd finish up with Rusty there. Twenty years' age difference isn't so much when one of you is twenty-five and the other is forty-five, but now it was like a thousand years.

The first thing I noticed was certain crazy things we'd done in our youth had gone missing in Rusty's head. He covered up real quick by answering, "Well, yeah, whatever" and such like.

Shirley Mae had been retired for five years and with Rusty's faltering help had their little place in town pretty shiny. She was sure wanting Rusty to retire with her, but for plain working cowboys, there was no such thing as retirement pay. Finally, Ralph Moon, the new foreman, had to let him go. Shirley was sure happy to have him home, even if he was getting a little forgetful a mite more than most. Rusty had gone to wrangle the horses every now and then without his pants on. And once he'd even gone out barefooted and no shirt. 'Course, he never forgot his hat.

A famous TV mogul and his movie star wife—at the time— bought the Ladder and were turning the whole damn thing into a buffalo ranch. That is right. Over two hundred thousand acres of buffalo. I don't have anything against buffalo. I just wasn't raised to work them. I was goin' crazier than I was natural born. That is crazy. I had to go.

Then, luck finally hit me right between the horns. A Texas oil man had bought a play-pretty ranch a few miles southerly from town and to everyone's surprise, his wife, Dottie Eastman, took to it and went and started raising and breeding Arabian horses like she'd been born to it. She wouldn't hardly ever go back to his Midland, Texas, headquarters with him.

One day, he had a hunting party of longtime, rich friends driving and climbing around after elk. Carl Eastman fired on a big five-by-six and just as the elk fell, so did he, both deader than a bleached cow skull.

I went over one week later. I sat in that big fancy kitchen and had coffee with that big fancy woman, stayed all day and stayed all night, and had me a top-paying job helping raise and train them Arab horses on this big fancy ranch before the sun came up that next morning.

A week after I'd been employed on the Dottie outfit, she took some meat out of the freezer and cooked us up the best damn elk steak I ever tasted. I was sure enjoying life like never before. I silently thanked old Carl Eastman for being such a good shot.

'Course, my tires was flattened a little every time I visited Rusty and Shirley Mae. He was always so happy to see me that he'd forget and crush my hand. He might be old and getting soft everywhere else, but those damn hands could still turn a chunk of steel into baking powder. But it was getting damn near impossible to talk about the old days and great times we'd shared. He would remember a snatch or so, then his eyes would go to a place unknown. Finally, it hurt my heart so bad, I told Dottie this would be the last time I could take watching him disappear like that. To her credit, she said, pushing at her dyed red hair, with those wonderful fifty-year-old blue eyes wide as a baby's, "No, darling. You have to see it through. He would, for you."

She was right, of course, and at that moment, I realized I had finally moved up from Suzie Lou.

When I got to their house and parked the pickup, I knew something was wrong. There wasn't anybody in the house and their dog was gone. Ol' Rusty had just wandered off out of town, walking across the foothills west toward the F-Cross Ranch and the Ladder on beyond. With the help of their little mongrel dog, Buckshot, Shirley Mae and several more citizens found him. I met them walking back into the edge of the one and only main drag of Hillsboro. Shirley Mae was holding his hand, leading him slowly along with the little black and white dog by their side. The rest of the town folks walked respectfully behind.

When she saw me, she smiled a tiny bit and said, "Buckshot trailed him . . . or I might never . . ."

I took his other hand and tried to visit on the way back to the house.

"That old bay horse is hiding in the outhouse," I told him. That's all. He didn't even know I was there or anywhere else as far as that goes.

It got worse almost daily now. One of their daughters lived in Portland with her husband and two grade-school kids. The other one was divorced in San Diego, working at a computer firm trying to support three stair-step boys alone.

They managed at great hardship to come for a couple of days, each a month apart. About all they could do was clean everything up and cook several meals ahead and put them in the freezer. Then they had to get to El Paso and take flights back home and hold their worlds together there. That's just the way of it.

I brought up to Shirley Mae about putting him in a good permanent care home in Las Cruces. I'd checked it out myself. Shirley Mae finally said "no" for the last time. "Not while I can move." A month later, she fell dead, just wore out. The girls came. The cowboys from all around came. Most of the town of Hillsboro came. We buried her up on the windy hill where all cow-mining towns have their graveyards. The wind blew like hell.

The daughters dressed Rusty up in a suit he'd only worn twice in twenty years. One held his hand on one side, her sister did the same on the other. He smiled and said something unintelligible every now and then.

Some black yearling steers with white faces lined up along the fence, all in a row, staring at the people at the cemetery. A red-tailed hawk shot down out of the huge sky, screamed once and whirred off out of sight over the hills.

We all went down to the S-Bar-X and got a little drunk telling great stories on and about Rusty's wonderful wife. The girls stayed home with their dad, and the next day, Dottie and I went with them to Las Cruces and got all the papers done to keep him there. I told them, "Don't let the nature of things ruin your families. Just come when it's really possible—not impossible. I'll go see him every week. All we need to know is how he's treated. He doesn't recognize any of us any more."

They took off to the El Paso airport, and I drove me and Dottie back to the ranch.

Dottie and I went to visit him once a week. I could sit there and tell stories about all the cowboy wrecks, all the drinking, all the rodeoing, and more, for awhile. Then his not hearing, not knowing, began to wear on me. I told Dottie not to come with me anymore. It was doing more harm than good. They kept him clean, but his pajamas were hanging on his bones where all those muscles used to be. He looked backward into his head, seeing nothing in front. I don't think he weighed a hundred pounds.

Then I started falling behind on my visits. I only went twice a month now, and feeling guilty about it. I hadn't been to see my best friend in a month. But somehow this day I felt better. I didn't dread it so much. Maybe looking at the varied landscape around the ghost town of Lake Valley caused this. It sure was beautiful with all the odd shaped little canyons and valleys that you come upon like a surprise present. The golden fall grass was up a foot high. It looked like patches of ripe wheat on the rolling hills, and what cattle I spotted were fat.

Just before I got to the three or four buildings on the left of the road, I could see a great grouping of those breast-shaped hills that were scattered all over this country. To the left, near the road, was the opening to the old Bridal Veil Mine that once had silver ore so rich you couldn't even blast it properly. They had run a rail line into the mine and backed the cars in, cutting the silver loose with double handsaws, dropping it directly into the ore cars.

On around past the three or four buildings, all on the left side of the road, if you looked carefully up on the right-hand hill, you could see another windy graveyard. A little distance on from there was Skeleton Canyon, where Victorio, Nana, and the great female warrior and medicine woman, Lozen, had lured a bunch of drunken miners and soldiers into a destructive ambush.

I wondered why I'd never really looked at all the detailed beauty and history here before. I decided right there that folks go all the way through their little lives and miss seeing the things that matter most.

Lately, I'd gone into Las Cruces on Saturday to miss the Sunday obligatory rush to these places of the old and the stricken. I was stopped at a red light near the university when I saw something that would make an old-timer pray for total darkness. The last few years, I'd noticed cell phones grafted on most folks' ears. A man stood there holding one in each hand, talking first into one, then the other, so fast it appeared he was watching tennis. By God, I couldn't wait to report this sighting to Rusty.

I'd usually arrive just before lunchtime and push Rusty in a wheelchair to the dining room to eat. Well, he had to be fed by the nurses, by hand, so I did that, too, when I was there. The only thing in his room was pictures of Shirley Mae and his daughters hanging just above the table by his bed. About a year earlier, I'd fixed a place to hang his best hat below the pictures. I was a little early for lunch, so I started off talking about the fun we'd had on our wonderful loco horse-trading trip. There in the wheelchair, he never even moved. He was gone way off in another world that didn't belong to me, yet.

Just the same, I went on about him tradin' a good-looking loco'ed horse for an even better-looking outlaw. I reminded ol' Rusty about what he'd said: "All right, it's a deal if you'll throw in a paid-up doctor bill with the horse."

It was time. I got hold of the wheelchair to take him to lunch. Suddenly he started whining and trying to turn his head. It wasn't a complaining whine—just a desperate one, a solid little cry from long ago. I thought he might hurt his neck straining back. And one fist— the bones still big, the only thing left on him that wasn't shriveled to mostly nothing—reached out for the wall. I was puzzled. But then without a thought I took his big old Stetson hat from the wall, placing it on his head as near as possible to the way he'd worn it all his life. Rusty's whining stopped instantly. He put both his hands back in his lap, leaning forward some as if he wanted his horse to move out.

I pushed him through the halls of smells you never forget. The old. The dying. The urine. We rolled on into the dining room. A couple of the service ladies who recognized me waved. There were others at his table. Some were awkwardly feeding themselves. Others were spoon-fed by impatient employees.

I pulled an empty chair over by Rusty, intending to place his hat on it. To my astonishment, he beat me to it. He set the hat upside down so as not to tilt the brim out of its natural line. Then Rusty settled down in the wheelchair, not moving anything but his mouth as I scooped the soft food into what seemed to me an untasting, unfeeling body. Afterward, I wiped his mouth and chin carefully and replaced the hat properly on his head at the exact right angle, and I pushed him back to his room.

I sat on the bed where the side bars had been dropped. Then I took his long bony hands in mine. I looked as hard as I could straight into his eyes. I strained. Nothing. Absolutely nothing.

Just as I was standing up, I thought I felt the tiniest squeeze from each of his once-powerful hands. But I got nothing else from any part of him. He had gone to the place beyond the planets. I got up and left. I knew I'd never see him again.

Back out in Lake Valley, I drove leisurely along enjoying the wonderful land all over again. Then I remembered that a large fifth-generation rancher had been unable to hold it together with all the bureaucratic conditions put on his lovely land. Impossibilities had descended from many sources. He either had to sell it or lose it, thereby becoming an old worn-out pauper.

Suddenly I saw the first development house going up on the fresh-torn earth. How had I missed it on the drive down this morning? How? Then I knew. I'd just on this very day learned to see without looking down at the ground for animal tracks.

A lost sadness covered me, and penetrated inside, seizing every particle of my being. Then I was no longer here. I was worse off than Rusty. Then from somewhere I realized he would never know about the residences and residents to come. He would never have to bear seeing this special landscape smothered with dwellings or know that the deer, the cattle, the coyotes, and the mountain lions would soon be gone to that other place he now inhabited.

My eyes blurred with wetness so thick I could hardly see the road. I wiped them with my shirt sleeve as clean as I could. At just that second I looked back visualizing both sides so gleefully thinking we'd skunked one another when actually we'd broken even, unknowingly trading one loco'ed horse for another. Then I smiled just before I laughed out loud so hard I damn near ran off the road and had another wreck.

MAX EVANS was raised on two different ranches, his father's and one owned by his widowed aunt, which he helped run. At age eleven he went to work on Ed Young's Rafter EY on Glorieta Mesa south of Santa Fe. By the time he was fourteen he was drawing regular cowboy wages and in all he spent seven years on the Rafter EY or being loaned by Young to many neighboring ranches as everyone did during the depression. In a story too long to tell here, Max got his own ranch over in the northeast corner of New Mexico in what he calls the Hi Lo Country. He ran that operation for eight years and also did day labor for big ranches all around him. Then he became a successful professional painter and metamorphosed into a writer. He has written twenty-four books, including *The Rounders* and *Hi-Lo Country,* both of which were made into major movies, and *Bluefeather Fellini,* which he considers his masterpiece. He now lives in Albuquerque, New Mexico.

Afterword
Cowboy Truths

CANDY MOULTON

The horse I guess mainly started it all.

Back in the fall of 1998, as the editor of *Roundup Magazine,* I called Max Evans to ask about an interview concerning the making of his book, *The Hi-Lo Country,* into a movie. It had been a thirty-six year process for Max and was a story about which Western writers would want to read.

We'd met a few times, Ol' Max and I, at writers' conventions. He is one of the Grand Old Men of Western writing; I a comparative greenhorn. I knew he could slug down the whiskey and I had loved his cowboy story and the movie of the same name: *The Rounders.* I got my interview about *Hi-Lo.*

As I wrote in *Roundup:*

> *I dialed his number and we spent more than an hour on the phone. If you've ever had the chance to visit with Max for even ten minutes, you know what my hour was like. He is such a man of the West it is incredible. He says what he thinks, profanity comes as naturally as downing a shot of whiskey, and he throws in these wonderful lines. Like this one: The horse I guess mainly started it all.”*

Later Max wrote me a letter:

"Nov—Something—98

Hello Candy M.,

I hope you guys have a good winter. That's the third time only—I've been interviewed by a real cowgirl. It was fun. . . .

Have fun for sure—
Ol' Max (the Mongrel) Evans."

I thought that was the end of it.

I figured we'd say "hi" at Western Writer conventions, maybe even sit at the same table with other friends and have a whiskey, but a few months later Ol' Max called. He told me about this cowboy anthology that he wanted to do. He asked if I'd work with him to pull it together. Is the outside of a horse good for the inside of a man or woman? If you don't holler out "yes" then you don't have a clue about horses, or men and women for that matter. In fact, if you don't holler out "yes" you probably didn't grasp what we wanted to do with this book and you never even got to these final words of mine.

When Max first asked me to be involved with this project, I knew immediately that I barely met his qualifications. Though I was reared on my grandparents' homestead, though I first helped with the branding gather at age four, began driving a tractor in the hayfield at age six, and first helped my dad, uncles, and cousins move the cow herd to summer pasture when I was nine, I don't consider myself a cowgirl. My sister could outride me as a kid and I know women today, like my cousins Georgia and Alice, who can outride and outwork me when they are half asleep and have their eyes shut.

But I am a daughter of ranchers and a rancher's wife. I've been kicked by cows and their calves, chased by mad bulls, and dumped off of my horse. There is something in the Western soil that tugs me. There are times when the power of the land is so strong as it surges through me that I cannot keep the tears from rolling down my cheeks. I know what it's like to stand with a witching stick in my hands and feel the pull of underground water.

Throughout my youth I sat around on Sunday afternoons at my grandparents' house listening to my Dad, my uncles, and my aunts— good horsewomen all—telling stories. They were cowboy stories that involved tying bulls' tails together, riding green broncs or runaway horses, and training the draft horses that my grandfather raised. And I've spent many hours in recent years bouncing over western trails on the seat of a chuck wagon pulled by Kate and Jim, a fine team of mules owned by my cowboy friend Ben Kern. So I figure I have eaten enough dirt, and slept amid enough cactus and rattlesnakes and small Wyoming scorpions to write about and know the Working West.

Even so, as Max and I worked on this collection, I found I needed a little help, and to Darrel Arnold of *Cowboy Magazine,* I must say thanks for helping me throw the loop and make the catch.

Cold weather had already painted the aspens and cottonwoods, the meadow hay crop lay stacked in round bales that weighed nearly a ton apiece as my daughter Erin stood with me and watched Bill and his son Bruce work the cows. The animals ran all summer up in Wyoming's Sierra Madre and now they were mixed. Some were Rominos's cattle, others belonged to Montie or Alice, a few might have been our own.

The cutting was superb as Bruce turned one cow—theirs—back into the meadow, and forced another toward the open gate. Bill spun to stop a breakaway mother. Twisting, turning, spinning on a dime, it was cowboying at its finest. That is cowboying in 2000, for Bill and Bruce didn't ride their quarter horses this day, their dogs didn't snap at an old cow's heels. Instead, the men were on their four-wheelers, the dogs must have had their toenails curled to hang onto the back of each machine as it twisted and spun.

But they got the job done, turning their own cattle back to pasture, the others on down country. I've watched Bill work cattle since I was a little girl when I made my own first roundup riding a horse belonging to my Uncle Rene. Bill was three years older and a seasoned hand by that time, riding and roping off of Brownie. Bill and I learned to ride out of necessity, and partially because our mothers used horses as babysitters. He lived on his grandparents' ranch; I on my own grandparents' homestead just a mile away. His great-grandmother was my grandmother, and we are the closest of cousins still living just a mile apart. Our sisters and my brother have moved from Beaver Creek; they aren't as near to their ranching roots as Bill and I. Instead, my own brother rides for a big outfit sixty miles to the north while our sisters teach school and work for the Forest Service.

As children we all rode to help our families. Gathering milk cows, pushing cattle from one pasture to another, taking them to the high mountain forest range each year. Our parents depended on us to do the work, along with other cousins, uncles, and friends. Like most ranchers they had little, usually no, money to hire help, sharing labor was the only option.

Like the boys in "The Stormy Blue Jitney," we longed for something to drive and took our turn in the field on tractors and old trucks transformed by our dads into hay sweeps. We heard our fathers fret when winter snow didn't fall as often and as heavy as it should, knowing the irrigation water would be short, and the hay crop, too. We watched our mothers deftly prepare a meal for their families and stretch it to feed twice as many when someone showed up at dinner time or supper time, a feat accomplished by adding another pan of biscuits and helping themselves to smaller portions of steak or stew. We saw them kill and pluck chickens, take weak calves or lambs into their houses for nursing and nurturing, raise a garden, keep the ranch books, can vegetables, make chokecherry syrup, sew clothes for themselves and their kids, and drive tractors or sweeps to harvest the hay crop when they weren't on their way to the parts store for repairs.

Only one time in all the years my own mother worked on the ranch, did she receive pay. Cattle prices must have been up that year, because Dad and Uncle Bert bought down coats for the entire hay crew: Mom, Aunt Phyllis, my brother, and I. We felt rich. It was the only pay I ever received for ranch work.

Ranchers are like that. They don't really ever have much money in the bank, it's all tied up in land and livestock and broken-down equipment. Women may not get a regular check for their contributions to a family ranch operation, but they feel the same pain as men when cattle get stuck in bog holes, when lightning strikes a huddle of horses, when grasses wither and die from lack of rain. They feel the same closeness to the land and have a spiritual understanding of nature's cycles. Whether they are looking to be Saved or waiting for the great Anticipation, they know some greater force is out there. It's like the power that's felt as you dig your bootheels into your own land for the first time, or the faith that's needed as you deal with the death of a child.

The loss of the Working West began decades ago but in recent years it has accelerated like a space shuttle launch. It has affected my family more than once; it could yet again.

My husband was a young boy when his grandfather's homestead was overrun by Grand Teton National Park, though the barn where he played as a child, where his father and grandfather cared for horses and cows, has become *the* icon for Jackson Hole. It is the barn with the Grand Teton range rising behind it that you see on jigsaw puzzles, real estate brochures, in video advertisements, and thousands of photographic images. Thinking they'd spend their lives ranching on land homesteaded by the Moulton patriarch, instead his parents had to put down new ranching roots out of Cody, Wyoming. In the 1960s that was still possible. Land values weren't so ridiculously high by comparison as they are now.

Today, when the Old Folks decide to sell out in order to take life a little easier, or when they die, it is becoming virtually impossible for the younger generations to take over the land and continue the ranching traditions. A million-dollar insurance policy purchased years ago to be paid to one sibling upon a parent's death so the other could have the ranch free and clear, now may not even cover the estate taxes. People who have made fortunes in dot com companies and other citified jobs can afford to pay millions for ranches that, in their best and most productive years, turn a profit only in the thousands. Without creative planning on the part of their parents, ranchers' sons and daughters cannot stay on the land, no matter how much they want to do so. And even those who manage it often find themselves, or their husbands or wives, taking a second job "in town." In my own community women teach school so their husbands can maintain family ranches. And some men "work out" and pour their paycheck back into cattle and equipment to maintain their own ranches, irrigating and haying or working cattle by night and on weekends.

It grieves me deeply to know that my grandparents' homestead is no longer worked by the family. Like so many other ranches in the West it is owned by a corporate rancher; a man who has little understanding of the pain and sacrifice, of the joy that went into its running for the nearly one hundred years my family had it. Fortunately, unlike so many other family ranches that have been sold to settle estates or divide property, it may not become a housing subdivision. The corporate owner not only has the money to pay the inflated values now associated with Western ranches, but also he has an affinity with the place that is the West. Some of the ranches he has purchased are in conservation easements, which means they cannot be developed and used for anything other than ranching and open spaces. None of those great old ranches that he now owns, which were forged by homesteader families, have been broken into subdivisions yet and with luck they will remain working ranches managed and worked by strong men and women. Today cattle drop their calves on the land and the ditches of my grandparents' generation still flow water over hay and pasture.

Nevertheless, there is a growing desire by young people, my own children included, to leave behind ranching roots and move to the city. The urbanization of our country, and particularly of the West, has happened before. Archaeologists and anthropologists who study the Anasazi marvel at that civilization. Those early people showed ingenuity, fortitude, and ability in developing their towns, the remains of which dot isolated canyons of the Southwest. The Anasazi culture had power and pride. There were great irrigation and road systems supporting the agricultural production of the times. But the climate began changing. Rains didn't fall to nurture crops. People began moving from their farms to congregate in towns, cities or urban areas. There they had difficulty growing and finding enough food; they depleted their natural resources. Eventually most of the Anasazi people died, leaving behind their crumbling communities.

As I watch the exodus of people from rural America and note the climatic changes of today's landscape, I wonder if we will let history repeat itself, if we will all move to the city and buy our food at the supermarket. After all, urban school children today think that's where milk and eggs and meat come from. They simply don't know about those of us who raise the cattle or grow the crops.

But even when I'm in my most pessimistic mood one thing always lifts me up: faith. Ranch people don't always make it to church on Sunday, though some do. But in every aspect of their lives they have a deep, spiritual sense of knowing that somehow things will turn out all right. That the rains will come, the grass will grow, that the storm won't take too many new calves or lambs, that there'll somehow be enough hay to last until the winter snow melts away. They have faith that a cowboy on his horse will find shelter during a blizzard, or that a woman will find wonder in the beauty of a weed. For them the land is their altar, the soughing of wind through the pines or aspens their organ.

It is an immense responsibility we of the Working West carry, to preserve the traditions of our ancestors and to maintain the hard lifestyle that has captured our hearts and souls. And one we carry with pride. The cowboys and cowgirls who preceded us on this Western land would expect no less.